SHOW ME A HERO

Philippa
Waterfield

SHOW ME A HERO

ADITYA SUDARSHAN

Rupa & Co

To My Mother

SHOW ME A HERO

1

"YOU BOYS AND girls are going to be the future.'

I must have heard those words two dozen times before I was eighteen. But, as with every other piece of immemorial wisdom that is handed down to us the minute we learn to read, it never occurred to me that it actually meant something. Not through my schooldays, which I seemed to spend entirely consumed in the weekly test and the daily game of cricket, and not through college, when there were other distractions. Oh, I know we all wrestle with Life and Love and the Universe through those long, humming hostel nights. I know it's often said that that's as good as it gets, and even now, there are certain brittle moods in which I don't disagree. But I've learned better in my heart, and I learned it from another person – and I'm not talking about a girl.

I'm not even sure whether to call him a friend. We had studied engineering together in Bangalore, but at the time I only knew him in the abstract. He was simply Prashant Padmanabhan, who lived in Delhi, and whose father was from Trivandrum. This I knew, not because his surname meant anything to me, but because once upon a time I had booked a weekend to visit Kerala, and someone had suggested that I consult him first. The trip never happened, so we never got talking and he remained in my mind's eye just the slight, though sturdy boy who sat near the back of class and giggled a great deal. It stayed that way until well after graduation and a certain Sunday evening, one eventful monsoon.

Three months previously I'd moved to East Delhi's Patparganj and gotten myself a single room in a horrible brown apartment – just one among countless others on a horrible brown street. My landlady was a difficult sixty-year-old, with two sons in America, whom she talked of constantly, and a husband I had heard was dead, whom she never mentioned. She never tired of telling us 'boys' that this rental business was her only source of income, and the way she ran it, I believed her. From the first time we met, I knew I was up against something formidable.

I had made an appointment by phone, and presented myself in person at the appointed time – three-thirty in the afternoon on a punishingly hot summer's day. Outside, the surface of the street shimmered in the sun. Inside, she reclined impeccably still on a sofa, while I fidgeted on a wooden chair and wiped my streaming forehead.

'Isn't it hot?'

She smiled at me half-mockingly. I looked over her chubby face, her sharply-lit eyes, the heavy figure in the saffron sari, and inwardly, I quailed.

'Yes.'

'Do you have a girlfriend?'

'What?'

Her plump smile broadened.

'Don't you understand the question?'

'Yes – well – I mean –'

'She can't spend the night.'

'No it isn't like that –,' I started to explain and then stopped myself, because it was really none of anybody else's business.

We were sitting in the drawing room of her ground floor flat. Four floors above us, just high enough for the vertigo to kick in, was my home-in-prospect. Mrs Ramdass had had a single large apartment divided into four quarters, one of which still remained available for a suitable boy.

'I don't allow any girls to stay,' she went on, warming to her subject. 'I don't want any complications. But I don't mind if they visit. You can have girls visiting,' she added magnanimously.

'I don't think I'll have girls visiting.'

'Why not?' she demanded suddenly. 'How old are you anyway? A boy your age ought to be interested in girls.'

Her beady eyes gleamed in a predatory way. The transformation from prudery to prurience was startling.

'I've been living in Bangalore,' I said decisively. 'I don't know too many people here. I won't have anyone staying over whom you don't want. Is that okay?'

Mrs Ramdass pursed her lips and I sensed that she was somehow wounded; my matter-of-fact candour had jarred against her developing familiarity. So she turned aggressive.

'There's one important rule. Keep your bathroom clean. I had a boy staying here six months ago – from Chandigarh – I can't tell you how disgusting it was. Nobody's going to clean up after you, just remember that.'

'I don't expect them to,' I bristled slightly, in spite of myself.

'Where are your parents?'

'They live in Dehradun,' I explained. 'My family home is there, and my grandparents aren't very well, so that's partly why my parents moved in with them. But we were all in Delhi before that – when I was in school.'

'Where in Delhi?'

It had been a posh, powerful locality in the very important part of the city. The house had come with my father's job, but of course, I had taken it for granted. Without the slightest compunction, I had had as sheltered and delightful a childhood as anyone could ask for, and now, for the first time, faced with Mrs Ramdass's sneers, I found myself apologising for it.

'Do you have a job?'

'Yes. I work in a . . . wildlife organisation.'

'What's that?' she asked suspiciously.

'It's mostly to do with stray animals. You know . . . the stray animals in the city? Well, anyway, there are plenty. This is a group that tries to take care of them.'

The landlady frowned, and I felt the first stirrings of a smile. I was always on a strong footing, defending my work to sceptical listeners, because nine times out of ten their scepticism began in ignorance, and dispelling that was a cheap and easy kick. In a city whose commerce I barely knew, among a populace infamously cunning and worldly, it was good to have something up one's own untried sleeve that they knew nothing of. Wildlife Alert was a small, passionate group of people – just like the brochure said – and I felt I had prospects working there. I had problems too, let me quickly add. A less-than-adequate salary was one. But at that point in time, the exoticism of the job was still dear to me.

'Will you . . . bring animals over?'

'No,' I assured her. 'Not unless it's an emergency.'

'I'll need the rent on the first of each month.'

'All right.'

I frowned at the change in subject. I had lost my momentary advantage, and before I could recover she was quoting a figure at me.

'Can't you make it less?' I asked helplessly.

She told me four different kinds of taxes that she had to pay, and then some 'local charges' which I did not even pretend to comprehend.

'Okay,' I agreed heavily.

The heat felt immense now. The slow-whirring ceiling fan was a futility. I glanced out through a window to my right, and my eyes hurt in the vibrancy of the sun. Outside, on a bright, blazing courtyard, a group of six or seven children were kicking around a football and hollering at each other in deadly earnest. The apartment blocks towered around them gloomily. A little further in the distance was the main road, and the relentless honking of the mid-afternoon traffic, making its presence felt. When I turned my gaze back, the interior was suddenly dark, and I felt quite giddy. Mrs Ramdass was saying something.

'Can't you hear me?'

'I'm sorry – I didn't.'

'I said – when are you moving in? If you're moving in right away I need a deposit, and you have to sign.'

Perhaps it is apparent now, that my first impression of my new home was far from positive. It really was a dreadful, dreary locality, and my apartment, a 'humble' abode. I had very little space of my own. I had a terrace, but there wasn't a view – just a bleak and greying sky above and below, cycle-rickshaws on the dusty tar. But although my sensibilities were spontaneous and could not be suppressed, I did not admit them, even to myself. I had determined, after all, to be practical – to make something of my 'Start in Life' – and for all its faults, this place was the best deal I had found. However strongly the heat in the air and the crowds on the streets assailed, I told myself that they were unavoidable discomforts, which it would be snobbish to decry.

The more I detested the things I saw, the more I admonished myself. It was in my mind that all successful men spent the first decade of their working lives in an obligatory 'struggle' against the odds, and so I even tried to extract a perverse sort of pleasure from all my inconveniences. Plus, now and then, when the day's work was done, my imagination would loosen upon me movie-like images of young, lonely men plunged into unwitting adventures, from which they emerged improbably and wildly triumphant. I am a straight-laced fellow by disposition, but I enjoyed those images. And every time I paid my landlady the monthly rent, I felt a little more vulnerable and a little more heroic.

Time flew — at first. My room, these apartments, this office — it was all new to me, and there is a certain pattern to the tackling of any fresh set of enduring problems. They are at first too daunting, then surprisingly yielding and then — when you realise that you are not in a sitcom and your first triumph is not the cue for a fresh episode — then finally, they are sobering. I barely noticed when two months of my life at Akash Apartments had passed, but as the third month drew to a close it settled upon me — unhappily -- that there were many more to come. Every morning I was waking up with an inexplicable foreboding, which stayed with me through the day's routine. It used to be a pleasant success to 'fix' my own breakfast, but I was getting bored of tea and toast and it frustrated me that I couldn't cook a decent meal. When I manoeuvred my father's Maruti out onto the choking roads, I did it with a deep-set trepidation. Previously, I had shuddered at East Delhi's impossible traffic and gritted my teeth during my long, daily commute to office. Then I had found, to my astonishment, that I could live with these things -- and now, with three traffic *challans* and the frenzied abuse of a near-miss motorcyclist behind me, I realised that I had to keep on living with them.

It was something similar at work. I knew the theory of the job well enough. I could use the buzzwords without batting an eyelid, and when I read about a problem, I cared about it. Add to this my native punctuality and general good manners, and it was no wonder my boss liked me. But I had spent several weeks admiring from a distance those who *did* – those who went on the midnight expeditions to 'rescue' some runaway python from some terrified house-owner; the men who brought bleeding, abandoned dogs home at night, and cared for them all through the following weeks until they were well again – or dead; the ones who knew the first names of the rangers in Ranthambore (and the poachers too). I knew that, deep down, I did not share their sensibility. Yes, I loved the documentaries on National Geographic, and I visited the zoo in every city I travelled to, and I'd read all of James Herriot – but when it came to dealing with the real, pulsing creatures – which was my job – I was nowhere. How long, I worried, can you conceal a thing like that?

We were doing a project on the dancing bears in India. The problem was how to separate the bears, whose lives were torture this way, from their owners, who got their livelihood this way – and still keep everyone happy. I'd written a report on the strategic questions – I'd moved between the library and the internet all the time I was writing it – and when my boss was done reading he called me into his office.

He was a kind, middle-aged man, who spoke average English. His office bore the stamp of his personality – sparse furniture and a great busy mess of papers.

'This is very good,' he said to me.

'It's very well-written,' he added.

'You have a future in this line,' he finished.

When I walked out of his office, I was literally shivering. I felt an immense, clinging shabbiness. The rest of the day I spent repeating those three sentences to myself until I had extracted from them every last drop of meaning, and finally I reached the conclusion that the man had been . . . sarcastic. Everybody, surely, could see that I was deadweight.

In retrospect, I put these apprehensions down to a guilty conscience – something like the murderer's guilty conscience in that story by Poe. But just like that fellow, I couldn't get rid of them.

Now, the customary cure for such crises is the company of 'those who care' – meaning, I suppose, family and friends and, if you should be so lucky, one other person. I don't dispute the general thesis, but it wasn't working for me. My parents telephoned every weekend. My mother would ask about my cold, if I had had a cold anytime in the previous three weeks, whether I was eating all right, and how my work was going. I would give her a monosyllabic assurance that did neither of us any good – but prepared the ground for the following week. My father, with whom I was willing to be more voluble, was usually even less so. But articulate or inarticulate, the shared parental worry loomed large over my affairs. I had no answer to the question: What, after all, are you doing with your life? And I didn't know whom to ask.

Just a year ago I wouldn't have had to look far. There she was, at whose ethereal feet I had laid the best dreams of my college years. They lay there still, but the feet seemed less ethereal, more clay – though I hardly liked to say that even to myself. Her name was Anita. She had long, wavy hair and a smile that I'd never seen bettered. She liked passion fruit and strawberries and the colour pink, and for a long time we had been very much in love. We were still together. Who knew me as well as she did? Who knew her as well as I did? But she was in Mumbai and I was in Delhi, and I don't think we missed each other. Oh, I thought of her a lot, but only when I was feeling low – and you don't need to be a believer to pray when you're in trouble. Many a night, when the dissatisfaction in my heart had grown too great, I called her, she said something soothing and then sure enough, I'd be all right – until the next morning.

But I won't extend this litany of woe. I did find somebody who could transform my mood in a fresh and decisive fashion. At the time this story begins I didn't know him very well or like him very much, but even then I found him interesting.

In my quadrangular apartment No. 504, three boys lived in the rooms next to mine. We shared a common space with a fridge and a television, and that was where we sometimes bumped into each other. (On the weekends Mrs Ramdass also turned up, reckoning the emotional high of her favourite soap worth the physical toll of the journey upstairs). One of my neighbours was an Assamese medical student called Kisle, who kept odd hours and kept to himself – he was not a type I was familiar with. Another was Arjun, a turban-less, Sikh 'techie' journalist who had close-cropped hair and the sort of hard-drinking, weed-smoking lifestyle that had long since lost its novelty in my eyes. The third was Animesh. Kisle was prone to unfathomable mood swings that manifested themselves every now and then in a great slamming of doors and guttural swearing. Arjun, expectedly, was a manic depressive – by turns unduly enthusiastic and greatly depressed. Animesh was always invariably at ease. In my early days at the apartment I wondered the most about him.

We had had one introductory chat when I moved in, but I must have done all the talking then, because I hadn't learned any of the usual details about him. It had occurred to me, though, that Animesh was a good-looking boy, albeit in a slightly feminine way. He was small-built, with large eyes and long lashes, and he had a certain deferential quality which was compelling – you wanted to know more about this person who did not seem to want to know more about you. Later, I reached the conclusion that he was – unemployed. In the morning, when I went to work, I sometimes caught sight of him just sitting by himself on his bed, and when I returned in the evening he'd still be there – unchanged, right down to the clothes he was wearing. He wasn't scruffy, though.

Our first proper conversation was on the same Sunday in July that I have been building up to. I had finished my routine phone call to Dehradun and it had been an especially torrid call. My parents' advice that I should get a proper, paying job was sounding more practical than ever, and I hated to hear it from them. Kisle-esque, I exploded into the living room.

'Hey!'

Outside my door was Animesh. The collision was inevitable. When he regained his balance, he smiled at me sanguinely.

'What's the matter with you?' I demanded.

His smile flickered worriedly; then became patient.

'I didn't expect you to . . . emerge like that.'

'I hope you weren't eavesdropping.'

'I overheard,' he admitted.

'What?'

'Unintentionally. I was doing a round of this room,' he traced a circle in the air with his index finger, 'and I paused at this point, just to think.'

'Just to think?'

'Yes.'

'What were you thinking about?'

He seized on the question with great seriousness.

'I was thinking about what it means to feel good about life in a place like this. I've got an answer too.'

Saying this, he caught my arm and propelled me into my room.

'It means building a sense of romance — against all the wretched odds. Come here.'

And then out onto my terrace. I barely had time to be offended at this casual invasion, before he was pointing intently towards the outdoors.

'Look at that. Just look at that.'

Reluctantly, I looked. It was the usual mess. On an intersection in the road that had no traffic lights, a phalanx of cyclists was advancing towards an opposing line of pedestrians, each on a collision course with the approaching cars. Meanwhile, the sides of a DTC bus were shuddering furiously, its engine going like a death rattle, and soon enough, the whole dilapidated monstrosity had launched into a semi-circular arc that threatened to sweep aside everything in its path. Into the afternoon air there darted a succession of swear words, but for them I was actually grateful, because much more disturbing than any casual abuse was the stoicism of the participants to this chaos. It was their calm assumption of inevitability, their cool tolerance of what was surely intolerable, which made me feel a sudden stab of fear. Of course, I had been in countless such snarls myself. But watching from the outside, it was always a miracle to me when they were finished, and what passed for peace was reinstated on the road. The sun hid behind a cloud momentarily, and then I breathed in heavily.

Animesh was grinning.

'These things were no trouble when we were children,' he said. 'I don't think any of us noticed the state of the city.'

'That's true,' I agreed.

'And so it's all right for the perpetual children too. Arjun, for instance. He has no trouble dealing with . . . reality, because it simply doesn't exist for him. It's all just a lark. He can go out for a drink every night and pretend he's in Manhattan.'

I frowned.

'What about Kisle?'

'Oh, Kisle *is* reality,' Animesh chortled, 'so no problem for him either.'

We went back indoors. He sat down on my bed, without an invitation. I stayed standing.

'I've been meaning to ask you,' I said to him. 'What do you do all day? Are you studying? Are you working?'

'I am researching,' he answered promptly.

'Researching what?'

He threw up his hands gaily.

'Everything.'

'Be serious.'

'I am serious,' he replied. 'I have a lot of very good ideas and I'm trying to make something of them. Tell me about your job.'

'You already know,' I said pointedly.

'Yes,' he went on, unabashed. 'Tell me more.'

I shrugged my shoulders.

'It had seemed worthwhile work. But it's not really progressing.'

'You want to do worthwhile work?'

I shrugged again.

'That's great,' Animesh said softly. He was looking at me afresh with those big, black eyes. I realised, with inward astonishment, that I was starting to enjoy the attention.

'What do your parents do?'

I told him.

'That's very good and proper,' he said lightly. 'But it doesn't excite you, I suppose. It doesn't hold you captive. I'm not surprised.'

Suddenly he said:

'In college, you were the president of your student body.'

'How did you know that?'

'I'll tell you in a minute. Did you like being president?'

'Well,' I considered, 'it –'

'I've heard you were great.'

'I was okay,' I shrugged for a third time, although I was very pleased to hear it.

'You like to manage people,' he was saying slowly.

I had the sense now that Animesh was speaking almost to himself.

'I heard you saying on the phone that you can't do the things the people at your office can. You sounded worried about that, but why should you be? Not everybody does things. Some people help other people do things.'

He stretched his arms out on either side and arched his back luxuriously. He was getting comfortable.

'Yes. And some people don't do anything at all.'

I couldn't resist that. But he was proof against sarcasm. He simply took my words at face value.

'I know,' he said eagerly. 'We understand each other.'

'I know a guy from school,' he went on immediately, 'that I'd like you to meet. Actually, you already know him. Once,

I mentioned you to him and he said you'd gone to college together.'

'What's his name?'

'Prashant Padmanabhan.'

'Yes . . . I don't know him well, though.'

Animesh got up from the bed. He was smaller than I had thought at first. He came up close to where I was standing.

'If you like to bring out the best in people,' he said to me quietly, 'then you're looking for a guy like this. And he's looking for a guy like you – believe me.'

'You sound like you're setting us up.'

'I absolutely am.'

The fading sun had bathed the room in a mellow shade. In the late evening light, the other boy's face had taken on a kindly hue. He looked momentarily very wise, and very sure of himself.

'I'm sure I'll meet him sometime,' I said hesitantly.

'He's coming over tonight. We were going to watch the match.'

'Today's Sunday,' I reminded Animesh. 'Mrs Ramdass will be here for her serial.'

'We can deal with her,' he answered smoothly. 'The three of us together can deal with her.'

I said nothing. Animesh went back to his own room and I spent the rest of the evening staring at the blank wall ahead of me and trying to guess the time. After an indefinite period, the interior started to grow dark and a mysterious melancholy welled up within me, dulling for a while the tight expectation in the pit of my stomach. But when the doorbell rang and I got to my feet, my heart was beating strangely fast.

2

IT WAS ONLY Mrs Ramdass, arrived earlier than expected. She entered at her own pace and beamed meaningfully at the both of us, as if to say that she knew our dirty secrets. Her billowing figure subsided onto the sofa in front of the television.

'Do you like cricket, ma'am?'

'It's a waste of time,' she spat back. There was a jingle of silver bangles and her forearm reached for the remote control.

'Today's a match,' Animesh continued brightly. 'It's a big match. It's a final. I've called a friend over.'

She nodded, unperturbed. The pictures on the screen flicked by, in time with the stabbing of her finger. A succession of aborted tidbits rushed into the room. The dead were piling up in another riot in Kashmir; an ex-chief minister was being tried for corruption; a young man, grinning incredulously, was about to win twenty lakhs – I wanted to see if he would, but there was no lingering; there had been a murder in a South Delhi home.

Then the channel with the soaps came on, and I lost interest. The landlady adjusted her posture confidently. She was that sure of herself; it did not seem worthwhile to interfere. I took Animesh aside for a moment.

'We can watch once she's done,' I said. 'She won't be long.'

He shook his head.

'She should get a television downstairs. She can't barge in on us every time, as though it's all up to her. We pay for this, remember? Besides, it's a twenty-twenty game. We'll miss the best part.'

Suddenly he broke off, rummaging in his left pocket.

'I've got a call.'

He moved away from me. I watched him saying something into his ramshackle mobile phone, and about then it occurred to me that Animesh was right. Having our landlady exercise a sort of feudal *droight du seigneur* over our television had been taking its toll on all of us, and yet no one bothered to stand up to her.

'Prashant's downstairs,' Animesh turned back towards me. 'Once he's here, he'll handle her.'

I made no reply. But as the doorbell rang for the second time that evening, I pictured to myself some bulked-up bouncer with a single-minded style and a set expression. Animesh's expectations of Prashant did not square with my remembrance of that unobtrusive backseat boy. I wondered suddenly if we had really been thinking of the same person.

The front door swung open loosely on its hinges. It was him all right. There was the same strong mouth and the same playful eyes and the same unruly black hair – he had lost weight since college, but these things had not changed. Even the silver frame of his spectacles was just as I recalled.

We had an awkward moment directly after the first enthusiastic greeting – I mean the anti-climactic falling off, which is inevitable when you never really knew each other. I had just thought of something to buoy the flagging mood when our attention was distracted.

Mrs Ramdass was regarding our visitor askance, and Animesh was introducing him to her with a visible smugness -- in the manner of one unveiling a trump.

'This is our friend, Prashant Padmanabhan. He's from Kerala. He'd like to watch the cricket match.'

'What does your father do?' She asked Prashant – in Hindi.

When he didn't answer immediately, she struck again.

'I know you're from Kerala,' she said with equanimity. 'But don't you understand Hindi?'

Prashant's features were shaping into an uncertain simper.

'I understand Hindi. I've lived in Delhi all my life –'

'-- Ma'am,' he added, and next to me I saw Animesh's brow furrowing.

'Watch in an hour.' The landlady sounded suddenly bored. She flicked her attention back to the screen. It was a final gesture.

Rallying hard, Animesh looked pointedly at Prashant.

'Didn't you want to watch now?'

'No, no, it's fine,' the other boy crooned, jiggling his head in the way that says that anything will do. 'Anyway it's only twenty-twenty. I like Test matches better. Besides, if the television isn't free –'

'I like your manners,' Mrs Ramdass announced, without taking her gaze off the screen. 'They're better than average.'

'Thank you,' said Prashant.

I intervened then.

'How about we go out somewhere?'

It seemed the only thing to do -- to cut our losses fast.

'We can watch in a restaurant -- a club.'

'Yes, let's do that,' Prashant perked up. 'I'll drive.'

Down in the parking was his black Maruti, the same colour and model as mine. By the time we had got into the car, Animesh's indignation had faded to bemusement.

'What's the matter, Prashant?' He struggled clumsily into the backseat. 'That was a pretty sorry display back there.'

'What do you mean?'

'Animesh thought you would get us the TV,' I explained. 'Our landlady takes over it like this every weekend.'

'I don't know her from Eve,' Prashant replied. 'How could I talk back to her?'

He started the car. Soon we were escaping down the empty Sunday streets. It was a still, hot evening, good for a late siesta and limbering up to a late night. As we gathered speed, a warm breeze rushed in through the window. I looked out at the dusty trees drooping forlornly in the direction of the ditch that passed for the city's river. We climbed onto the bridge that would take us to the other side — the nice part of town.

Behind me, Animesh shifted on the upholstery.

'I've seen you before, talking to strangers,' he said reproachfully. 'You weren't so timid then.'

'When did you see me?'

'At Kunal's party, last winter. Remember the guy who wanted to take your photograph?'

Prashant's forehead creased in thought. His mouth closed hard and tight. Then his face cleared and his lips curled at the corners.

'I must have been drunk.'

The car accelerated over the bridge. I reached for the radio. The first three channels were playing something jubilant and unmelodic. Bryan Adams was on the fourth and I stopped there. I've always liked him, but I was surprised that nobody else protested. The upbeat *When you're Gone* came streaming into the warm interior, and trailed out of the windows into the night.

Just at the peak of the bridge's ascent, there is a point where the 'whole city' appears on the horizon. When we reached that point, I looked. In the clear night, the far-off lights were glowing brightly and the fast-moving vehicles were on full beam; for a moment it did not matter that there were power cuts in great swathes and no skyscrapers. We were headed to some place with crowds and also space; some place expensive.

'What are you doing nowadays?' I asked Prashant.

'Nothing really,' he said heavily. 'There's a chance – my father – I might get a job with the science ministry.'

'That's fantastic,' I said.

Prashant was concentrating on the road. For a little while, I watched the rhythm of his feet on the pedals, and how he manoeuvred the wheel and the gears. There was a grace to his movements, which was a masculine grace – careful but controlled, inhibited but confident.

Animesh was leaning forward from in between the two front seats, the way that I used to when I was five.

'Imagine there's a man on the street and you have to get his money,' he started without a prelude, 'which is the problem for most people.

'Now you could rob him. In one way or the other, more or less subtle, more or less vile. Or you could do something that makes him so grateful that he takes out his wallet and pays you.'

He looked at us, each in turn.

'Those are the options. And what do you think most people make of them?'

A bemused silence greeted the question.

'I'm asking the two of you.'

'Well,' I considered gamely, 'I guess . . . I don't know. I think most people try to be useful. And some succeed.'

'Prashant, do you –'

'I think most people are . . . hyenas.'

He said it with a certain dry simplicity.

'And they live off the lions.'

When we were close to the marketplace, Animesh's phone buzzed inaudibly once more.

'It's ten overs left in the first innings,' he reported. 'Let's get there fast.'

'There' was nowhere at the time, but after a frantic scurry through the grungy and yellow-lit lanes of Khan Market it materialised; a new lounge-bar called Calabria. Thick, stylised metal doors barred the entrance; a thick, suited man was at the door; the concealed interior gave off a sense of dense and throbbing activity. We passed through, into the darkness and up a flight of slow-winding stairs.

Inside the club, there was a steady beat of music playing. This was a new track – one of the horde of trashy and transient numbers that are always swamping the airwaves. No doubt the songs were the usual fare at this place, but tonight they were incongruous against the telecast. A large screen on the left-hand wall of the room was beaming the cricket, shorn of sound and harsh on the eyes. It was like a shoddy movie screening in a very smart hall.

With a very smart audience. When we found a table and my eyes adjusted to the lighting I looked around. There was one group of teenagers, in football jerseys and Bermudas and overflowing animal spirits, who treated this place with a casualness that struck me as vaguely offensive. There were two families my parents' generation, trying unsuccessfully to affect an easy good time. But they were too old and their children were too young. The rest, I guessed, were 'young professionals' – people like us.

Of course I noticed the girls. They wore spaghetti tops, and, if not skirts, then embroidered, shiny jeans with ostentatious belts. They were pretty, but there was blankness where there should have been character in the expressions that they wore, and so they were not beautiful.

For one happy moment, my mind dwelled on my own far-away girl. Her soft, quizzical glances, her eternally kind smile — those would have stood out in this crowd.

'What will you drink?' asked Prashant.

'I'll have a beer.'

He told the waiter, and ordered vodka for himself. Animesh wanted lemon juice.

'You have the most set tastes of anybody I know,' Prashant chided him. 'It might cost you ten bucks on the street or eighty in here, but it's always the same thing.'

'Alcohol clogs my mind.'

'All the more reason.'

A collective cry went up in the room. I turned my head sharply towards the big screen. It was the first over of the second innings; India had a hundred and eighty to chase, and our latest, greatest hope to fill the opening slot was being stared down by four Australians, with a fifth rushing into view.

'What happened?' I asked aloud.

'I don't know.'

'Give it to those cheats!'

To my right, a big-built boy in spectacles was pumping his fist savagely.

'What happened?' I tapped him on the shoulder.

'What?' He half-turned his head and I caught a breath of beer.

'What just happened?' I asked patiently.

'He nicked it, but the umpire didn't see. Now they're sledging him for not walking. I say, treat those cheaters just as they would treat you.'

'Of course.'

The drinks arrived, and my attention was distracted.

'Nobody walks,' Animesh was saying solemnly. He lifted his glass of juice and took a pensive sip.

'He can't bat though,' said Prashant. 'Cheers.'

Our glasses clinked.

'He may as well have walked. Just watch.'

Uncannily, the batsman was caught at first slip ten minutes and three runs later. He departed to jeers from the opposing team, the crowd in the stadium, the crowd in the club.

'A batsman like that,' Prashant was looking flushed and quite pleased with himself, 'inspires no confidence. He doesn't look like he's going to score runs and it always looks like he's going to get out.'

'But it doesn't *feel* like he's going to get out,' Animesh said slowly. 'You don't care one way or the other. The special players are the ones you're afraid for.'

'There hasn't been one like that for ages,' I said.

Meanwhile, Prashant had started on another drink.

'What will you have?' he asked me again.

'I'm not done with this.'

'Well, get done.'

'I didn't know – in college – did you go out often?'

'You didn't know anything in college.'

He was grinning lazily. He adjusted himself loosely in his chair, and took another deep draught of his drink, which finished it. Now, his eyes were not focused on any one thing; they were panning all across the interior, taking in the view.

Suddenly his gaze stiffened. Beside me, Animesh cleared his throat.

'If there was sound,' I heard him musing, 'we'd have had the Aussie commentator saying its okay not to walk because you take the rough with the smooth – the smooth with the rough, I mean. And the Indian commentator would have been squirming with delight at the "win at all costs" attitude of our youngsters. Idiots,' he finished evenly.

'What's wrong with that?' I narrowed my eyes. But when Animesh started to reply, I didn't hear what he was saying. My attention was still on Prashant, and his was on something, or someone, at the far corner of the room.

Through the shadows, from in between the tables, two people were approaching – laughing and leaning on each other with his eyes on her and hers on Prashant. That is how it appeared from a distance. When they were one table away I saw the girl make a brief movement with her shoulder, and suddenly I realised that she was shrugging the boy off. With the greatest possible delicacy, she was letting him down. He clung on though, stupidly, uncomprehendingly. From the glaze over his eyes, I figured he was drunk.

They reached where we were sitting.

'Hi Prashant,' she said, 'I need a little help.'

'Sheila . . . who's your friend?'

She was of a middling height, diminutive really, with an oval face so bright it might have been lit from within. I noticed that, but not her clothes, or any other physical feature. She had a style that precluded scrutiny.

'Hey man, why don't you ask me instead?'

We all frowned. Sheila's companion had returned his right arm to his own side. Him I saw clearly enough -- he was tall, unshaven, dressed in deliberately untidy clothes, which were nevertheless as dandyish as any black-tie affair. He had what they call 'big hair,' and a muscular frame, but the way he stood now, restless, childish, shifting his weight from one foot to the other, made him look curiously unfit. He had the body of a bully, and a manner to match.

Prashant continued speaking to the girl.

'Come, join us.'

'I'm with a group,' she said lightly. 'The thing is, I've got some money riding on a question, if I can answer it. We're having a quiz amongst ourselves.'

'How cute. And money -- how grown-up too.'

'Don't condescend. It's fun.'

'Well, what's the question?'

'It's so simple -- that's the embarrassing part. They always kid me for not paying any attention to the matches, and now someone wants to bet on it. So, do you know who scored the most for Australia today?'

'I didn't watch,' Prashant apologised.

'Oh,' she made a disappointed face, 'I thought you would have for sure.'

'Something came up. Who're "they" anyway?'

'I'll introduce you.'

'You can start with him.'

The large boy had been standing back contemptuously. Now, he leaned his upper body forward.

'My name's Roshan,' he drawled.

'He's a friend of Madhav's,' Sheila explained calmly.

We all went over together to the other end of the club. As we made our way, a little distance ahead of me, I heard Prashant telling her –

'Here's a question you can ask them back, which is just as easy, and I promise nobody will know the answer.'

'Sheila!' cried a feminine voice.

On a triple-segmented sofa turned at right-angles, two boys and two girls were sitting around a wide wooden table. The tabletop was a happy mess of bottles and glasses and plates of food, and an ashtray twirling smoke.

'You're so . . . blatant.' It was a pleasant voice; weary and amused. It belonged to a dark, solemn-faced girl, whose arm was wrapped around the sofa in a proprietorial way. 'Your answer won't count now you've cheated.'

'I didn't find out,' Sheila answered promptly. 'But I'll double the stakes and ask a question back. And if Gitanjali doesn't get it, anybody can try.'

Her confidence was charming. Next to her, Prashant was smiling hard and I did not think he could help it. The others made space and we joined them. I looked discreetly over the new faces; there was Gitanjali, the girl who had spoken, and to her right a youthful-looking boy with a scared expression. Opposite him, fairly dwarfing him, was an elegant clean-cut figure gazing pensively at the ceiling, and now and then at Sheila. The fourth of the group was a tall and very fair girl with an aquiline nose.

Sheila spelled it out slowly. 'Who is the best batsman to play for India in the last ten years?'

There was a confused pause. Gitanjali arranged a lock of hair across her forehead, and looked oddly into space.

'That's . . . not a proper question. Vivek, is that a proper question?'

Vivek, the timid-looking boy beside her, was unsure.

'I mean, it's subjective,' he started. 'There's been no one really good either,' he said thoughtfully. 'Maybe Sharma – or Tiwari.'

'Hey, there's no answer to that,' Roshan snorted. 'You lose, sweetie.'

'She doesn't lose,' Prashant spoke up suddenly. 'The answer's easy, but I'm not surprised no one remembers. It's Ali Khan. There's no other name.'

Roshan laughed in a slack, extended way – the sort of laugh that is half-mockery and half-boredom, and not contagious.

'Ali Khan – that freak-show! And he's ancient – how *old* are you?' he sneered at Prashant. 'Madhav, you remember Ali Khan?'

The elegant one smiled slightly. I figured he would be six feet standing up. His hair was cut short against an angular face. His eyes had a quality of abiding appraisal; it was hard to think of them animated.

'I'm not really a cricket fan,' he said, in a rich and mellow baritone.

Suddenly the fair girl – her name was Preeti – burst into giggles.

'Nor is your . . .' she cleared her throat with meaning. 'I bet Sheila's never *heard* of him. And look how shamelessly she's asking!'

'She's the consummate actress,' chimed in the baby-faced Vivek.

Soon they were all joshing her. Animesh and I were only watching, but Prashant was fidgeting. All the while, he was making steady headway into another glass of something, but his attention was broken up. I had the sense he was trying to take the reins of the conversation, or at least take a part in it. He was leaning forward from the edge of his seat, nodding a little at intervals, guffawing hopefully when the others laughed. His mouth opened and shut on more than one occasion. But the group of six was caught up in its own talk, and nobody was paying him any attention.

That included Sheila. She had brought the three of us here, and there had only been a perfunctory introduction, but she wasn't taking care of us any further. I didn't mind that myself; I could settle back against the cushions and watch the big screen, and I think it was the same for Animesh. But it was bothering Prashant. He was listening in unhappily.

Somebody asked:

'How much do you owe me now, Sheila?'

'Oh, be kind. I'm struggling for my rent.'

'*The landlord says your rent is late. He may have to litigate,*' Vivek was singing tunelessly. '*Don't worry, be happy.*'

Gitanjali frowned. 'What about those threatening letters you've been getting? You should tell Mr Kapoor about those.'

'Oh they've stopped,' said Sheila. 'It was the postman's mistake.'

'I thought that was quite serious,' Prashant butted in. He was looking steadily at Sheila. She regarded him sideways with a doubtful expression.

'No . . . I didn't say that. It only happened once, anyway.'

'I thought it was something serious.'

'So *that's* what you tell your other friends,' Roshan laughed. 'That you're getting death-threats — like a real *filmi* heroine.'

Once more, there was laughter, and Prashant was left unsmiling.

On the screen flashed figures that said India was losing badly. We were six down with more than half the chase still to go. It was going to be an early night at the Wankhede.

'Hey Madhav,' Vivek perked up. 'It's S.P. Singh coming in to bat. Give us your imitation.'

'Yeah, do that,' Preeti implored.

'Sheila wants you to. Don't you, Sheila?'

The girl raised her eyebrows coolly. It was supposed to signify that it was all the same to her, but it was the first affectation that night that she had failed to pull off.

'Not tonight, boys and girls,' Madhav leaned back on the sofa.

'Oh come on.'

'You're so *good* at it.'

'Thank you.'

'Hey come on.'

'I'll do it.'

Now he had their attention. With a dramatic gesture Prashant gulped down his drink, and before I knew it, he was rising to his feet.

'What's he doing?' Animesh whispered.

'How should I know?' I muttered back.

He took several unsteady steps back from our table, until he was within touching distance of another. From there, two muscular and unforgiving-looking teenagers were regarding him warily. He took no notice of them.

'This is S.P. Singh, taking strike,' he announced cheerily. His voice was slack and too loud.

'He's had too much to drink,' Animesh sounded worried. 'I should have stopped him earlier.'

Ahead of us, Prashant was now jabbing an imaginary bat into the surface of an imaginary pitch. He straightened his back, wiggled his hips, then glowered down at the imaginary bowler and made the notorious 'bring it on' gesture with a single toss of his head. Behind him, the teenagers grimaced at each other through the clouds of their cigarette smoke.

I suppose, if he had been sober enough to carry it through, and less self-conscious, it might even have been a funny performance.

'Are you watching?' he called out unnecessarily.

We were all watching. Vivek was open-mouthed, and trying to appear indulgent. Madhav was inscrutable, but, I figured, unimpressed – and Sheila was the same. Roshan was on the verge of saying something.

Preeti's white face was visibly shocked. She leaned over towards Gitanjali, and I caught snatches of her speech.

'– shameful . . .

'– totally drunk . . .

'– friend of Sheila's; I'm not surprised.'

Gitanjali was nodding all the while, but her reaction struck me as more complex. She didn't find Prashant's act funny – nobody could have – but there was something in her eye that was far from disapproving. It was a kind of admiration.

'He's a friend of mine too,' I heard her say.

'Man, why don't you sit down?'

Roshan walked over to Prashant and put a patronising arm around his shoulder.

'Come on back.'

'Oh but I've just begun. It gessmuchbedder . . .' Prashant stopped, momentarily disoriented. He looked around with owl-eyes. 'Once he has his first play and miss, it gets much better.'

'It's all right,' Roshan was guiding him back to the sofa. 'Look – there he is on the screen. Look – isn't that cool?'

This was cheap and meaningless. But Prashant looked and I winced on his account.

'Next time, you can do Ali Khan for us,' Roshan was grinning cruelly. 'Nick it when it matters and walk.'

Prashant's indignity was amusing to Roshan. The rest had better grace; Madhav even changed the subject. But I saw Sheila staring down at the floor. A flicker of hurt passed across her vivid features. When Prashant finally sat down next to me, I gave Animesh a pointed look.

'I think we should leave.'

'Yes it's all over anyway.' He looked regretfully at the screen. We were eight down, and even in this frenetic format of the game, where the shift in advantage could be so quick as to be almost imperceptible, numbers nine, ten and eleven promised nothing.

'Prashant, shall we leave?

'Prashant, I'm talking to you.'

Prashant's chin stayed buried in his chest, but he raised his right hand, as if to say: give me a minute. I wondered if he was aware of the spectacle he had made of himself. Sitting there, I suppose, he was feeling the fiery whips of humiliation – unless the alcohol had doused them altogether.

He looked up, slightly confused. Then a kind of calm settled slowly over his face. He turned towards Roshan.

'I'll do Ali Khan,' he said decisively. 'I'll do him so well I'll make *movie* 'bout him.'

'You will? Wow, man, that's great.'

'It will be. It will be . . . great!'

'Sheila, I didn't know your friend here made films. I'd have been nicer to him.'

'Come on, Vaibh–. An'mesh, stop . . . slothing; I've to drop you home.'

Prashant smiled at me then. It was a golden smile. For the three seconds of its duration it cast off the sodden drunk completely.

Then he stumbled to his feet so much off-balance I had to clutch at his arm, or he would have fallen on his face.

'We have to pay first,' I reminded him.

Later, he stopped suddenly at the exit, putting me immediately on alert, but this time he had better control of his movements. He flung a final glance back across the room. It wasn't intended for Roshan or for any of the others.

'Sheila, I like you to be my lee'ing lady,' he called out very loudly, so everybody in the room could hear.

'I'll phone you,' he added, sweeping past the door. Animesh and I followed him out, and into the de-populated night.

3

IN THE DAYS that followed, I was unusually busy. My report on the dancing bears had been such a hit that I was asked to adapt it for a chapter in a new book my boss was editing. Of course, it was a kind of honour, and it allayed my fears that the powers that be at Wildlife Alert were on to me, but I half-wished it hadn't happened. In its own way, the prospect of the sack had been a heady one; instead I found myself more entrenched than ever. There didn't seem to be any alternative though, so I set about burning the midnight oil.

Going to work early and coming home late, I didn't get a chance to have a proper conversation with anybody – not even Anita – until a full week later, one balmy five o'clock in Patparganj, when Animesh knocked on my door.

'I'm here with Prashant,' he said simply. 'He's downstairs, getting the air in the tyres checked. If you're not busy, let's sit for a bit.'

The compensation of an always-crowded locale is the heightened charm of the occasional quiet moment, and this was one of them. In another hour and a half, the avalanche of office commuters would be upon us, but that Monday, after a week's strenuous editing, I was home early. In the gathering twilight the sky was a dull yellow, dim enough to look anywhere without blinking and bright enough to keep the street lights from switching on. There wasn't a breeze, but it wasn't hot either. Animesh and I pulled three cane chairs, of the British Raj sort, out onto my terrace. While we waited for Prashant, the two of us sat listening to the sound of our voices, which we lowered, so as not to spoil the mood.

'I've been meaning to ask you all this while,' Animesh said. 'What did you make of Mr Padmanabhan the last time we met?'

I resisted the instinctive grimace. I had not enjoyed the aftertaste of that night. Perhaps I am overly proper, but exhibitionism and showmanship are things I have always been distrustful of. It was one of my conceits — that I took plain-speaking over polish, whether or not the boy was downstairs.

'I don't know. To be honest, I wasn't impressed.'

'No?'

'No. I don't know why you were so keen that I should meet him.'

Animesh nodded sagely.

'This is why. Because you're able to see what's wrong.'

'So can you. So could anybody. He was making a fool of himself.'

I said it with more feeling than I had expected to. I think a part of me scorned Prashant, not for his having got so drunk, but for his having got so drunk on so little.

'You're right, but that's an incidental failure. It comes with his style.'

I gave the other boy a sceptical look. He went on placidly.

'Prashant likes melodrama. They all do, actually. They're all looking to be actors, you know.'

'He isn't.'

'He isn't, but Sheila is. And the group she was with is. They just finished at the School of Drama. That's why Prashant's film might actually be a chance for them.'

'Prashant's film?' I frowned. 'Wait. You don't mean —'

I had a point to make. I had had some experience, in my time in college, of dilettantes whose favourite pastime was shooting their mouths off, but it seemed to me that in the real world, real achievement belonged to the workmen. My ideal was the uncomplicated way of the folks at Wildlife Alert.

'He was too drunk,' I said severely, 'to know what he was saying. He was shouting across the club, and I wouldn't be surprised if they don't let him in the next time. People who are serious about doing things — they don't *talk*. It's that empty vessels business all over again.'

'Then what's the need for wedding vows?' Animesh asked unexpectedly.

'What?' I grimaced.

'Why do people have wedding vows? Why go to the trouble of telling the whole world how your heart feels, if all you're doing in the process is illustrating its emptiness?'

'Look . . .'

'Vaibhav,' Animesh grinned at me. I made a resigned expression, and let him go on.

'The nicest thing about Prashant,' Animesh was saying, 'is that he isn't a fraud. He says things only so that he can go ahead and do them. It gives him a sort of drummed-up courage.'

'What are you anyway — his manager?'

'I'm just someone who likes to see things go right,' he answered lightly. 'You're the manager.'

The steady crunch of wheels on gravel floated up to my terrace. It was Prashant's Maruti, manoeuvring its way to a standstill just inside the gates of the apartment block. I watched as the subject of our discussion waved the car door shut and patted down his pockets, then turned briskly in the wrong direction.

'Hey!' I shouted, but he was out of earshot.

Fifteen minutes later he had made the two-minute elevator ride upstairs. He was wearing a plain dark T-shirt and blue denim jeans.

We hadn't been sitting outside five minutes when he turned to me.

'I'm sorry about the other day.'

'It was nothing.'

'That's true,' he agreed unexpectedly. 'But some people mind. The thing is, I only drink in company and only for other people's sake.'

'How does that work?'

'Oh, just to give them a good time. I'm always in control, you know.'

'I see. . . .'

'But I was thinking about that night later,' he said, 'and I realised how silly I had been.'

'Well it's physiological, really –,' I started to say in mitigation of his drunkenness, but he was going on speaking.

'I mean – the question I had thought of,' he explained. 'The question about the best batsman of the last ten years. I should have known they wouldn't allow it, even though there really was only one right answer.'

'How about you?' he asked me softly. 'Do you remember Ali Khan?'

Did I remember Ali Khan? The truth is that I follow the sport just as keenly as the next man, but until Prashant had brought it up in the club, I had quite forgotten the name. Since then, I had let my mind wander back to the time when Ali Hassan Khan had opened the batting for India and I had realised with a start just how recently that had been. I suppose it is common knowledge that public memory is short, and less obvious that so is one's own.

'He was loose outside the off stump,' I offered the conventional remark.

Prashant seized on this in a way I did not expect. He leaned forward from his chair, glaring at me as though he had spotted something contraband in my eyes.

'You mean to say, he was caught behind a lot. Which opening batsman isn't? Which batsman at any position isn't?'

'Well, he was great for about two years,' I said in conciliation. 'But after that – I don't know, there were too many controversies. And he stopped being consistent.'

'He lost some form. That's normal. That's a kind of error that isn't actually an error – otherwise we wouldn't say that stuff about it being human to err. He would have been fine if the critics hadn't started swarming about him like flies.'

'You sound quite . . . affected.'

'I just think it's ironic, how someone who isn't a man gets to vilify someone who is a man, for not being a superman. I'm talking about the critics.'

He paused for a moment. Outside, the main road was beginning to rumble. The hitherto stray horns would soon become the norm, and it would be hot under the lights. When Prashant spoke again his voice was calmer – and more purposeful.

'You may have forgotten everything else about him. But don't you remember the World Cup?'

Of course I remembered. When I had made the effort to recall Khan, it was the first memory that had sprung to mind.

I had turned eighteen that summer. I was going to Nainital to visit my grandparents, and all through the ten-hour drive, I had fretted because their house, though old and lovely and full of memories, didn't have a television. But as it turned out, the neighbours' did. So I spent most of my days with the neighbours, which my mother didn't like, but which everyone else understood. The World Cup justified a falling-off of filial piety. And India had made the semi-finals.

Come the thirteenth of March, and we lost the toss. The opposition, again, was Australia, no longer the inevitable champions but still, on most days, good enough for us. It looked like it was going to be one of those days, when they marched in their fifty overs to two hundred and seventy-three for the loss of six. I forget if anybody bowled well; I remember Samuel Clarke scored a lucky hundred.

Then it was our turn. In the narrow 'TV room' of that tiny house with the mud flooring and the flag-stoned roof, the first innings had drawn a reasonable crowd. But with India batting, it had doubled. As our openers walked out onto the pitch at the Wanderers, the air was chock-full of expectant human breathing. Outside, the night lay cold and silent, with dots of light speckling the mountainside. Inside, a flurry of conversation and activity was subsiding to a hush as the players assembled.

One of my uncles had been in attendance. He was a man who boasted an encyclopaedic knowledge of the game, which no known encyclopaedia had ever corroborated. He quoted statistics with a brazen disregard for the facts. He also prophesied frequently, and always ill. I mention this because the hoary old line he announced that night, as though it was his own, stayed with me until much later. 'India will snatch defeat from the jaws of victory.'

From the first over, it was clear that Khan was in touch. He played a quick inswinger off his pads for two, and then a square cut past point for four. All his famously correct technique was in evidence, and unlike the last Indian batsman feted for technique, Ali Khan had a strike rate too.

But the reaction of the crowd was mixed. The applause was less spontaneous than when the other batsman took guard, and that was testament to the extent, by this time, of Ali's notoriety. It had been one thing after another and throughout, the tall, moody opener had remained unapologetic. I think the match-fixing affair, for one, had only just blown over.

Gradually, as the night wore on and wickets fell at the other end, it became clear whose shoulders the team's hopes rested on. Push had come to shove and now the Indian supporters had cast aside entirely their grievances with Khan. Now, only cricket mattered. The cheers for a boundary were resounding; the hush at the fall of a wicket, the shrieked anxiety of a near run-out or a play and miss – it was an atmosphere that permeated through a million television screens into a million drawing rooms. I think it was the fortieth over when Ali reached a hundred, and the forty-seventh when he lost his ninth partner.

We only needed five to win when McDermott ran in to bowl the first ball of the fiftieth. The commentators were treating an Indian win as a sure thing, and I remember hating them for it. My fearful imagination reminded me how many ways there were for a batsman to be out.

McDermott bowled a bouncer, which took everyone aback. It took Ali completely aback. He fended at the ball as it went past to the keeper. I was on my feet shouting no-ball, because it had looked high. But the Australians were appealing.

'Not out!' declared my uncle, and still they were appealing. The cameras swivelled towards the umpire.

My eyes bored into his right arm. It was tucked behind his back – *Stay that way*, I willed it. In those fearful seconds many jumbled thoughts raced through my mind –

He's an English umpire and aren't they all racists; they crack under the pressure when the Aussies appeal; he'll give it out just to complete the drama. Everybody is drawn to the affirmative; he won't say 'No'.

He did say 'No'. The pleas of the Australians expired slowly; they turned to each other in disbelief. The broadcaster's feed fastened on the stick-thin McDermott. I watched the open-mouthed disappointment draining slowly off his features. He wasn't looking in the direction of the camera.

His dulling eyes brightened inexplicably. He raised both arms upwards and bellowed. He disappeared into the circle of whooping, yelling yellow shirts.

The cameras panned furiously, trying to find out what had happened. They took a long shot of the pitch and the players, and we all saw Ali Khan tucking his bat under his arm and beginning the long walk back to the pavilion.

In the quiet stadium, the self-absorbed cheers of the Australians had sounded eerie and wrong. Amidst the shock, their shouts were sacrilegious. It was only when Ali had reached the edge of the ground, with our number eleven trailing confusedly behind him, that the crowd resuscitated. At the steps to the dressing room he raised a hand to wipe a tear – the cameras caught it, the big screen gobbled it. There was a smattering of applause, then soon it was general, and I think, and so did the South African commentator, that most of it was for Ali.

Metaphorically, the applause for him continued well into the following weeks. I don't know how much of it was sincere – there were so many competing emotions involved and walking, though the umpire hadn't given you out, was hardly even expected of a batsman. It was an old tradition, part of the so-called 'spirit of cricket,' that the game's administrators talked of constantly, and most others ignored.

For his own part, the batsman made no comment. When India played its next series at home against the West Indies, his name wasn't in the squad of sixteen. It was reported that he wasn't fit. He retired a year later, eulogised afresh as 'the gentleman cricketer'. Then, he faded altogether from the popular imagination.

Prashant was still regarding me intently.

'Yes,' I said, 'I remember.'

'My uncle,' I went on, 'never believed that cricketers should walk. He used to say that the only duty is to abide by the umpire's decision. You know you have to go when you're actually not out but declared out. So why shouldn't you stay, when you're actually out but declared not out? It's just the rub of the green – one way or the other. I kind of agree with that.'

Prashant gave me a scornful look. Then he set about arguing.

'That's only because you haven't really thought about it. If you know you're out, and you still stay, it's cheating, and all the sophistry in the world can't change the fact. Batsmen are expected to pay for the umpire's mistakes, but they're not expected to take advantage of them. That's fundamental to who a batsman is, and who an umpire is.'

An immediate annoyance surged through me. I resented this categorical opinion. Annoying also, was that I couldn't find an answer to it.

'Ali Khan was a batsman who understood that.'

Prashant was going on speaking; his eyes were shining. He may have shot down what I'd said, but I sensed now that that wasn't his idea. His idea was creative.

'You know, Vaibhav, most batsmen walk. Now and then, when it's convenient, when the stakes aren't too high. But how many could walk at the moment Khan did? It takes rare courage to do a thing like that.'

'Or rare stupidity,' I muttered under my breath. What I said out loud was:

'Well, he got plenty of praise for it, didn't he?'

'Yes!' said Prashant triumphantly. 'Plenty of praise. But all the wrong *kind* of praise.'

'What do you mean?'

'I'll tell you,' he promised eagerly. 'I'll explain. It's a little complicated, but I'm going to put it all in the movie, so –'

But I was sniggering now. 'Your movie,' I said. 'Oh yes. You really want to make a *movie* about him, just for that one incident?'

My face was cast in a deliberate sneer; I meant to be provocative. But Prashant seemed not to notice; a tide of enthusiasm had swept into his voice.

'Not only that incident. That's only . . . illustrative. But, like everything else about him, it's very misunderstood.'

In the face of his continuous enthusiasm, I felt my mockery slinking away. I looked doubtfully at Prashant.

'I didn't know,' I said, 'that you were interested in movies. In making movies.'

'Oh, I've always been,' he practically blushed. 'I used to well, never mind.'

'A sort of secret love,' Animesh interjected. 'Movies are his girl.'

'Oh, shut up,' Prashant retorted.

'How much headway,' I inquired, 'have you made on this?'

'Well I've written out a script — most of it, I mean. It's nothing very detailed yet.'

'Written, produced and directed by — Prashant Padmanabhan!' Animesh announced. 'He wants it all, that boy.'

Prashant flashed him a dirty look, and then turned back towards me.

'It's going to be a pretty solo thing — out of necessity — but really, making a film is a collaborative business. And I'm not so good at things organisational. I'm a little wishy-washy sometimes.'

'Get some help then,' I said carelessly. 'Get yourself a team.'

'Exactly.'

There was a pause, during which I felt something was brewing.

'Would you be interested?'

'What do you mean?'

'I'd just feel more comfortable if you were on board. You've got the . . . Midas touch.'

'No, I don't!' I exclaimed, astonished, but also, in spite of myself, pleased.

'You're right,' he apologised immediately. 'That was a silly thing to say. It's really that in college I thought you were a great president. I was telling Animesh about you. If you could help me manage this film — I mean, most of all, the people I'd feel a lot more confident about it.'

And now, having previously lauded myself many times for my steady level-headed style, I confess to a near-complete helplessness against flattery. It was my turn to blush.

'I'm busy through the week.'

'You don't need to be there all the time. Come on the weekends.'

'I didn't realise you were serious about this. When you mentioned it that night.'

'He thought it was the vodka talking,' Animesh explained.

'But apparently you always do the things you talk about,' I gave them both a dubious look.

'Oh, that's not true,' Prashant laughed. 'But I never do the things I don't talk about.'

'Anyway,' he added, just in time, 'enough about me.'

It had already occurred to me that Prashant's vanity was too much on display. But there was something impressive about his unabashedness. He was talking to the two of us the way I could only imagine talking to a girl.

'If you come over right now, I could show you,' he suggested suddenly. 'My plans for the film, I mean. It's all there at home. There are some things I think you'll find interesting.'

The previous evening, I would have refused the invitation without a second thought. But just at the moment I couldn't think of anything waiting on my desk the next morning. And more than that, I suppose, I was still tingling from his praise of my presidency. I thought to myself: he wasn't likely to get anything done on his own, this kid who couldn't hold three drinks or find his way upstairs.

'All right.'

'Good,' he said calmly. 'Shall we go now? It'll be late before we know it.'

Prashant had stood up as he was speaking, and now he was looking out over my shoulder. I followed the line of his sight. The street below was thickening with traffic. From the distance an extended piercing sound approached, growing steadily louder and more urgent. Soon, a lone motorcycle came into view. It swerved its way through the collected cars, buzzing all the while, like a mosquito.

It was getting dark too. The bulbs in the flats across the street were glowing. The street-lights were all lit, and everybody's headlights were on. The sky was a murky haze of dim reflections, clouds, and dust.

'I'll drive,' Prashant offered.

'We can both drive.'

'It's not necessary. I'll drop you back. I'm in New Friends Colony – that's not too far. And I know a quick way there.'

A door banged loudly inside the apartment. I turned, startled – I was still not completely inured to Kisle's ways but the movement reminded me that there was a third person present on the terrace. Animesh had been an observer for most of the conversation. Now it was ending, the two of us were leaving and he remained sidelined, shifting in his chair. I gave him a quick, questioning look. He was pretending to be content to study us from a distance, but there was a flicker of a frown about his brow.

'How about you, Animesh,' I said. 'What are your plans now?'

He opened his mouth a fraction; then looked at Prashant. The other boy, still standing, had lowered his gaze. He was glowering at his toes. It occurred to me suddenly that they looked a lot like brothers, and Prashant, with the added height and the sturdier figure and most of all, the authoritative air – like the elder brother.

'Yeah you can come along too,' he said tonelessly. What he hadn't said was more eloquent.

'I . . .' Animesh's large eyes were confused for a moment. His seamless self-possession was briefly interrupted. Then he said, grandly, 'I can't come.'

'Why?' I asked.

'I have to work.'

'What?'

'I have to work.'

I just looked at him. But he didn't bat an eyelid.

4

THERE WERE NO quick ways to anywhere at that time of day. When Prashant's car was brought to an inevitable standstill at a junction not far from my apartment, we rolled up the windows and he pressed the button for the air conditioner. Immediately life improved. I stared out of the glass at a bearded man in tattered clothing, proffering his one good arm to the traffic. He was coming our way.

Five seconds later, he tapped on the driver's side and bowed tragically. Prashant cranked the window down.

'No, I'm sorry, I can't give you anything.'

'It's for my children,' said the beggar, in tired and plaintive tones.

'No.'

'God will bless you. You will succeed in all that you start.'

'I really can't.'

'You will marry soon.'

Prashant was looking uncomfortable. He frowned and said 'No' a third time, but the other man kept reciting his piece. I figured he wouldn't stop until someone acted decisively one way or the other.

'Here, I've got a coin,' I arched my back, stretching for my wallet. 'Just get it over with.'

'But I don't want to give him anything.'

They were still going back and forth when the light turned green. With a final shake of his head Prashant put the car into gear.

I looked at him. He needn't have allowed the intrusion of the night's heat and the old man's wretchedness. There were easier ways to deal with beggars. But as we started forward, I held back a momentary urge to laugh at Prashant. The lines of concentration had faded from his brow. He looked oddly self-assured.

On a blessed flyover, where the traffic was quick, we talked about movies.

'I bet you watch a lot of movies,' I said.

He shook his head.

'Hardly any. I watch a few movies again and again.'

'Such as?'

'*Unbreakable*. *A Few Good Men*. Everything by Hitchcock and everything by Chaplin. Oh, and *Casino*. That's by Martin Scorsese and it's got Robert de Niro and Sharon --'

'I know it.'

'Well, that was the movie that made me want to make movies. You remember the scene when De Niro's character sees Sharon Stone's character on the floor of the casino – and she's been cheating another guy of his cut of her winnings and she's so unconcerned she starts to hurl the chips up into the air? They turn the sound off and the camera's on De Niro's face and then the music starts. It's a great scene -- emotionally.'

While I tried to recall the scene, he turned his head towards me for a full two seconds, the way you shouldn't when you're driving.

'Because earlier,' he said, 'I used to worry that movies couldn't really convey emotions. None, except the most superficial. The way I looked at it, the interesting emotions don't always broadcast themselves on our faces, or through our gestures, or even our speeches, so how can you communicate them through pictures?'

'I suppose that's true,' I said.

'And that's a pretty unassailable problem. It's one of the real limitations of movies. But *Casino* made me see that it was sometimes enough to hint at a complex emotion – there wasn't a need to explain it, like you would in a book. You leave an impression on the minds of the audience, and then they can go home and think about it.'

'I thought a picture was worth a thousand words.'

'It is. But sometimes a thousand pictures aren't worth a word. You just,' he shrugged, 'have to know when.'

'What about Hindi films?'

'The very old ones,' he said with aplomb, 'I haven't watched. The ones they made when we were growing up, I hated. And I don't much like the new ones either. They have about as much emotional intelligence as the WWE. They're made for children, you know, and I'm not six years old any longer. Everything is set up in terms of the most childish emotions: it's either shyness, or petulance – or tantrums –'

'– or love?' I suggested.

He grinned.

'Not love. Our love stories are a misnomer. They're too . . .'

'What?'

'I don't know. But whatever they're about, it's not love.'

It seemed to me his judgments were too many, and too cavalier.

'I think you're pretty harsh. Maybe you're missing something.'

'Well . . . maybe I am.'

'Yeah,' I mocked his tone. 'And maybe pigs have wings.'

'What? No, no,' he giggled. Then he became serious again.

'No, I mean it. Perhaps you're right. Anyway, I do like some of our comedies. They're better than Hollywood's. And as a rule, we have better taste. The most formulaic of our films aren't as tasteless as the trashiest of theirs.'

'What about other films? Foreign films – I don't mean American. The European – the Japanese greats?'

'I haven't seen them.'

'You do know,' I told him, 'that the movies you said you liked aren't exactly . . .' I hunted for the right word. 'I mean, they're . . .'

'They're common as muck,' Prashant smiled. 'I know.'

Five minutes later, we had reached the colony where he lived. The little car went past a brightly-lit marketplace that had a man selling a shock of red roses upfront, and then turned into a dimmer, cozier side-lane. A gang of stray dogs watched us go by, and one of them started a conventional protest.

I was looking out at the houses we were passing. They were tall, spacious, private buildings. The glitter in their windows was warm, and I imagined delicate and chatty parties playing out indoors – but it was also unrevealing. The curtains were beautiful, but drawn, and not a whisper emerged into the moonlit night. There was a box for a guard in front of each house, and most of the gates were too high to see over. 'Beware of Dog,' said the sign on one wrought-iron affair.

Prashant's home was the last in this lane that ended at a rusted railing that bordered a municipal park. It was a white brick house, with a long, cobbled driveway, upon which, in single file, three cars were parked, one of which, I could see, was a Mercedes.

We entered the premises. To our right was a well-grown garden separated from the road by a low wall. A small pomegranate tree stood at its centre, with several birds' houses hanging off its branches. Beyond the tree was a strange structure, not unlike a kennel, built from shiny wooden boards and panes of glass, with a stylised, sloping roof for cover.

I followed Prashant down the driveway, then through a doorway. We arrived in what looked like the living room. 'Sit,' he said. I lowered myself onto a sofa. He turned away briskly.

'I'll just be back.'

When he was gone, I looked around, taking in the surroundings. The room had a dining table, laden with chrysanthemums, and on the far side of the table, a staircase that disappeared into the ceiling. Above my head hung a golden chandelier, casting its yellow blaze over a mantelpiece arrayed with glittering glass crockery. I turned to my right and came face-to-face with a large brass statue of Ganesha seated on the floor. A little way above and to its left was a gilded portrait of a mustachioed man with a dangerous look in his eye, who, I suppose, was a relative. Underneath him, thankfully, the green of the garden showed behind sliding glass doors. It lent some sense of space to the chock-a-block interior.

All the same, I didn't rise from where I was sitting to take a closer look at anything. I didn't feel up to it. Instead, I let my fingers drum lightly on the glass-topped coffee-table below my eyes.

A middle-aged woman wearing her hair in a bun emerged into my peripheral vision. I smiled cautiously at her.

'I'm Prashant's friend,' I explained.

She said a hurried hello.

'Have you had something to drink?'

'No – but I'm fine.'

'Oh . . .'

Her expression was kindly, but more worried than the facts warranted – which worried me.

'Will you have . . . juice?' she said hopefully.

'Okay,' I shrugged.

She turned on her heel with some relief, and went the way Prashant had.

Two minutes later, two figures came into sight. Prashant was holding a thick paper envelope under his arm. He was walking a little distance ahead of a small, wispy man, who was carrying, with excessive concentration, a tray and two glasses.

'Sorry, I'm not such an attentive host.'

'No, I was fine. I met your –'

'My mother. Well, gulp it down.'

I took a deep sip of the orange juice. The thin man lingered indulgently, until Prashant gave him a hard look.

'So,' I said grandly. 'Tell me about your film.'

But Prashant wasn't listening. He was staring at his own glass with a troubled expression.

'What's the matter?' I ventured.

'Nothing.' It was a patent lie. He looked suddenly disgusted.

'There's only one ice-cube in this. I had asked my mother for three. What's the point of one ice-cube? It's the most useless thing. I've told her so many times.'

'It's just incredible,' he went on with a curious catch in his voice. 'The tray is full of ice-cubes. Why be so stingy? I've told her so many times.'

I smiled slightly. Then I stopped smiling when I realised he wasn't play-acting.

He got up from the sofa without another word. I stayed where I was, but I followed him out of the room with my eyes, and after that my ears were unconsciously on alert.

'– *the matter with you?*'

I heard him say. And after a shocked pause, I heard him say again:

'*Every single time!*'

He hadn't been shouting; the urgency in his tones was what had carried to the drawing room. When he came back to join me he didn't shy away from anything, but he didn't apologise either.

'I just get irritated sometimes,' he sat down heavily. 'Nobody gets under my skin like my mother.'

I didn't say anything. I didn't want to know.

'I don't know why . . . even the smallest thing, it just sets me off.'

He was speaking thoughtfully now, as though he and I were discussing this, which we were not. I stayed silent.

'Anyway, let's go outside – I want to take you outside.'

'What's outside? This is a nice place,' I lied suddenly.

I felt a perverse desire to obstruct him further. I couldn't make any sense of his outburst and I wanted to register my own protest; to stand for my right as a guest not to be privy to the house's scenes.

But he was quite calm again now. Some sediment of self-awareness had stopped him from tipping off into unbearable rudeness. Now he was bringing to bear the full force of his charm to tide over his mistake – and all without an apology.

He was smiling at me, and it was hard to dislike him when he smiled.

'The summerhouse is outside. It's the advantage of having an architect dad. They're always rebuilding everything, but sometimes they come up with good ideas. That's where I work. I only came here for these.' He held up the envelope.

Ten minutes later he had emptied out its contents onto a high table in the room in the garden. I sat next to him, staring through a tinted sheet of glass at the pansies and dog-flowers in the flower-beds outside.

It was only a solitary room, and it was smaller than I had expected. It had an air-conditioner, a desktop computer with all the appendages, a video-camera on a ledge in a corner, and a tripod underneath. It had the table and two chairs, and many tangled clothes heaped in a corner. The walls were two-thirds glass, opaque from the outside and transparent from within, and one-third painted white boards.

Austerity clung to this room, just as riches had to the living room. It occurred to me that for all his public showmanship, Prashant had a spartan sense of style. Not that I wasn't comfortable – quite the opposite. In the cool, treated air, my mind felt calm and powerful.

'Take a look,' Prashant tapped my shoulder.

'Letters,' I observed.

'Because he doesn't use e-mail.'

'He?'

'Just take a look!'

He was full of energy now. He was arranging the papers, from one end of the table to the other. I picked up the first sheet. It was dated in the February of that year.

'This is a long time ago.'

'I'm not so impulsive as you think! Go on and read.'

'Dear Mr Ali Khan,' I read to myself:

'My name is Prashant Padmanabhan. I am twenty-three years old. I live in Delhi.

'I was a great fan of your cricket. I believe you are the best batsman in the world in the last ten years and would have been recognised as such, but for the perpetual controversy that dogged you.

'I want to make a biographical film about your life, on and off the field. I have written a script, which I would be glad to send to you, should you like to see it. I would also like your permission to make this movie.

'I realise you must get a lot of fan-mail, but please do write back to me, because without your permission I cannot shoot the movie.

'Yours sincerely,

Prashant.'

The response was a month later. I had to concentrate very hard to make sense of the flying scrawl.

'Dear Prashant,

'I have no desire to be the subject of a home video.

'Thank you for your letter.

Ali Hassan Khan.'

'That's pretty curt,' I said.

'But to be expected,' Prashant nodded. 'I didn't let it end there.'

'Dear Mr Khan,
'I had written to you in February about a film I wanted to make.
'It won't be a minor event, if it happens. It's true that I'm an independent filmmaker without sponsors, but I have backing. My aunt is Mrs Shanta Padmanabhan, who you may have seen on television or read about. She'll be able to ensure plenty of publicity for the movie.
'Also, I know how to make an excellent film on a small budget.
'I'm sending you the script for the movie along with this letter.
Prashant.'

'Where's the script?' I demanded.
'All in good time. Read further.'

'Dear Prashant,
'I've had enough publicity in my own time, and with due respect to your aunt, I don't respect journalists.
'It may not be possible for me to read your script. I am quite busy with my work here. Please apply your film-making talents to a different subject.
'Regards,
Ali Khan.'

'What work does he do anyway?' I asked.
'He coaches school kids in Meerut. He's been doing it ever since he retired.'

'How did you know that?'

'It's not a secret. Now see what I said next. This was the money shot — just a sec.'

He pushed his chair back and reached for a switchboard on the wall behind us. I turned as well. Through the darkened windows at my side, I could see the flaring white orb of the moon casting its sheen over the surrounding sky. But the clouds were thickening even as we sat, and no silver blaze reached the summerhouse.

A tube light winked instead, confident of its prowess. By its encompassing glow I read the next letter. It was a long one.

'Dear Mr Khan,

'I am putting into this letter the heart of the movie. I hope you'll have time for it.

'I believe that you are an anomaly, and I believe you suffered for that reason, and that is the single point I intend to make through the course of my movie. I believe that you played the game at a time when there was a dearth of heroes, and not just in our cricket team. Your contemporaries settled always for second-best and second place.

'You really believed that you were as good as anybody else. You really believed you owed yourself fulfilment. You are a Muslim by birth, but you never had any sense of identity with your community. You lived alone with your father in a big city from the time you were seven years old. You were an individual — that was all. When you became famous certain Muslim leaders chafed at your refusal to pay homage to them, or to adhere to the religion. You drank. You didn't pray. When they protested – you didn't apologise.

'You did not play cricket out of a desire to represent the country. You played cricket because you didn't know what it was not to play cricket. The Indian team meant to you the best eleven cricket players in India – nothing more political and nothing less sincere. At the world championship in Australia, you joked that you'd rather have the sponsor's logos on your gear than the national flag, because its colours didn't go with the uniform. You played the tournament, and as it happened you did not do well. But even when the whipped-up frenzy of the mob stoned your house, partly for that comment, and, I think, mostly for your failures, you didn't take a backward step, and you did not apologise.

'At first, the media loved you – I mean the more high-brow sections of the English media. They thought you had transcended things like nationalism and patriotism and loyalty, which are words that discomfit them. You were, for a little while, their darling – the flag-bearer of individual self-aggrandisement. Then you did the interview with Shekhar Sen, who thought it was a compliment to tell you that. You told him it wasn't. And after that you told him what you thought of him. The media's love affair with you ended that day.

'They started labelling you. They called you condescending to your opponents, and perhaps you were – to your white opponents. But you were condescending where others were servile, and that was the difference. You weren't sheepish about winning, and you weren't overjoyed about winning. You took it for granted. When you were punished by the referee in New Zealand for walking off the field after Alex Jones abused you, you got no support from the Indian journalists. Your confidence was new and startling to them. They took the side of their old masters, and they denounced you. You took the ban, and you didn't apologise.

'When the allegations of match-fixing arrived, I thought they would finish you, and yet you survived. Just at that time you were making too many runs to be touched. But the moment they were all waiting for came at last. Your form faded – the knives emerged. The critics cut you no slack whatsoever and you could not cope.

'Even before the World Cup, it was clear you were going to be dropped after it. You were so brilliant in that semi-final; at least you left on a high – of sorts. But you should never have left at all. That hackneyed expression holds arrow-true in your case: you were a genius before your time.

'Mr Khan, I think your story is an important story and I know how to tell it, so that everybody will watch it.'

'Wow,' I said, astonished. 'You really feel strongly about this guy.'

'It's just a whole lot of truth on one page,' Prashant answered drily. 'It never does ring true. Read some of your old love letters.'

'What?'

'Read some of your old love letters,' he repeated patiently. 'The point is, I knew what I was doing. Look how he responded.'

'Dear Prashant,

'You can make the movie, but only if I'm involved in the process. Tell me when you are beginning shooting, because I would like to be present for that.'

'I thought he was too busy!' I exclaimed.

'Too busy for this?'

Prashant was smiling, with a kind of compassion.

'He says he's had enough publicity, but that's not the point. He's never had the right *kind* of publicity. Everybody wants to be understood, Vaibhav. Ali Khan's no different.'

I read the last letter.

'You've told him to come this month.'

'We'll start this month,' Prashant nodded. 'I've got a script; I've got my camera –'

'That's a video-camera,' I said absently. 'Don't you have film?'

He shook his head quickly, still smiling.

'Film is expensive. And more complicated. I have all the editing software on this computer.'

'It's all right,' he continued aggressively. 'I'll use video cameras and the software for now. It doesn't mean I don't want the studios and the bright lights – eventually.'

He laughed then.

'I don't plan to stay independent any more than I plan to stay single.'

This easy intimacy I found faintly offensive. Instinctively, I rebuffed it.

'That's good to know,' I said curtly. 'How about the cast?'

'I'm . . . trying to get it together,' he replied. His manner had grown withdrawn. I regretted my snub.

'Well, that shouldn't be a problem. You wooed Ali Khan pretty skilfully.'

But Prashant responded deliberately graciously, and it was I who felt accommodated.

'That was easy — because I really am a fan. I think when you want to woo somebody, all you have to do is believe every word you're saying.'

'That's not true,' I said doubtfully. I hadn't got Anita so easily.

'Well, no,' he agreed. 'That's not enough. But it's the minimum. Beyond that you have to make a lot of inspired guesses.'

We sat for a while without saying anything. My stomach growled.

'I was wondering,' I asked anxiously, anything to suffocate my hungry complaint. 'Why don't you involve Animesh in this? He seems a . . . smart guy.'

'I don't know,' Prashant was looking amused. 'My feeling is that Animesh is likely to slow our progress. He's fun to listen to but when it comes to *doing* anything . . .'

'Yes, I want to know that. What does he do all day?'

'Hasn't he told you? He writes essays.'

'You mean he's a journalist.'

'Oh, no. At least, he says "Oh, no" when somebody tells him that. He wants to be an essayist after some old mould which is apparently now forgotten. He hasn't published anywhere yet.'

'Between the two of us,' Prashant said in a kindly way, 'if Animesh was a stock I wouldn't be buying.'

Music burst out suddenly; Frank Sinatra's *New York, New York*. I glanced, startled, around the little room.

'Hello,' I heard Prashant saying.

He had got up and walked a little distance away from me. He was curling his head into his cell phone in a self-conscious way. Across those five metres, I couldn't hear what he was saying.

When he had finished, he looked down at the device for a few unnecessary seconds and then looked up at me with a just-shaken- off sheepishness.

'That was Sheila. She's coming over. You – remember Sheila? From the night at Calabria?'

'I remember,' I said. 'Does she live close by?'

'Kind of. She said she was in the area. She should be here any minute.'

He was peering out the glass pane with a newborn worry.

'I think I'll leave now,' I said. 'I should be getting back.'

Prashant looked at me confusedly. I gave him a pointed look. His face cleared.

'She's coming about the film,' he explained. 'I have to sell the idea. You need to help me.'

I stacked the letters onto the table, and rose to my feet. It had gotten cold in the summerhouse, and more than that, the air felt stuffy. Beyond the gate to Prashant's drive was the rich, lit street, and the pouring moonlight and all the empty outdoors.

'All right,' I said. 'But let's wait outside.'

5

So FAR, I was simply going along with Prashant's programme, still uncertain of my role in it. But his correspondence with Ali Khan had impressed me. Cutting through celebrity to reach the individual is a difficult mental feat and I thought he had managed well. The letters between the two figured in my mind as part of the slow stitching together of thought into actuality – which, I knew, was how Things Got Done. Khan's real-life presence was a heady prospect too, so much so that I did not yet believe it would happen. I had the sense that Prashant was earnest enough to warrant my indulgence, but how far was he going to go? I didn't know.

And at that moment, I didn't care. My immediate idea was mundane and well within grasp. I wanted something to eat.

Outside his gate, Prashant and I looked down the deserted lane, waiting for our visitor. We didn't have to wait long; the splash of a headlight announced itself against a far house, and then the vehicle turned into view. My eyes were momentarily dazzled. When I could see again I saw a sleek Lancer, gliding through the blackness.

A door slammed and Sheila got out of the car. Its engine stayed humming.

With the added poise that comes from being already at the scene, I studied her calmly. She stood on the passenger's side of the car and waved us towards her.

'Aren't you coming in?' Prashant took a step forward.

'Gitanjali's here,' she answered gaily.

The car was still going and two of my old neuroses were coming over me: I hated to keep anybody waiting and I hated to think of an engine running down.

'We'll go to Illusions,' she promised. 'Don't say maybe.'

That was a nice Italian restaurant in a market in Greater Kailash I. It made my decision for me, and I started forward at about the same time as Prashant.

Gitanjali was in the backseat. The two of us shoved in beside her and I thought I saw her set her face when she saw I'd got in first.

Sheila stayed outside until everybody had settled down. Then she leaned into the seat next to the driver. Her legs stretched out lazily and her elbow balanced against the armrest. She tilted her head sideways and smoothed a lock of her hair. She wasn't bored, just very practised.

I caught a familiar face in the rear-view mirror. Madhav's half-closed eyes saw through me and beyond, into the empty street. He started to back the car up for a three-point turn all the way around.

I looked at Prashant. I expected a comment, or a frown, or some show of disconcertment. But he didn't catch my eye. He was looking patiently into his lap, and it occurred to me that perhaps this spur of the moment jaunt was only the usual. Perhaps it was always the case, that everybody was invited.

Suddenly Prashant's face turned up to mine. His spectacles, which had fallen a little way off his nose, reasserted themselves.

'Don't worry, I'll drop you home.'

My neck snapped back as the car pushed off from a standstill.

'You drive too fast,' Gitanjali admonished.

We drove fast all the way to the marketplace. Madhav could do things with the steering that I hated myself for not being able to condescend. He parked the Lancer in a spot I would have thought too difficult for my Maruti.

As we emerged into the night, Sheila turned to me, beaming.

'Don't you love going out at the end of the day?'

I murmured my assent, but I knew she wasn't listening. Her proud and constant smile was meant for the world, not me.

'It's like the sweet at the end of a meal,' she said.

It was a nice night all right. There was rain in the air above – the first rains of the season, perhaps – and below, trapped in the razzle-dazzle of many bright hoardings, the pavements shone beneath our shoes. Our group pitched forward towards the canopy of the Italian place. We divided in several telling ways. Sheila walked in front with a long skirt dancing about her shapely legs. She had Prashant and Madhav on either side of her and Gitanjali a little distance behind – closer to me than to the others, and trying, I thought, to change that.

I heard a few snatches of the conversation up ahead. Prashant and Sheila had their heads close together – Madhav was listening in, not taking part.

'You know, you've got a name like a cat,' Prashant was saying snugly.

'What do you mean?'

'Sheila. It sounds so . . . curled up, and . . . comfortable.'

'Oh, it's not the name. It's just me.'

'Are you comfortable? Right now?'

'I was, in the car.'

Their voices drifted away as they hurried along. Suddenly, I felt too much of a straggler.

'Do you do much theatre – Gitanjali?' I called out loudly.

Unwillingly, the girl slowed her pace.

'No – there was one time in Chennai, that's all.'

'So you're all a bunch of out-of-work actors?'

'I've got training in design too,' she frowned. 'That's probably more my thing, to be honest.'

'It's a sort of classic type,' I went on earnestly. 'You know – the out-of-work actor. It's something literary.'

I saw a spasm of confusion pass across her features, and I thought for a moment she was going to set me down as just another oddball. Then suddenly she pushed her hair back and her face smoothened.

'All right,' she said. 'I'm not one though.'

I looked at the dark, grave girl and tried to think of something agreeable to say. Nothing came to mind and so I flung my gaze about, searching for a prop. Ahead of us, far above the restaurant doors, loomed a billboard for the latest Bollywood movie. It was a commercial disaster, that the critics had panned, but my opinion of it was not the general opinion.

'Have you seen that one?' I said. 'I liked it!'

Gitanjali raised her head politely. 'I've seen it.'

'People say it's boring, but doesn't it have these wonderful moments?'

'Uh-huh.'

'Like at the reunion of the long-lost brothers, when the first thing the elder one says to the younger is: "That's my shirt you're wearing." In that accusing tone. You know – just small things, but so true!'

Dimly, I was aware I was getting carried away. But Gitanjali's gaze hadn't wavered from my eyes, and with a slow, settling surprise I saw that she really was paying attention. She really was listening. I persevered excitedly.

'It's like — I sometimes feel like when somebody says one nice thing — just *one* truly simple, nice thing — it makes up for everything. For that one thing I want to forgive them all the rest.'

Breathlessly, I finished, and then I waited for her inevitable bemusement to show. She couldn't have understood; I had hardly been clear.

Instead, she nodded.

'I know . . . little things go a long way.'

The way she said it, it seemed the most obvious truth in the world. That made me smart, because it hadn't seemed so obvious to me, and for a moment, despite her agreement, I felt like protesting. I didn't, though. Within me, there tossed a reluctant respect, a confused admiration.

We walked together in silence, the rest of the way into the restaurant.

Illusions knew better than to style itself as particularly authentic. It had a bright, cheerful, bustling interior. It catered to my crowd, which cared for plushness and pasta, but not for protocol. I sat straight down when we found a table, because I wanted to get at the menu. Prashant and Sheila were hovering above me, but it was Madhav who tapped my shoulder.

'There aren't enough chairs,' he said distinctly, 'for all of us to sit.'

'Oh,' I leaped to my feet, burning red. 'I'll get another.'

I looked around. The room was packed, but a waiter was approaching. He understood from six feet away and moved delicately to a table in the corner, that was surrounded by three chairs with only one occupant.

He was about our age, and apparently lost in thought. The waiter bent to say something to him, which he fully ignored – then a little louder, which he seemed to catch – and nod at. Our table was pointed out to him and he shifted his chair around to stare. at us. He was wearing a dark-blue shirt that looked familiar; he had crisp, neat hair and large eyes and long lashes –

My eyebrows darted up of their own accord.

'Animesh!'

'It is Animesh,' Prashant said thoughtfully. 'What in the world . . .'

I was surprised to find how glad I was to see him. Of course, I was doubly surprised to see him in the first place.

'What are you doing here?'

He came towards us unselfconsciously.

'Why?' he answered casually. 'Isn't this a public place?'

'Don't be a fool, Animesh,' I said with unnecessary vehemence. He reacted good-humouredly.

'It's actually my favourite restaurant.'

'But it's so far away – from Patparganj,' I objected.

'All the same, it's my favourite.'

'I thought you wanted to work.'

'I am working.'

'Stop talking,' Sheila interrupted. 'And come join us. The more, the merrier.'

Her voice was urgent, tense, with a certain subdued excitement. For a few seconds then, I found myself staring at her. I wasn't insensitive to her clear, bright face, and the controlled *joie de vivre* that seemed to shoot out of her brilliant and narrow eyes. Sheila wasn't my type of girl – I sensed that immediately. Very likely she was too complicated for me. But she was an authentic type. Her whole manner radiated a wholesome niceness, that hinted at a subliminal passion, that was tantalisingly exclusive.

Before dinner, nobody spoke about Prashant's movie, and during dinner, nobody spoke at all. Afterwards, Prashant cleared his throat.

'We've got some things to clear up – for the cast.'

Next to me I heard Gitanjali draw a patient breath.

'These are the substantial roles,' he continued, businesslike. 'Ali Khan, his father, his coach in school, his wife, the bookmaker in Barbados, the Imam in Delhi, the president of the National Flag Association, two journalists and one match referee. The rest are minor parts, mostly teammates and opposing teams.'

'I guess we can get that many people?' Prashant looked at Madhav.

Madhav inclined his head thoughtfully to his right.

'We can,' he said, 'provided they're interested.'

'There's the bunch of you at least.'

'Provided we're interested.'

'Who's going to play Ali?' Sheila asked suddenly.

After a few seconds' silence Prashant answered.

'I thought – Vivek.'

I recalled to myself the blanching boy from the night at Calabria.

'Vivek?' Gitanjali was wincing. 'He's not –'

'He's a very good actor,' Prashant said quietly. 'I've seen him perform.'

'I suggest Roshan,' Sheila said flatly. 'He *looks* the part. And he's the only one who can actually bat for real. He just needs to be himself, and he'll seem realistic.'

It sounded well-meant advice, the way she had said it. It didn't warrant, to my mind, Prashant's forceful response.

'That's totally wrong,' he shook his head firmly. 'That's a totally wrong way of casting.'

Sheila bristled gracefully. Prashant continued.

'You put people in a movie so that they can act, and be somebody else. You don't put them in a movie so that they can be themselves. Then it's not art at all – it's just a gimmick. I know it's fashionable and it has a kind of infantile appeal – like any gimmick. But I'd rather have a guy who looks nothing like Ali Khan and understands what Ali Khan represents, than somebody who's the spitting image and a complete idiot.'

This roused Madhav briefly from his usual impeccable state.

'That's not the way Tarantino does it. Or Marlon Brando. Or –'

'I don't care. I don't want to make their mistakes.'

'As you say, Mr Director Artist,' Sheila said evenly.

Prashant stared moodily around the table. I sensed he wasn't winning the confidence of his putative crew.

'Look, Roshan isn't fit for any role except an extra's. I'm sure you guys agree with me,' he added improbably.

Nobody objected volubly, although Madhav had closed his eyes in a resigned way. Then Gitanjali said:

'Prashant, the audience won't care whether the person on screen is acting, so long as he looks right. Suppose someone big-built like Roshan would convince them more easily than Vivek? What then?'

'Yes,' Prashant agreed suddenly. 'The audience wouldn't care, but I would, and I have to think of myself first. I want to be able to direct an actor, not push around a prop. I want to – I should stop saying I,' he broke off with a laugh.

Madhav looked at him derisively.

'Yes, you should.'

Look,' Prashant resumed, 'it wouldn't be fair to Roshan either, to use him for what he can't help, rather than what he can do.'

'It'll be a good role for him,' Sheila insisted.

'Why're you so keen on him anyway?' he turned on her, jovially; unexpectedly. 'I thought he was just "a friend of Madhav's".'

Her features froze. They looked at each other; he with his questioning, playful eyes that could never sustain any real length of anger; she with a stony, judgmental gaze that was all the more disturbing for the tenderness that had gone before. In a staring match between these two there could only ever be one winner.

Gitanjali sighed a second time.

'Listen, Prashant,' she said in a kindly voice. 'Are you really going to make this movie? I mean, I, for one, have no problem with these decisions, but we'll all have to put other things aside for it, and I just hope you . . . know what you're doing.'

Prashant sought me out then. He bestowed upon me a special, understanding smile, as though he and I were in on a secret joke and it was time, at last, to share it.

'I certainly do know.' He almost winked at her.

'We'll send it around to the film festivals,' his voice was growing eager. 'It won't be just any old amateur movie. It's going to create a splash.'

'Who'd you know?' Madhav asked wisely.

'It'll create a splash on its own strength,' Prashant maintained.

'Plus, there's my aunt,' he admitted. 'She'll push it like crazy.'

Madhav half-swivelled from where he was sitting. He had on an amused expression, but there was something mean-spirited behind the amusement.

'Sheila keeps telling me what an independent, self-reliant soul you are. Doesn't it sting to stoop to *sifarish*?'

Sheila half-opened her mouth to protest the transferred compliment, but Prashant was looking at Madhav.

'I don't mind using my advantages,' he answered calmly. 'I don't believe in pushing my back up against a wall, just for the sake of appearances. If I have support, I use it.'

'Is that why you still live with your parents?'

'That's not – yes.'

'Still tied to Mamma's apron strings?'

Prashant smiled a tense, controlled smile. The barb had stung, but he was swallowing the hurt.

Madhav smirked.

'Be careful. You'll always need to eat. You may not always have the silver spoon.'

The waiter came to clear the table. Amid the clatter of plates and glasses, I felt the mood change. The aftermath of a good dinner was really too pleasant an occasion for hostile talk.

Prashant sensed this too.

'Vaibhav, tell them about the letters. They don't know yet.'

I told them. Gitanjali was the most visibly struck by the news, but it was striking anyhow.

'He's really coming down? Wow! How old is he now?'

'Forty-four,' said Prashant.

'You didn't need his permission,' Madhav pointed out, 'to make this movie. He might hamper our . . .'

'Our objectivity? I'm not worried about that.'

'We can use him,' Prashant went on, sensing the threat and seizing the moment, 'for interviews, and maybe some of the later scenes. We'll make it nice and simple. It'll be simple shots, and smart editing. For example — here's an idea I had.

'There'll be shots of Ali playing cricket with his school friends in some *maidan* — there's one not far from my house that'll do fine. We'll have the camera trained on the length of the pitch and show the shot; then we zoom it further into his face. He'll be smiling back at the bowler — all brash and chatty. Then we take the footage of an international game ten years later, and he'll be playing the exact same shots — just like in his schooldays. But when the camera zooms in, there isn't the ghost of a smile.

'We'll intersperse the school day shots with the TV footage. It'll go to show the things that don't change when a player matures — and the things that do. What do you think?'

His manner was the opposite of desperate. He held our attention in a matter-of-fact way — just a professional talking things over. Everyone exchanged glances — I looked at Animesh. The way the conversation had panned out, it was practically impossible to resist the conclusion. Prashant hurried to it.

'Is Monday a good day to start? Can you guys check with Vivek and Preeti and the others?'

'We can check,' said Madhav slowly. Sheila waved down the waiter, and soon it was time to fuss over the bill.

Afterwards, when we went outside, I found myself shivering. An unseasonably cold wind had struck up. A drop of water struck the bridge of my nose. It was starting to rain.

Animesh and Prashant were next to me. The others had retreated beneath the canopy of a nearby bookshop. I saw Sheila take a box of Classic Milds out of her handbag – I recognised the label from my college days – and after that, the three of them shared a communal sixty seconds of lighted matches and jutting cigarettes.

The three of us stayed out in the drizzle. We made our way to the parking.

Between the marketplace and the rows of cars, we stepped across a pavement upon which an impromptu human settlement had established itself. I hadn't noticed it when we arrived – perhaps it hadn't been there – but it was hard to miss at the moment. A woman with long filthy hair and a colourless sari was stirring a greyish liquid in a saucepan over a flame. All the while, she was barking instructions to a naked infant sucking his thumb – whether from habit or from hunger was an open question. I averted my eyes because it wasn't a pleasant sight.

Not ten metres away, a Mercedes turned in from the road and almost ran me down. It flicked on to high beam and a steady horn blared, until a scraggly parking attendant had hobbled his way across. That wasn't a pleasant sight either.

Amid these contrasting hostilities, we waited near the parked Lancer, with the rain dripping off our hair.

'I think Gitanjali likes you.'

'What?'

Animesh had said it. He was nodding wisely to himself. Prashant was smiling too. I thought of making some counter-insinuation about Sheila but then I decided to let it pass. I didn't know enough of the relations between them.

'So, you've got your actors,' I congratulated Prashant instead. 'That's a big step. Good luck for the movie.'

'Thanks,' he replied, 'I couldn't have convinced them if you hadn't been there.'

'I didn't do a thing.'

'Yes you did. When I tell them something they're sceptical. When you tell them they're interested. These are film and drama school graduates,' he explained. 'It's hard for them to stomach taking orders from an outsider. I know I'm going to have trouble with them through the course of this thing — it'll keep bubbling up — and when it does I need someone who can smooth things over.'

After a moment he said:

'I hope you don't think I'm patronising you.'

Should I have thought that? I don't know. My opinion of Prashant was still unformed. Instinctively, I felt he was too grandiose — surely, sooner or later, he was bound to trip up — and yet, I couldn't dismiss him as just another small-minded go-getter. The self-promoters of this world don't wait on other people, and Prashant was looking at me now, waiting for my reply.

Eventually, as I tended to, I reserved my judgment on the real question, and let a certain reckless impulse make my decision for me. What did it matter, I told myself. It was no big deal anyway.

'Weekends,' I promised. 'I'll come to where you're shooting on weekends. And we can be in touch otherwise too.'

'Let us know when Ali Khan arrives,' Animesh interjected smugly. 'I've never seen a real-life hero in the flesh.'

So there was an 'us'. Prashant didn't protest, and I was a good deal happier because it seemed to me only fair that Animesh stay involved, given how enthusiastically he had brought us together. Animesh may not be any good in a pinch, I thought to myself, but he wouldn't need to be. The movie was going to be just a harmless diversion.

Looking back at it now, I couldn't have been more wrong on every count.

6

MEANWHILE, I HAD other things to think about. The next three weeks went by, and Prashant didn't call. In that time, I almost forgot about his movie. The work-a-day routine was pulling me under, and I spent my days barely aware of how I was feeling – until my mother asked and I found myself annoyed, and Anita asked and I found myself cloying.

In those days, the very elements heightened my moodiness. The change of season was imminent, and the transition was not smooth. Like a bucking, rearing horse, protesting at being manoeuvred, the weather could not be predicted. The days would start out muggy; the skies would turn overcast, the long-expected rains would not come, the evenings would be cool. In the evenings, at least, I felt the urge to be social, but since I had such few friends in the city, I spent them all on the Internet instead, people-watching. Already, my classmates were spread across the globe, and Facebook was flooded with photos from places a long way from Patparganj. But it wasn't what I'd never had that made me ache with self-pity. It was what I'd had and lost. It was the college photos, the classrooms, the corridors, the ground outside the boys' hostel. They were all lovelier in the remembrance than they had been at the time – and perhaps that was the trick I was missing. Still, I would raise my eyes from those memories to the four walls of my room, and wonder why life had cheated me.

On one such evening, I searched out the Facebook profiles of the drama school crowd. I saw that Sheila hadn't specified her 'relationship status'— which didn't surprise me. Then I went back to Anita's profile and saw that she hadn't either — which did. I also saw that it was her birthday in two days' time. I had clean forgotten, for the first time in four years.

She liked gifts, and I had bought her something every year. So, that same evening, I made the trip across the river to a confectionery store I knew, at a well-heeled market in the heart of South Delhi.

By the time I had finished there, it was twilight. In the shops and on the streets, the lights were glowing hardily, while the sun faded and the air grew still and burnished. I stood beside my Maruti, watching the cars turning into the parking, with their headlights blazing fiercely. Soon, it would be dark, and the market crowded with shoppers and the roads clogged with traffic. At such times of transition, I had felt, in the past, a certain breathless enthusiasm, waiting to be swept up into the bustle of the night, but on this evening my mood was melancholy. Watching the impersonal march of the world, I felt small and vulnerable. I wished that it would stop. And that was when I saw Gitanjali.

She was walking down the pavement in front of the shops, clutching her bags unassisted. My voice emerged with a jerk.

'Hey!'

'Oh hi!'

'What are you doing here?' we asked in unison.

I told her. 'I was about to leave,' I explained.

'Me too.'

But in the anonymous, menacing swirl of people, Gitanjali's presence seemed to me a sign — and you don't turn your back on serendipity. I felt the evening air pressing around me, close and confidential. I wanted to talk.

'Listen,' I said. 'If you're not in a hurry, how about we have some coffee?'

'Okay,' she agreed.

'Great.' I moved to help her with her bags, but my hands were trembling and I took them clumsily. The impulsiveness of the encounter, foreign to my nature, had sent nervous energy coursing through me. In my eagerness I chided her. 'Vegetables! How plebeian.'

'Fruits too,' she corrected demurely. 'You get some nice things here. I don't live far, you know.'

Later, when we were indoors, my adrenaline settled and steadied me. My mind felt calm and alert.

That evening, conversation came easy. The coincidence of our meeting had lent it a peculiar intimacy. I had the strange sense that Fate was on my side, that it had spiralled me to a place where the usual rules didn't apply, and I could say anything to her and it wouldn't be remiss. Sitting in the warm, well-lit cafe, I confessed candidly.

'The first couple of times I met you, Gitanjali — I was afraid you thought me a real bore!'

'It's just how I look,' she sighed. 'It's my expressions. I look too serious.'

'No you don't,' I disagreed gallantly. 'Not too serious — just more than most girls.'

'I ought to look happy-go-lucky,' she mused. 'You know — carefree, tripping down the road with a small and strappy handbag. I don't even like handbags.'

'Oh, I know that type,' I said hotly. 'They're all very well to begin with, they sweep you off your feet, and then later –' Here I paused, astonished, because I realised I had in mind Anita.

But it wasn't long afterwards that the conversation turned to my gift-wrapped present. Gitanjali seemed happy to listen, and I found myself talking about Anita freely and without reserve.

'I was crazy about her,' I confessed. 'Before I met her, I never really thought it was true: the things they say about – about love. The poets and the writers and all that. I never really thought much about it. But when I met her I knew, and I didn't just know – I *felt* – like nothing I'd felt before. Stop grinning!'

'You're sweet.'

I blushed awkwardly. I was surprising myself, with my openness. 'Well – anyway that was a long time ago. Nowadays it seems pretty different.'

'Long distance is tough,' Gitanjali murmured.

I shook my head. 'It's not the distance. The distance is probably what's keeping us together.'

Then I shaped to shrug my shoulders and click my tongue and change the subject, because even to my own ears I was sounding cryptic. But Gitanjali was nodding; her sympathy was encouraging, and I went on talking.

'We liked the pursuit,' I explained. 'That's what we liked. Even when we were a couple, we always had this sense of mutual longing, and I was always chasing and Anita was always leading, and we were both happy. And now I get the feeling she's gotten tired. Now, when I talk to her on the phone, she's . . . clinging. We both are,' I admitted. 'But I, at least, don't know how to handle it.'

'Go on.'

'For example, she keeps asking me to "say something nice".
So I say: "I got a raise", or "it rained last night" or "tomorrow is
a holiday" – and then at the other end, I hear this disappointed
silence.'

At that, Gitanjali laughed. Her dark eyes, shining suddenly,
fixed me with a warm and maternal tenderness. Her voice bore
a cheerful admonition.

'Say something nice,' she told me, 'doesn't mean say *anything*
nice. It means say something nice about *me*. It means – give
me a compliment.'

'Why doesn't Anita just say that then? Why doesn't she
just say – give me a compliment?'

'If she had to say that, she'd feel like crying.'

'What?' I protested. 'Why? Explain. I don't understand.'

'I can't explain,' Gitanjali answered frankly. 'You're expected
to understand.'

For a moment I was silent, and confused.

'But,' I started again, 'what if I can't think of a
compliment?'

'Then,' she said, 'if you can't say something nice, don't say
anything at all.'

Her rich and patient voice seemed to breathe new life into
these hoary old platitudes. I sat back, mulling over her words. In
the meantime, a waiter approached and we ordered two coffees
and a cheesecake to share. When he left, I smiled.

'This is so lovey-dovey, isn't it?'

I saw Gitanjali's eyes, suddenly panicked, leaving mine.

'The time after you order,' I explained hurriedly. 'Just after
you order is a comfy feeling.'

'Oh . . . that'. She relaxed visibly. 'Yes, it is.'

We ate and drank in a peaceable quiet. Within me, the gloominess of an hour ago had disappeared. I watched Gitanjali slicing the pastry with a frowning concentration, and a thrill ran up my spine. She was someone new, with powers and perceptions unknown to me. An interesting stranger has infinite promise, and in that moment, the girl across the table appeared to me a kind of oracle. With a burst of eagerness, I sought her opinion on another, troublesome subject.

'What do you think of Prashant?'

'We're friends. Family friends, you know. My parents know his parents since before we were born, so . . .'

'Why,' she added casually. 'What do *you* think of him?'

'I don't know,' I admitted at once. 'I didn't know him much in college – and now I'm not sure I like him.'

As she waited, I struggled to explain myself.

'Prashant is just so . . . he's so confident. He's got such strong opinions about what's right and wrong, and what's the proper way of doing things – like the other day, when we were talking about the movie.'

'Uh-huh,' Gitanjali nodded. Her serious eyes were regarding me closely.

'And . . .' My mouth hung open; my right hand stayed poised in mid-air, while I searched for the words, 'I know I'm not like that. I'm not so sure of myself. I don't know what I want from life or even who I *am*. When I hear him holding forth, it just bothers me – to be honest, it makes me feel inferior. You know what I mean?'

'Yes.'

'You've felt inferior too?'

'No!' she laughed.

I must have looked puzzled, because she took it upon herself to explain.

'Partly it's Prashant's fault,' she said, 'because he is sometimes too opinionated. But mostly it's your ego.'

'My ego?' I was astonished. My own view was that I didn't have enough of an ego.

'You're being too macho. Conversation isn't a competition. When Prashant gets on one of his pet topics, what I do is, I *listen*, because he is usually interesting, and if I agree I agree and if I disagree I disagree. Instead of feeling sidelined, try and admire the fact that he doesn't mollycoddle his friends. He isn't scared to speak his mind to them.'

'But his manner – those airs – don't they get to you?'

'Male plumage,' Gitanjali replied drily. 'We've learned to look beyond that. Maybe it's easier for a girl.'

I was struck by this. 'Well I'm a boy,' I pointed out. 'So what's a boy to do – faced with all that . . . plumage?'

'Get in touch,' she said, 'with your feminine side. Shall I tell you one sweet thing about Prashant?'

I waited.

'He's always able to say something nice.'

When we left the cafe the sky was dark, and the market bright and bustling. Gitanjali's car was parked behind a stall selling paperbacks and magazines and newspapers. For a little while we browsed distantly – and I winced as usual at the headlines. In Bihar, a college lecturer had had acid thrown at him for preaching the Bible. In Punjab, there had been yet another 'honour killing'.

Gitanjali looked at her watch.

'I should go now. Here – I'll take those – thanks.'

With the shopping bags weighing her down again, she looked small and burdened, and suddenly vulnerable. I stepped forward impulsively.

'Will you be okay — driving back?'

'I should be. I've been chased by drunkards a couple of times, but at this hour it'll be fine.'

'You've been chased?'

'More than once,' Gitanjali nodded, 'but not so early. Closer to midnight. That's why my father obsesses so much, and now, when I'm out late, I always get someone to follow me home. More for his sake than mine, but it's true,' she shrugged. 'Delhi's unsafe.'

'Delhi's unsafe,' I echoed automatically. 'Yeah — but I didn't know these things actually — I mean I know they happen, but I didn't know —'

'That they happen to people,' Gitanjali smiled. 'Of course they do. This is nothing — I've had a lot — staring, pinching — the whole nine yards.'

'The whole nine yards . . .'

'Not the *whole* nine yards!' her eyes widened quickly. 'But it's pretty bad.'

Listening to Gitanjali's matter-of-fact talk, I felt a hot flush of embarrassment.

'I always thought,' my voice dropped apologetically, 'that women exaggerated this stuff.'

'You must have been speaking to the wrong women. Well — I'll see you later, Vaibhav. It was nice running into you.'

As she turned to go, I murmured something that was inaudible even to myself. She looked back with her eyebrows raised politely. I summoned up my courage.

'Why don't you give me your phone number?'

'Because I don't want you stalking me.'

'What? Hey –'

Then I saw that she was laughing. I shook my head in mock-exasperation, but when the formalities were over and Gitanjali's car had pulled away, I was still smiling.

In the aftermath of our meeting, the night felt cheerful and vivid with possibility. I lingered awhile, letting my gaze wander as it pleased. Ahead of me, a crowd had gathered outside a popular Punjabi restaurant whose doors flapped continually with the traffic of its patrons. From the pub alongside, I saw the smokers emerging anxiously for their fix, and a paan-wallah, strategically positioned, dispensing the cigarettes. Meanwhile, all the while, the cars were bearing down in single file – now the Honda at the head of the queue stopped to honk at a sweeper at work who lumbered back and forth, bear-like and oblivious. The honking grew louder and more strident, and I grimaced and looked away.

I was thinking of Prashant. Gitanjali's words of approval had heightened my interest in him, fashioned him in my mind as someone compelling. A sudden, irrational fear gripped me – a powerful premonition that if I lost touch with Prashant, I would miss something important. I wondered to myself what had become of his movie.

～

A few days later, I found out. I was reading the morning papers in my office. The city pages were bursting as usual with violence and corruption, but there were three column inches of something different.

'Retired Cricket Star Back in City for Shooting of Bio-Pic.'

Reading the report, you would have thought that Prashant's film was the most anticipated event in Indian moviedom. Immediately, I picked up my phone.

His disembodied voice was as excited as I'd ever heard it.

'Vaibhav! Did you read the paper?'

'Yes, just now. That's why I'm calling.'

'Isn't it great?'

'You mean he's here? Have you started shooting?'

'Just a few shots. So far, so good.'

'And I've met him,' Prashant added proudly. 'He likes the script.'

'When are you working next?'

'The coming Saturday – at noon – there's a sequence I can do close to my house. Can you come?'

'Sure.'

'Great. Oh, and one more thing,' he said.

'Let's try to keep this low profile, okay? I didn't think I'd need to say this, but my aunt has got a little carried away with the coverage. I don't want the whole city thinking about our film. Khan shouldn't be mobbed every time we step out.'

That evening, when I returned home to the apartment, I saw from the staircase that the front door was ajar. I heard a familiar voice carrying all the way outside.

Inside our living room, Animesh was sitting on top of the sofa's backrest with his feet on the cushions. He had an open newspaper balanced clumsily on his knees. He was reading out aloud, to an audience of two.

On a chair in front of the sofa was Kisle, with his chin in his palms and his eyes fixed on Animesh. Arjun, whom I'd never before seen staying still for two minutes together, was coming close now. To keep up appearances he was half-sitting, half-lying down on a small *takhat* we'd had put in a month previously, with half his overt attention on the television screen. But you could tell from the crease on his forehead and the slight cock of his head that he was listening too.

'"And the shooting for this unique tribute to a much-misunderstood man is already underway,"' Animesh finished triumphantly.

'I'm part of the movie crew, you know,' he looked around, smirking.

'So is he,' he waved graciously, as I walked into the room.

'Oh really?' Arjun stared at me appraisingly. 'Not bad, dude. You guys acting?'

'We're part of the production,' Animesh answered blandly. 'We're the brains behind the whole thing.'

'Animesh,' I said edgily, 'can I talk to you for a second?'

Kisle turned in my direction. On the rare occasion that he voiced an opinion, he did it forcefully.

'Ali Khan was useless.'

'Don't be silly,' I retorted.

'He couldn't baa,' he continued, in the peculiar accented English that he'd picked up from Star World. 'Shashikanth Choudhury was way be'er.'

'No he was not!'

'And way be'er looking,' Kisle added, as though it followed naturally. 'Ali Khan was an arrogant guy who never won us any matches.'

Unconsciously, against my better judgment, in spite of my planned restraint, I was drawn into an argument. Soon the three of us were prattling away, with Arjun providing the occasional smarmy interjection. His conceit was that he didn't care for cricket anyway. Finally, the quarrel broke up, and I was able to get a private word with Animesh.

'What are you doing?' I demanded.

He looked immediately injured.

'I was just reading them the paper. Haven't you read it?'

'We've all read it. Prashant asked us to keep a low profile on this.'

'He should make up his mind.'

~

Nor, in the days that followed, did Prashant's aunt stay her invisible hand. Come Saturday, I read another enthusiastic piece in the arts supplement of *The Hindu*, recalling and extolling Ali Khan's 'defiance of religion' -- that, anyhow, was the author's interpretation.

It was close to twelve o'clock when Animesh and I reached New Friends Colony. The tall houses looked different in the day, plainer and less opulent, perhaps because the beating sunshine allowed for no glitter. I saw Prashant's Maruti standing outside his gate, as before, and the three fine cars inside as before. When we rang the bell, the inconspicuous man who had brought me the orange juice emerged into the driveway and pointed us to the park.

By the standards of my own neighbourhood *maidan*, it was a neatly kept affair. There was more grass on the ground than dust. A water sprinkler worked quietly in a corner. The benches did not look treacherous. In the evenings, I imagined, the place filled with joggers and furtive couples. But at this time of day, it was deserted -- save only for the 'crew'.

They were not an inspiring sight. At the back of my mind, I think I had had a pretty fixed notion of bright lights mounted on cranes, and expertly decorated sets. Instead, there was a camera perched on a tripod and Prashant waving his arms about at a group of milling figures.

All the same, he looked happy with what was happening.

'I'm just taking a few close-up shots,' he explained to me. 'It's a fight Ali got into in the twelfth standard, where the other boy kept calling him a pig and he was amused because he thought it was quite a decorous word. He didn't realise it was supposed to hurt him. That's how vague his religious identity was.'

'How do you know this?'

'He told me. Just a sec.'

He moved over to talk to Vivek. I looked around, squinting in the sunlight. Animesh was gazing about him with a beatific smile, and in the group of other faces, I recognised Madhav. There weren't any girls.

'Hey you!'

A shadow fell over me. Roshan was advancing.

'Did you decide who plays who?' he demanded.

I grimaced. 'Excuse me?'

'I don't have to do this, you know,' he said bitterly. 'I've got a lakh a month waiting for me — *a lakh a month*, just waiting for me! I don't have to waste my time on any two-bit movie!'

I wanted to say congratulations, but he was too big and menacing. He had on a leer, which brought out all the bully in him.

'I'm only doing this for kicks. Tell Prashant not to get too big for his boots.'

'Why don't you tell him yourself?'

'Because he said *you* were in charge of all grievances.'

While I wondered at such an obedient rebellion, he continued venting his ire.

'Have you ever met anyone so full of himself?'

It wasn't a bad question really.

'Prashant's problem,' Roshan growled, 'is he doesn't see what a loser he really is. He's good at a few things and he lives in his own world which he's the king of – and he doesn't know the ABC of real life. You know why he resents me so much?'

'I don't know. Do you know where Ali Khan is?'

'Because for all his supposed smartness he still can't get any.'

Roshan left me – and then I spotted him. Several metres to the right of the camera, almost hidden by the trunk of a tree, was a man sitting on a bench. He was wearing a loose white shirt and plain brown trousers, and if I'd passed him on the street, I wouldn't have given him a second look. But he was in the right place, at the right time.

'Animesh,' I said tensely. 'Look – is that Ali Khan?'

Animesh looked. 'Yes.'

'He seems. . .'

He seemed old. Gone was the lithe frame, the Tom Cruise cheeks, the Bret Hart hair. His face had filled out; his eyes had slanted in. I thought he looked tired from all the standing around.

The session's shooting took longer than I had expected. The scene was not complicated but Prashant insisted, I suppose reasonably, that nobody would come back later if he missed an angle. When the shoot was finally over, the crew began to leave the park, and it was then that we were introduced to Ali Khan.

I think it was the sheer ordinariness of that meeting which made it so surreal. The man in the white shirt nodded gravely at Animesh and me in turn but we were both too tongue-tied –

at least, I was – to produce any memorable greeting. It was difficult to speak to Ali Khan without seeing yourself speaking to him – under open skies in a public park on an occasion that was no occasion. Oddly, it made me think of the first time I had telephoned Anita, and realised that 'Hello' worked just as well with her as it did with every other mortal.

Prashant himself suffered from no such uneasiness. I was struck by how fluently he carried on the conversation – this same boy whom Mrs Ramdass had run into the ground. He even got us all to exchange telephone numbers.

'Are you two also actors?' asked Khan.

His voice was deep, but mellow. He spoke his words slowly, as though he knew from experience that there was always time to say everything that you wanted.

'Not actors – we're –

'They're just here for autographs,' Prashant laughed. 'I hope they don't bother you.'

'I'd be delighted. Nobody's asked me for an autograph in years.'

'They will after this.'

Khan smiled. It came and went in the flicker of an eye, but for that instant it was the old, television smile – the smile that was also a challenge.

'You have great expectations,' he said.

'I've got a great story,' said Prashant.

'You're twenty-four,' Ali Khan set his face, with grim humour. 'You don't know yet that nothing happens the way you imagine. Not one thing. I didn't either, when I was your age, but if you're the same at forty as you are at twenty, then you've wasted twenty years of your life.'

Prashant smiled absently. I had been listening closely to what Khan had said, but I didn't think Prashant had really heard a word.

'Come see today's footage,' he offered. 'This is the advantage of video.'

I remember it was as we gathered around the camera, that a raised voice shattered the still noon air.

'What's going on here?'

On the other side of the railing, on the far side of the park, five men stood watching us. They were young men, probably not much older than me. A sixth, more middle-aged figure, was making his way inside, spurning the zigzag entrance for the direct leap across. He had a thick, ugly moustache that was prominent even from a distance.

As an abstract type, these men were familiar; as personal experience they were not. I looked at the greased hair, the cruel lips, the skin-tight black jeans. I thought of the headlines on the city page every day – a brawl here, a murder there – gangs that dealt in petty violence.

My eyes went racing about the park. The sun shone from end to end, on unpopulated earth.

However, there were still the four of us. And it was broad daylight. So I breathed relatively easily, with only a muffled heartbeat sounding out my tension.

'What's going on here?' the stranger repeated.

He wasn't far away now. He had his hands in the pockets of his jacket, which worried me. His feet were splayed a little way apart, and he didn't bridge the ten metres that still separated us. In the background, I saw the other five beginning slowly to move.

Prashant stepped forward. He had on a dutiful, tolerant expression, as though some slightly amusing chore remained to be completed.

'We're just talking. We were shooting a movie before.'

'Do you have permission for a movie?'

'What?'

'This is a government park. You can't do commercial business here without permission. Have you got permission?'

The five were coming up slowly. They were of varying shapes and sizes, but they all wore the same scruffy bad taste with the same unabashedness. I watched one of them swivel his head and spit emphatically into the ground. On their faces was the cheap superiority that those who are poor and have nothing to lose feel for those who are well-to-do, and careworn.

'Hey,' Animesh piped up, 'Prashant, just ignore them. Just –'

Prashant told him with a gesture to shut up. The sun was bright; his house was next door; it was not possible that anybody could be an enemy.

'I didn't know I needed permission,' he said in a contrite tone. 'I'll check up about it.'

'You do that,' the other man said encouragingly. 'I'll keep the camera till then.'

My stomach tightened. Dimly, I noticed heads nodding in the direction of Ali Khan and the men talking to each other in low tones. 'Is that really him?' I supposed, was the gist of their discussion.

Meanwhile, Prashant's manner had altered a hundred and eighty degrees. The casual threat to his camera had caused him to abandon sweetness altogether.

'Who are you anyway?' he demanded. 'I don't have to tell you anything. Get out of here!'

He added a few mild expletives. In his speech, Prashant had adopted the language and the accent of the men he was berating. His customary even tones were trying hard to be uncouth, and he was stumbling over Hindi words that were unfamiliar to him, and very familiar to them.

'What did you say?'

'I said, who do you think you are?'

The leader of the pack pulled out a knife from within his jacket. He let the sunlight glint off the serrated blade, and then put it back inside. He stared at Prashant with an insolent and animal challenge. His lips moved; he was swearing now, in soft, dangerous tones.

Ali Khan stepped forward and put a hand on Prashant's shoulder.

'It's all right. I'll speak to them.'

'I'm Ali Khan,' he informed the group. 'Who sent you here?'

It doesn't sound like much when you put it down so plainly, but the knife had changed everything. I had lost my sense of place; the wide expanse of the park was shimmering at the edges of my vision. There wasn't anything else – just this ten-foot-long corridor of dry ground and sporadic grass, with me at one end and six armed men at the other. The man with the knife was still muttering coarse insults. My ears were stinging.

I had retreated behind Ali Khan without the slightest sense of shame. I wasn't thinking of how I looked.

The men were regarding him with a uniform frown. Then one of them came out with a curious question.

'Which of you is Prashant Padmanabhan?'

'It must be him,' another called out, pointing correctly.

They went back into a huddle of sorts. For the first time since I had spotted them, I felt my muscles relax – very slightly. It occurred to me that the cause of their confusion was Ali Khan's presence. I caught a few snatches of what they were saying to each other.

'He's not alone.'

'Boss had said –'

'Is that Khan?'

And then, reassuringly –

'Why'd you take the knife out? Are you crazy?'

Khan was regarding them patiently. He asked again –

'Who sent you here? If you tell me who your boss is, we can speak to him ourselves, and sort things out.'

He was being very polite. He made it sound like a perfectly reasonable suggestion.

'Your boss must have a problem with this movie. I understand that. We can settle it directly.

'It's always better to settle things through discussion,' he added philosophically. He hadn't altered the pace of his speech one iota from when he had been introduced to me and Animesh. It was just as measured, and unruffled.

The gang-members were still grimacing.

'Are you actually Ali Khan?' One of them asked doubtfully. He looked the youngest of the lot, and perhaps he didn't even remember the face from television.

'Yes.'

'Then what do we do?' This to the man who had shown us the knife.

'We forget it,' was the answer. 'I don't want to waste my time here.'

Nor did he want to retreat without a parting offensive. The mustachioed man wagged a finger at Prashant.

'You watch it. You're just a kid. All this has to go,' he waved the finger at the mounted camera.

Then he turned to stare at Khan.

'Mr Arindam won't let this happen. He hasn't forgotten anything.'

I watched the men disperse. They didn't all go the same way they had come, but no one lingered either. When the last figure had disappeared into the side-lanes of the colony, I felt my breath returning.

I looked at Prashant. His eyes and mouth were visibly twitching. A stranger coming upon us then might have thought that he was struggling to hold down laughter, but I knew better. He was resisting an impulse to burst into tears. He caught my eye and we shared an embarrassed moment of communion. We had both just been deeply afraid.

We took up the video equipment. On the way back to Prashant's house, I glanced at Khan. A tense, grim smile was playing about his lips. Before I could, Prashant asked him.

'Ali,' he said, 'do you *know* those men?'

7

WE TALKED IT over in the summerhouse. For four people it
was a small space, but Prashant said he liked the privacy. He
sat on the swivel chair in front of the computer, which was, in
a manner of speaking, the head of the room. But we all more
or less deferred to Khan.

'You shouldn't have lost your composure,' he was cautioning
Prashant. 'When you're talking to men like that – there is a
technique.'

'I've never met assassins before. How can I know the
technique?'

It occurred to me that Prashant was a difficult person to
talk down to – however nicely you tried. He had a rough,
egalitarian manner that jarred against anybody's assumption of
authority. On terms of equality, I thought, he and Ali Khan
would get along very easily – but those were unusual terms to
set up across the span of a generation.

Khan went on in his own measured way.

'You must not imitate their way of speaking. They know they
sound coarse. They will not like you any better for mimicking
them. They will respect you, on the other hand, if you maintain
your gentlemanly ways. Fight with your own weapons, not
your enemy's.'

'If you can talk with crowds,' Animesh weighed in with a mumbled line, 'and keep your virtue; or walk with kings — nor lose the common —'

'Who were those men?' Prashant asked impatiently. 'Where did they come from?'

'There's a slum in Shalimar Bagh,' said Khan. 'Most likely from there.'

'They live in a slum?'

He sounded so incredulous; I felt suddenly annoyed.

'There are slums in this city, Prashant! Just because you can't see them from here doesn't mean they don't exist!'

'I know there are slums,' he snapped back.

'The men are only pawns,' Khan continued forcefully. 'If Arindam Yadav so decided, he could have their shanties demolished. They depend on him and he uses them.'

'Yadav,' said Prashant. 'That's the guy they were talking about. Who is he?'

'He is many things. A pimp, a sycophant, a DDA official. He's also a party worker.'

'For what party?'

Ali Khan named a prominent one — on the extreme right-wing.

'I see,' Prashant frowned. 'They . . . don't like you, of course.'

Animesh and I were looking puzzled. Prashant explained for our benefit.

'When Ali made the joke about preferring the sponsor's logos to the national flag, this was the party that had organised the protests. Their idea was to portray him as an India-hating, money-mad mercenary. He was the "non-patriotic Muslim" — remember that catch phrase?'

'There is so much jingoism surrounding the game,' Khan was smiling wistfully. 'I used to find it funny. People don't realise that a sportsman needs to love his sport. It may help a little if he loves his country – but that's all.'

'I guess,' said Prashant, 'they figured there were votes to be got from your downfall. They made you out as a public villain. Anyway, that's what we're up against.'

He settled back in his chair, as though naming the enemy had taken care of it. But I was on pins and needles. The very idea of an enemy was alien to me. Even in my own society, among people I called my friends, I made it a habit to avoid confrontation – so how could I have sought it out from strangers carrying weapons?

'But what's their problem with this *movie?*' I demanded. 'For all they know, we could be agreeing with them.'

'They're deluded,' said Khan drily. 'But they aren't fools. They've read the papers.'

I gave Prashant a knowing look.

'This is what comes of pushing the publicity!'

I expected him to agree. Instead, he shook his head firmly.

'This is no reason to stop publicity. I thought Ali might be swamped by autograph hunters. That was my concern. But I'm not going to stop talking about the movie – or stop my aunt talking about the movie – just because some people don't like it.'

'What I don't want is men with knives,' he went on thoughtfully. 'I'm not made to be in fights, you know. I wear glasses, and the worst thing about glasses is, they go flying at the first punch. Plus, I have a weak skull. A doctor once told me.'

It seemed to me our conversation was growing too flippant. Surely the situation warranted more urgency.

'Let's call the police,' I said suddenly.

For an instant when I said that, I saw something in Prashant's eyes that mirrored my own apprehensions. Then it stiffened. Then it relaxed.

'Well, that gang didn't do anything,' he said flatly. 'If they had, it would have been different. But there's nothing to tell the police – when it was over so soon.'

'Mr Khan,' I turned to him; of course, his experience ought to dictate our actions.

'Do you think we should call the police?'

Gravely, Ali Khan inclined his head.

'Not at this moment. Let's ignore them – to begin with. Just try to get on with the shooting. But if any of you are threatened again, call the police – and call me too. The movie is more important to me than it is to any bunch of goons.'

As he spoke, in that relaxed, resonant voice, I found myself looking at him afresh. With age, his mouth had puckered slightly and the once-proud cheekbones were gaunt and hollowing. But what was lost in vitality was gained in gravitas. It was a measure of Khan's self-sufficiency that he could take his place among us young men with no demands at all; it was equally a measure that he could have our attention when he chose.

'What about the media reports?' I said. 'The media coverage that Prashant's been arranging – you think we should just lie low now, Mr Khan?'

'Vaibhav,' Prashant chided, 'let's not stop before we've started.'

'I'm only saying –'

'It's just one small incident.'

'Look, I don't know about you, but I didn't like what happened today, and I don't mind saying so either.'

We went back and forth like that for a little bit. We had both been truly worried in the park; but Prashant had shifted his mood since then, and I had not. He seemed strangely at ease now.

Khan put his palms on his knees and leaned forward, as a signal that he was getting up. We stopped talking and looked at him. He gave us a quick, encouraging smile.

'You're all in charge. I'm only here to watch.'

The afternoon sun had passed its peak by the time Ali Khan left. Prashant walked over to one of the tinted glass windows of the summerhouse and flung it open, letting in a cool breath of overcast sky. For a few minutes, Animesh and I sat in silence while he fiddled with the video equipment and the desktop's CPU.

'Hey Prashant,' I said eventually. 'It's pretty strange, isn't it? Having Ali Khan over just like this. No fanfare at all.'

'It was bound to happen.'

Prashant was bending gracelessly over the wires at the back of the computer. When he stood up again, his face was bright with triumph.

'What I like is, he's not come loaded with expectations. He knows this is an amateur bunch and it's not going to be a Hollywood production. He doesn't have any airs.'

'You're pretty pally with him, though,' I spoke out suddenly.

'I'm pally with everyone.'

'Yeah, but "Ali"? That's Mr Khan to you, you know.'

There was an edge to my speech, and that was because the point had bothered me. It was such a different behaviour to what I was used to. My boss at Wildlife Alert called me 'beta,' and I couldn't imagine how he would react if I answered 'Bhairav.'

'Look,' Prashant folded his hands demurely in his lap. 'Cricketers are used to their fans *knowing* them. And, in any case, people don't mind being treated as equals.'

'You don't treat people as equals,' said Animesh. 'You treat them as grist to your mill.'

But his voice was mellow, and he was regarding Prashant with an almost maternal indulgence. It struck me, as I looked at them, that for all the put-downs Animesh suffered at the other boy's hands, it was he who held the reins of their relationship.

'You both know,' said Prashant, 'that I worship Ali's batting more than anything. I guess that's why I'm making more of an effort -- not to let myself come under his thrall. We have to make this movie objectively, don't we?'

I wasn't convinced, but for the time being, this settled the point. Through the balmy early evening, we basked for some time in a comfortable silence, until I turned my head and saw Animesh's lips beginning to twitch.

'By the way, Prashant,' he said innocently. 'Where'd you steal that gesture from?'

'Which gesture?'

Animesh was grinning. I looked questioningly at him.

'That cute little gesture, with your hands in your lap,' he went on patiently. 'You've picked it up from someone, haven't you?'

To my immense surprise, Prashant's cheeks were turning pink.

'I don't know what you're talking about,' he lied.

Animesh said nothing. I only watched.

'I mean, yeah, Sheila does it too. Can we watch the footage now?'

～

But the following weekend, he did not change the subject. We had finished a scene in the driveway of Ali's old house in Jangpura, a peeling building covered with bougainvilleas, that was now a PG accommodation for female students. When we started the proceedings, the more enthusiastic among them had come out to watch, which was a nice thing all round and the kind that stays with you. Hours later, back in the summerhouse, with the shadows lengthening, our conversation turned to women.

I pleaded guilty in a perfunctory way. But when Animesh probed, I felt something suddenly terrifying about the idea of discussing Anita. So, out of character, I challenged Prashant.

'Well, what's the deal with you and Sheila?'

He blushed, just as he had the time before. But this time he let the moment linger. There was a little sigh, a little smile. When his brow contracted, I thought his hesitation lay within him -- the way mine did -- but then he shot a glance beside me.

Moments later, Animesh got up.

'I should be going. I have some things to finish.'

I looked at him in surprise. I was quite happy to sit there myself, with the breeze blowing into the quiet room and the weak sunlight fading gently -- and a confession on the horizon. But I thought perhaps I should follow his lead.

'Well I guess I'll go too,' I started to say; then I spotted Prashant's expression.

'What's the hurry?' he said. 'Do you have something to do as well?'

'No.'

'Then it's just your conscience telling you that if, of all people, *Animesh* is busy -- you can't possibly not be.'

We laughed, all three of us. Animesh motioned at me to stay put.

Later, it occurred to me that he had left us deliberately. Perhaps he knew that so long as he was there, Prashant wouldn't drop his guard. Male confidences are sidelong affairs, and nobody who thinks as directly of another's welfare as Animesh did of Prashant's can ever be a confidante. They were, as I said, a bit like brothers, but you can't play all the roles -- it is the social doctrine of the separation of powers.

For myself, I am a reticent person, and especially so in matters of the heart. I couldn't imagine speaking to another boy as candidly as Prashant spoke to me. Inwardly, I was prepared to disapprove of him from start to finish – but when he began to talk it didn't turn out that way. There showed, in his whole manner, an incredible confidence that I was interested, that I wouldn't merely laugh at him, that I wouldn't think him pathetic. I found myself listening with an almost breathless interest.

The summerhouse was dark and cool, as we sat together, staring out at his garden.

'I once read,' he told me, 'a story about a painter. He would draw the face of a woman, again and again. The same face, and it was nobody he'd ever seen. It was the face of his wife and he hadn't yet met her.'

It had been, he said, something like that. One day, three months ago, Gitanjali had invited him home.

'I've got a friend staying with me too,' she had added incidentally. 'Her name's Sheila. You've met her.'

'I have?' Prashant had wondered.

'Yes – on my sixteenth birthday. We played dumb charades.'

When he tried to, Prashant remembered nothing of how the other girl had looked; he carried only a vague impression of brown hair and a tomboyish manner. But now, on the night before he was to meet her again, he found that he could not sleep. At intervals he would slumber, and then awaken desperately – with her name on his lips.

Why? He didn't know. There was no reason. But his heart beat a steady drum-roll of anticipation. Across his mind there flew a montage of soft, falling curls, and passionate smiles. He felt a sweetness so sublime that tears pricked at him. And all this with nothing more than a name – only a name to breathe, and hug, and cry into the sheets.

Chasing after imagination's seven-league boots, life had broken all precedent and taken the lead. The next day, Sheila had come down the stairs of Gitanjali's duplex in Asiad, one dulcet step at a time, with a carriage so self-possessed he could only stare in wonder. That evening, Gitanjali had thought Prashant curt and unsociable, but he had really never been happier. There was a music that was born in his heart, and he only wanted a moment of solitude to listen to the rhythm, and find the words – and then sing it to this miracle girl.

The soaring fancy of his ambition came to ground at last. She agreed to meet at a restaurant in Panchsheel. It wasn't, however, a date. There wasn't that culture. The city that abounded in furtive fornications and cacophonous weddings had little encouragement to offer its lovers. Like many others, before and after him, Prashant had blurted out in desperation what ought to have emerged as surefire magic – and had promptly been thwarted.

'I realised then,' he said to me with a rueful smile, 'that "I love you" is the least effective line ever invented.'

There had been a solemn week or so after that, when the skies had seemed black and pitiless. But he had been in love before. He knew that you must always knock twice: that rejection is only rejection if it is twice over. So he made up his mind to persevere.

It was hard work though. Sheila seemed to move perpetually in a swirling circle of other people. In trying to take her aside for himself, he felt as though he was swimming always against the current.

Of course, she liked him. He had a mien that other men didn't – a certain invincible dreaminess. But she was not so weak as to give up her heart to a man who merely, sincerely, wanted it – however grand the sweep of his thoughts.

Sometimes she would laugh: 'You're certainly earnest' – and his heart would leap because he thought he was winning her. But the truth was, his reverence exercised a high strain upon their fledgling relationship, and Sheila was bearing the brunt of it. She wasn't seventeen any longer – she didn't have the energy to humour him. She would have dropped him long ago, if he had not the occasional, interesting ability to laugh at himself.

'I think her idea was that I knew nothing about women,' Prashant admitted. 'I wanted to put her on a pedestal and she wanted to be taken care of.'

He lost tremendous ground, he told me, one rain-swept afternoon at a market near her home. A little bit of success had gone to his head.

They were sitting in a place that sold ice cream and iced tea. The sky outside thundered gently, and she sat close to him, with their feet just touching under the table.

'I don't know why I'm feeling homesick,' she had complained. 'All through college, too, I was away from home and I never felt like this then. So why now?'

As he recounted the incident, Prashant looked at me with a remembered pride.

'I explained it to her,' he said quietly, 'and she hadn't expected that I could do that. I told her how college is such a structured time – and life after it isn't. Life after it is when you feel the real sting of things. It's when you're out in the world and everybody's going about their business and nobody's bound to care any longer – that's when you feel it.'

Later, they took a walk, an aimless, contented stroll down washed and sparkling roads. The birds were singing in the treetops, but it seemed to Prashant that their own happiness needed no words. So he hoped the time was right to speak.

'Why,' he asked her, 'do you keep me so much at bay?'

To similar pleas on previous occasions, she had merely smiled and said nothing, but now he saw, with a jolt of excitement, that she was giving the question thought.

'Do I do that too much?' she said softly.

'You do. Oh, you do! And you mustn't!'

'You mustn't,' he repeated, tingling with anticipation, willing her closer. Then it happened. She slipped a soft palm into her handbag and produced a box of cigarettes. She lit one.

'I didn't know you smoked.' His voice had emerged strangely high-pitched.

'Yeah, sometimes.'

With a strange, mounting frustration, he watched her puffing self-absorbedly.

'Well it's a stupid thing to do,' he retorted bitterly. 'You'll be addicted before you know it.'

She laughed. 'I don't get addicted to anything.'

'That's what you think. It's not in your control!'

He was swinging freely now, damaging further the moment she had tarnished. But she should have come to him, she should have had the courage, and instead she had chosen to indulge herself, to feed this petty habit.

'And it's terrible for your health!'

'Well, I'm not scared,' she said facetiously. She took a long, languorous drag. He thought of which trashy siren she looked like when she did that. It twisted his heart to see on her, that cheap allure.

'I'm not scared about my *health*,' she went on, with the cigarette between her lips. 'Come on, we're all young here.'

His moralities creaked in protest at her manner. Inexorably, his mood soured.

'You're being an idiot,' he said viciously. 'You're not scared only because you don't see anything to be scared of. You don't see your lungs or what's happening to them. Don't give yourself airs. It's not because you're brave.'

She held her lower lip abstractedly. She snuffed out the cigarette and put it back in the box.

'I won't smoke in front of you – if it'll save you your peace of mind.'

Her voice carried a vast condescension. It lashed at him as though he was an errant child. He flailed out again, furiously.

'I said – lose the airs! Why don't you go running into the middle of the road when there's a bus coming – if you're not scared!'

He didn't know how high he raised his voice. She didn't look at him. At a bend in the road she took a turn back.

'Where are you going?'

She didn't reply.

'Where are you going?'

She walked straight home.

Somehow, Prashant had recovered. Partly because he took a lot of the blame – but mostly because he didn't take it all.

'I realised just in time,' he said to me again, 'that "please forgive me" is the most aggravating line ever invented.'

He hadn't lost her. He had understood, instead, that she was not beyond reproach. Some of the naiveté of his worship faded – for which they were both thankful. But in its place, there settled in him a deep conviction of her extraordinariness. She wasn't simply slack, like so many others. She wasn't just another eager young thing desperately seeking her place under the rising sun of misunderstood womanhood. She was different from all of them – better than all of them.

She had no scruples, that was all. She denied herself no pleasure that she really wanted – and if she couldn't get it she would flay you with her self-denial. She had a brick-hard selfishness – the same selfishness that had made her walk away from him that day in May without a single explanatory word.

What saved it for the two of them was an unlikely compatibility, begot from contrasting sources. His internal rules were always proud; her unscrupulousness was always regal. She did as her tastes dictated, and yet, with rare exceptions, her tastes matched his conventions. So they got along.

And so they'd been getting along – with their hearts still hanging in the balance.

'It's just unrequited love,' Prashant summed up. 'I mean – as the world has it.'

For a moment, the wrinkles around his eyes told of his strain, and I wanted to tell him that everything was going to be all right. Then he smiled, humorously, resignedly, and I let it go.

As we watched the sun beginning its slow dip into the west, a thought occurred to me.

'Don't you . . . have competition?'

'Of course,' Prashant grinned. He looked at me steadily, face-to-face.

I felt suddenly very comfortable. This was my sense of how men talked about love. Love was a fine, manly battle, fought for a golden prize. It wasn't our way to kiss and tell, or gossip in details. It was the broad spectrum of the horizon we were looking at, with shaded eyes and a steady resolve.

'There are two guys, basically,' he said warmly.

'That I know of,' he added, 'Madhav and Roshan.'

'In that order?'

'In that order. At least, I hope so.'

'Why's that?'

A grimace went stealing across his face.

'Roshan is . . . scum, really; he hasn't got a chance with her. He could never be anything to her and he knows that. What he wants is different.' Prashant stopped heavily.

'You've only just met him,' I objected. 'That night at Calabria was the first time you met him.'

'Oh, I know the guy,' Prashant said airily. 'It's all over his face, and his walk — his whole demeanour. I guess pretty good, you know.'

'I couldn't stand the thought,' he said stonily, 'of anything . . . casual happening to her.'

'What about Madhav?'

'Madhav,' his lips curled into a smile of genuine, unlikely pleasure. 'Well, she likes Madhav, and I know he likes her too. He's all right, Madhav. Very dignified guy.'

I could see, from the way Prashant was speaking, that other men bothered him not to the extent of their worthiness but to the extent of their unworthiness — measured, of course, by his own standards. It wasn't the possibility of never having Sheila that stabbed at him; it was the possibility that he'd never had a clue. He had invested in her so much of his ideas of right and wrong, and men and women, that her romantic fate was a trial of his convictions.

Suddenly, he became serious. 'I don't mind competition,' he said. 'Because . . . because I believe there are two kinds of people in the world. There are those who take care of other people, and there are those who need to be taken care of. I've always felt like I'm the first kind. So I don't mind – I can be nice to those two guys. I should be nice to them. Even to Roshan. I've got to be all-comprehending, all-forgiving. There should be nothing that can throw me off balance.'

As he was speaking now, Prashant's whole face had lit up. The sweep of his emotions showed in the tremor of his voice. Amidst all the revelations he had made to me that evening, it was this that brought the colour rushing to his cheeks. Then, he caught his breath.

He went on, more measured.

'You don't fight anyone directly, not unless you're a child at this. The only person you deal with directly is the girl, and whoever deals with her best, must win. It's the battle of the sexes, you know.'

'You need luck too.'

'I don't believe in luck.'

'I mean,' I added testily, 'you need to be the right type. Otherwise you've got no chance, no matter how brilliant you may think you are.'

I felt my own wisdom deserved to be recognised.

'That's equally true.'

This mollified me. I asked him pleasantly –

'So how come you're directing the same girl you're in love with? That looks to me like a clear conflict of interest right there. Not very professional.'

I had said it half in jest, but his face darkened as I spoke, and now he nodded gravely.

'It's tricky. Hers is the only troupe I had access to, and I couldn't very well exclude her – not for a reason like this. Besides, she's a good actress.'

'Oh it's nothing,' I assured him. 'Don't worry. All the best directors do it.'

We both smiled, and it was about then that a knock sounded on the door of the summerhouse. That was the end of our conversation.

~

The frail figure of the servant appeared at the threshold. Prashant looked warily at him.

'What is it, Rajendran?'

'Somebody had come, sir.'

'Who?'

'A man.'

'What man?' asked Prashant, with threadbare patience.

'He left something and then went away.'

Prashant clicked his tongue, and then his agitation came bursting to the surface.

'Why didn't you tell me? I told you already, if anybody wants to see me, come and tell me – or call me if I'm not around. Don't send them to the park like you did the other day!'

The other man performed an exaggerated bow and said something to the effect that Prashant's wish was his command.

'Didn't you ask who it was?'

Listening to the questions, an idea appeared to occur to Rajendran. His sallow, beseeching face perked up.

'Perhaps it was the postman. This is what he gave me.'

Prashant took the proffered envelope. 'You can go now.' He pushed the door shut; it herded out the sunlight.

'That guy gets on my nerves,' he declared. 'All that fake ignorance – anything to avoid responsibility.'

I watched Prashant extract a single sheet of paper from the envelope. Standing beside him, I couldn't resist a glance over his shoulder. On a dimly typed form, an untidy hand had scribbled out a string of words, above an official-looking stamp. I narrowed my eyes, trying to make sense of the legalese.

After several seconds, Prashant said uncertainly –

'It's some kind of summons.'

'A court summons, yes,' I was still reading.

'It's for you,' I explained. 'Someone's filed a case against you.'

'A case?'

'Yes.'

'An actual court case?'

'Yes,' I told him. 'The hearing is this Saturday. What's it about?'

'God knows,' he said distractedly. 'How should I know? This . . . summons doesn't say – does it?'

We looked at each other with bemusement and a growing consternation.

I checked it again.

'It says it's a suit for a preventive injunction. That means an order to stop you doing something.'

'Well?'

'What are you doing that someone wants stopped?'

8

THE SUMMONS WAS only in Prashant's name, but Animesh and I decided we'd go as well – for company's sake and for curiosity's sake. At nine in the morning the following Saturday, Prashant came to pick us up from the courtyard of Akash Apartments. We departed in his car to disapproving looks from Mrs Ramdass. She'd been seeing a lot of Prashant lately, and despite their cozy first encounter she didn't appreciate frequent visitors. I think she was afraid we were becoming a sort of gang.

On the way to the Tis Hazari Courts, I asked Prashant:

'What do your parents say about this?'

'My parents,' he sighed wearily. 'They don't know what to make of it. My father told me two of his classmates are lawyers. He's busy tracing them. My mother thinks I'm stuck in some Hitchcockian plot. She's imagining the iron bars cropping up around her beloved son.'

He smiled thinly with his eyes on the road.

'Well, I'm imagining that too,' he admitted.

'You don't yet know what it is,' I reminded him. 'Besides, it's a civil case. So put to rest the iron bars. There's no danger of prison.'

'I guess . . .' he said worriedly.

'I *know*,' I assured him. 'I did a month's correspondence in law.'

'A month is a short time,' said Animesh balefully, from the backseat.

I gave him a dirty look. 'This is basic.'

He was trying to catch Prashant's eye in the rear-view mirror. 'Speaking of Hitchcock – you haven't told us what your parents think of your movie-making. Do they talk about you in low tones and stop suddenly when you enter the room?'

'They're okay,' said Prashant grimly. 'They're better than some. I'm keeping them at bay for the time being, and they're letting me do that. I guess that's something.'

Animesh nodded sympathetically, 'It's hard for parents,' he said. 'It's hard for that whole generation. They're a generation that built nothing that wasn't borrowed. And here you are declaring an imagination of your own. It's like a declaration of war. It's a metaphorical glass of wine you're dashing in the faces of your forefathers.' He chuckled obscurely.

I felt suddenly moved to object.

'No,' I said. 'No. Whatever happened to standing on shoulders and seeing further? Our parents' generation did a lot. We've got more luxuries now than they ever –'

'I don't buy that,' Animesh cut in. 'They had enough. They should have done something of their own. And if they had nothing of their own then they should have done nothing. But they compromised and they did things they didn't believe in and so they did them half-heartedly. Hence this mess.'

His outspokenness surprised me. I had gotten used to listening to Prashant, and looking at Animesh. Whatever gifts for abstract thought the other boy employed for his alleged essays had so far remained hidden.

We were driving past a row of electronics and car repair shops on a congested North Delhi street. Somewhere amidst the dust and the fumes, I spotted a billboard that looked like Switzerland. So did Animesh.

'And now,' he went on, 'they're escaping to their luxury homes.' Suddenly he smiled. 'But you know what?'

'I think we're reaching,' said Prashant.

'They still won't feel at home.'

Tis Hazari loomed before us — a massive grey box slotted into multiple levels and dotted through with windows. On a level with the highest of these was a walkway in the sky to the metro station. A steady stream of pedestrians was crossing there, above our heads, and down below was a road worse than any near my apartment — a thing I would not have thought possible.

The car bobbed and jolted along the potholes. For long minutes, we inched our way forward amongst the crowding cycle-rickshaws, until finally a turning presented itself below a rusted iron archway that announced the City Civil Courts. We parked outside and walked into the compound.

It was my first glimpse of a district court in all its confusion. Armies of lawyers were hurrying in every direction, jabbing and pushing with elbows and shoulders, while their retinue gave chase. Nobody simply walked. There were lines of stalls stacked with stationery, dust-laden cars that bullied their way through the crowds, and typewriters clattering freely. The ground was dirty with litter and spittle, which the men strewed as freely as flowers. There was the thick odour of perspiration, growing thicker and stronger as we entered the courthouse.

Prashant gripped the scrap of paper tighter between his fingers. In all the shifting chaos, those summons were our only certainty.

'Court No. 323,' he said grimly.

We climbed up three flights of gloomy stairs, just in time to hear the name of the first case on the day's roster being bellowed out into the *paan*-stained corridor. In waiting was a group of lawyers, whose attention was continually distracted by the ringing of their phones, and a sorry herd of litigants squatting in pockets along the floor. But I only had a brief look at them because minutes later, the man at the door was calling out Prashant's name. We pushed our way inside, brushing past him unavoidably but apparently unforgivably.

'Watch it!' he railed. 'Look where you're going!'

Inside, five or six lawyers sitting in rows of chairs turned to frown at us. Too late, it occurred to me that we might have dressed more formally for the occasion.

Animesh and I hung back; Prashant stepped forward to the bar of the court. Directly above him now was the Hon'ble Justice V.T. Sharma, and standing over the judge, a liveried attendant who was armed, like the doorman, with a gaze of bright malevolence.

Meanwhile, our opponent had appeared. An old bearded lawyer, in stiff coat and trousers, who carried his papers in a folded plastic bag. He moved with slow and careful steps to join Prashant at the bar. Then, once he had settled there, he slid a set of sheets across its shiny surface and bowed low.

'My Lord,' he intoned, 'I have served the defendant.'

'I don't know what the case is about,' Prashant said confidently.

That did not seem to matter. The judge, at any rate, did not raise his eyes. His mouth worked, but I couldn't hear a word, until he broke off to ask a question.

'Do you have a lawyer?'

'Do you have a lawyer?' The standing figure couldn't stand the suspense.

'N – no.'

Prashant raised his eyebrows hopefully, but nothing more was said to him. The judge finished his mumbling, and the other man shouted out a date in October, and then another set of strange names. Two of the seated lawyers sprung from their seats as though stuck by a pin, and rudely, desperately, Prashant was pushed back towards the middle of the room. There was a clash of voices; a scuffle of papers, and then the lawyers' heads were bobbing up and down in eager agreement with whatever fresh and inaudible utterance his Lordship was engaged in.

Prashant returned to our side, clutching the plaint. We spilled out into the corridor and made our way to a corner where the crowds didn't reach. Animesh and I looked over his shoulder, and we all read what was written.

The gist of the plaint was that one Mr Saeed Ibrahim had reason to believe that a movie was in the process of being made, which threatened to disturb communal harmony, and injure the sentiments of the Muslim community, not to mention his own. He wanted a court order to stop the shooting.

'It doesn't even say what it is that he thinks will be offensive,' I pointed out.

'He doesn't know the script,' said Prashant.

'Then the case should have been thrown out. It's premature.'

Bending over the pages, I saw a shadow fall across them. We looked up at once. It was the bearded lawyer.

'Hello,' he said, 'I am Saeed Ibrahim.'

'Hello,' said Animesh.

Close up, the man's beard and eyebrows were still forbidding, but his mouth pouted in the endearing way that infants and the aged have in common. That, and a certain kindliness in his eyes, surprised me. He was smiling gently at Prashant.

'I wasn't expecting someone so young.'

'I'm sorry to disappoint you,' said Prashant stiffly.

'Have you ever been to a court before? This must be all new to you.'

Prashant stared back at him.

'There's nothing to it.'

'Why don't we talk about this?'

'I don't have anything to talk about. I've only just got these papers.'

'Can we at least sit? I want to explain.'

'Explain what?'

'The case. I'm not trying to harass anybody. Are these your friends?'

There was no magic in his words, but his manner was winning. He hadn't once brandished in our faces his superior years. He hadn't called Prashant 'son,' and he didn't look like he wanted any honorific for himself. Freed from all heavy-handedness, the natural authority of grey hair weighed upon us painlessly.

We went with him to a large and empty canteen in one of the compound's few airy spaces. It was a cheap, grimy, efficient place — I suppose it had two things in common with the rest of Tis Hazari. We settled down at a rickety table covered with a laminated table-cloth. Animesh and I watched the other two talk.

'I always say things should be resolved through discussion.'

Ibrahim's wisdom was uncannily reminiscent of Ali Khan's speech in the park — which was ironic, given what came next.

'Ali Khan never understood that.'

Prashant was swirling the liquid in one of the steel glasses that a hurrying waiter had plonked down before us. He took a speculative sip.

'What do you mean?'

'Khan did an advertisement for a liquor company.'

'So what?'

For an instant the old man's eyes flashed.

'Young man,' he said, 'I am not dictating to you. But for us, what is prohibited is prohibited. Khan ought to have been a public role model. Or stayed a private man. He chose to be a public menace. And he never apologised.'

'I understand your sentiments,' said Prashant. 'But I thought we were going to discuss your case against me. And I haven't done any advertisements – for anything.'

'I know,' Ibrahim smiled warmly. 'I am only concerned about your movie. I would not like Khan's wrongdoings to be glorified.'

'So you filed a case against me?'

'Not against you – against the movie.'

'The movie's hardly begun, and I'm here. Just what do you know about the movie anyway – sir?'

'I told you, I'm concerned. I don't know. I anticipate. Given what I read in the papers, it seems you are planning a tribute. Khan does not deserve a tribute.'

Prashant looked at me, and then at Animesh. His face hardened.

'That's my decision. It's got nothing to do with you – or what you think.'

'Listen to me – just one moment, young man.'

We had asked for tea. The cups arrived, to give the steel glasses company. I took a sip. It was all just warm, mildly-flavoured milk.

'I don't want anything,' the old man started promisingly, 'except that you should give me an undertaking not to shoot any scenes that justify Ali Khan's breach of Islam.'

Prashant looked back at him wonderingly.

'Did you ever file a case against *him*? At the time of the . . . breaches.'

'That's what I said,' the lawyer continued patiently. 'He was a very stubborn man. He refused to apologise. He didn't settle it.'

'What happened to the case?'

Ibrahim pursed his lips from behind his beard.

'In those days he was famous. The High Court stopped my case.'

'Well, Mr Ibrahim,' Prashant shrugged, 'I'm not famous, so you may have better luck. I can't agree to your interference in my movie.'

'All I want is an undertaking -- and I'll withdraw the suit. Otherwise . . .'

'Otherwise what?'

Ibrahim drained his tea in one long gulp, and then burped with satisfaction. 'Otherwise it continues.'

My face flushed. I looked at Prashant. Something haunted had crept into his eyes. I thought of the clogged road outside, the narrow, filthy corridors inside and the pathetic pleaders with their clinging clients filling to bursting point the whole vast Tis Hazari. It was the close of summer now, but even so, the courtroom we had been to had stunk of human sweat. Who would ever come here who could possibly help it? 'Prashant . . .' I started to whisper.

But once again, his mood was changing. The apprehension that he could not conceal was altering slowly, dissipating slowly. His voice was clear and level.

'I'm not giving you any undertaking. I guess we'll meet on the next date.'

'Compromise! My dear son, compromise! Don't be stubborn!'

Prashant looked at the old man with amazement and contempt.

'You file a case against me. You file a *case* against me without knowing a thing of what I'm doing. You drag me here just to satisfy your little ego, and then you ask *me* not to be stubborn.'

'I'm a lawyer. We all fight the way we know.'

'You're a lawyer − so you should know better.'

'Don't take that tone with me, son. I was in uniform before you were in liquid form!'

Animesh chuckled. I threw him a furious look.

That was the end of the meeting, though. To clear our heads and bolster our moods, the three of us walked to the metro station. According to Animesh, there was a McDonald's at the next stop.

Inside the slow-rocking, fast-moving train, I sat and stared at the endless sky, trying to imbibe its empty calm. Meanwhile, Animesh was summoning up a desperate cheeriness.

'This is all good for the movie, Prashant! We can use it for more publicity!'

'We don't need more publicity.'

'However,' Prashant's voice grew interested, 'it's true, we can use it. It's all proof of Ali Khan's controversy. I could give Ibrahim a mention in the same movie he wants stopped – how just would that be?'

He was smiling to himself the rest of the way, full of his own ideas. When the train shuddered to a halt, we made our way to the restaurant. Over a fast-food lunch, we talked a little more about the script, and now, across the cheerful orange tabletop, Prashant's eyes were glowing with excitement.

'I'll tell you what's interesting,' he said. 'Today, what everybody remembers of Ali is just that World Cup semi-final. He walked; the Aussies won; he retired, much lauded, into the sunset. End of story. Except it isn't really. Because, have you ever considered: *why* was he was so much lauded? Why wasn't he ridiculed? Or simply ignored? Do you remember, Vaibhav, that evening at your apartment when I said that all the praise Ali got for his walk was the wrong kind of praise?'

'I remember,' I said. 'You told me it was complicated, but you were going to explain what you meant.'

'I'm explaining now,' he said. 'My explanation is, that Ali's detractors found it a rather *soothing* event. All their aggression had failed to break him – but their condescension might still bury him. And this walk of his was a perfect opportunity. I mean – they could hardly have attacked him for it. It was a self-inflicted wound. You look very petty to kick a man when he's down. But on the other hand, why do you need to? You can simply raise the fellow to his feet, and give him a wash and a change and a fresh set of clothes. Your cut of clothes. . . .'

There had entered Prashant's voice a grim, steady conviction, and just a hint of bitterness.

'So,' he continued, 'they made him into a sort of *sentimental* figure. The reformed profligate, brash and independent to begin with, but bowing at last to authority. I guess for some of them that meant the authority of tradition, and for others it meant the authority of the West. But the basic image worked for them all: here was an overly-proud man, undergoing a much-needed penance. Give him a pat on the back, and then we can forget about him.'

There was a little silence then, while Prashant took a sip of his drink, 'You've given this a lot of thought,' I said.

His eyes contracted happily from over the rim of the cup. Then he put it down, and raised a cautionary finger.

'But look!' he exclaimed. 'Look what happens at the slightest glimmer of the possibility that Khan might be brought back into the limelight. That he might be shown for who he *really* was. The right-wingers get their knives out, the Islamists file a case –'

'Islamist,' Animesh corrected.

'Same difference. The uneasy peace is shattered, and suddenly Khan isn't just a goody two-shoes. Which he really never was. In his time he got under *every*body's skin, and that means the people who spend all their time fighting *each other*. The saffron brigade, the Islamist radicals, the self-loathing, irreligious elite. They all had a gripe with this one guy. Because he stood apart from them all! Because he was a slave to none of their masters!'

Prashant was smiling again – and this time with pure delight. Involuntarily, I had inclined my head; I was considering him as one considers a painting, and about then a thought occurred to me: he loves his work.

'Ali walked in that semi-final,' I listened to him saying, 'because he had a personal code of honour, and neither the result, nor anybody's opinion mattered more to him. It was an act of self-expression: supreme self-expression. Not self-denial. It was a martyrdom, not a suicide. And yet, that's the story people want to believe, because they want to believe they finally got his measure. That the prodigal son came home at last, settled down, gave up his dangerous ways, became one of them. I'm going to remind them it wasn't so.'

I nibbled cautiously at my sandwich. I was beginning, for the first time, to understand how serious Prashant was – about his movie, and about himself. All this while, I had thought of him as essentially an amateur, and of this movie as essentially just good fun. It didn't sit easily with my way of thinking to give him or it any more importance. He was too young; this couldn't possibly be his time to make it. How could he have anything mature and lasting to say, when those necessary years of struggle had never happened for him?

But we take from other people the notions we are too timid to articulate for ourselves – and then suffer a swift compensatory shame. If Arindam Yadav and Saeed Ibrahim treated the movie seriously enough to stir into protest – then it dawned on me that it might be more than a mere novelty.

'Are you going to shoot that walking scene afresh?' I asked him. 'Or use footage?'

'The footage is iconic,' he said. 'If I can get the rights, we must use it.'

'You know,' he added suddenly. 'As things stand, the script doesn't have the walking scene at all. I haven't been able to decide where to put it. It's like the country names on a map – it's so big, you overlook it. It's so central.'

'And you've understood it so brilliantly,' Animesh said stolidly. Prashant gave him a suspicious look.

We 'rode the trains' for a while after that, because the metro, so clean, so swift, was still a novelty. It was almost early evening by the time we had meandered our way back to the parking at Tis Hazari.

In the car, the two of them picked up on an old topic. I thought they'd forgotten all about it.

'Vaibhav, did you get Gitanjali's number? I can give it to you if you like.'

'Vaibhav, have you met her since that day?'

'Look, he's smiling!'

Link me to anybody and I grin like an ape. That's how it's been since I was fourteen. Of course, ever since Anita and I got together, I've had an easy way of defusing such teasing – but sometimes, for the sake of the other person's conversation or because the insinuation is flattering, you don't want to nip it in the bud. This wasn't one of those times.

'You know I've got a girlfriend.'

'Just the one?' Animesh looked concerned.

'Oh, give him a break,' Prashant said casually. 'He's got a girlfriend means he's got a girlfriend. There's an end to it.'

'Prashant is our last moral young man,' Animesh replied sarcastically. 'Our only saviour against the onward tide of Roshan Menons.'

The mention of that name turned Prashant's lips downwards. His eyes closed on the road, and he didn't answer back.

We were passing a stretch of intersections not far from our apartment. Cellophane bags and old wrappers tumbled in the wind, as we cruised from signal to signal.

'I'm only joking,' Animesh explained.

'No, no,' Prashant shook his head vigorously. 'That's all right. I know Roshan doesn't know anything. He's got no mind of his own; he thinks the way he's been told he should think. It's just that there are so many people to tell him he's right, and so few . . .'

'Go on,' Animesh smiled.

'Why shouldn't I?' Prashant half-turned his head to look at the other boy – the same habit of his I'd noticed before.

'There are just a few good men,' he shrugged. 'Always have been, always will be.'

Sitting next to him, I suddenly started to resent him. Just a moment ago, I had been the centre of attention, and much too soon it had swung away – and in his direction, who got so much of it anyway.

'Girls can be just friends too,' I said loudly, and then went on talking to stave off the fast-approaching blush. 'Since you guys asked, I have got Gitanjali's number. I talk to her quite a lot too. I think she's very sensible.'

This was all true. Since our evening at the cafe I had called Gitanjali a few times already. We had struck up a pattern where I did most of the talking – and she got the last word. She was an easy, uncomplicated confidante.

'She's like a sister, really,' I continued thoughtfully.

'Like a *sister*?' Prashant rolled his eyes.

'Yes. Not that I expect you to understand. You know what your problem is?'

'I don't –'

'You're just too sure of yourself.'

'I don't thi –'

I saw the car. I screamed.

He slammed the brakes. The car continued swinging into our path from the right-hand side of the intersection. Its back kept getting bigger and bigger in the windscreen. For an instant, I thought we'd halt in time. Then the jolt of the impact happened.

Prashant swore – gently. It would have been nastier if we'd been going faster, but the collision had been front to back, not sideways on. I didn't think either vehicle could have suffered much damage.

In any case, the other was larger and heavier. It was an SUV, a big-built Sumo. It had rolled on a little distance ahead. Prashant slipped the Maruti back into gear.

The door on the driver's side of the Sumo flung open. A man got out.

'Stop the car,' I said. I looked at Prashant; his face was unmoving, abnormally paralysed.

'No . . . Nothing's happened.'

I peered through the windscreen at the bumper of the other vehicle. It looked fine to me, not that that meant much. Prashant kept the Maruti crawling forward, towards the waiting driver.

When the figure of the man appeared at his window, he slowed the car further. My sight was obstructed, but I caught a glimpse of a white, sweat-stained shirt, filled out by a paunch – and then a clean-shaven, puffy face bending down to look Prashant in the eye.

'Get out of the car.'

'Nothing's happened to your –'

'Please get out of the car.'

The man had on a fixed and inscrutable stare. I couldn't decipher his expression – it could have been anything from deep-seated anger to poker-faced humour to a simple desire for conversation. It was that inscrutable. But the Maruti was still dribbling onwards.

'Just pull over and let's talk to him,' I suggested.

'Yes, just to pacify him,' Animesh agreed.

Prashant ignored us. He looked out of the window once more and told the other man decisively.

'Nothing happened.'

He pressed the accelerator, a little quicker than he should have. The car sprung forward, a little jerkier than it should have.

I turned around in my seat to watch the driver of the Sumo take a half-step forward and then pause. I saw his lips move.

The road ahead was clear, and soon he was only a speck in the mirror.

'It's okay,' Prashant assured us.

'This kind of thing happens,' he went on talking. 'If you stop for every little bump on the road, you'll never get anywhere. People should learn to take a few knocks without making a big deal of it. Anyway,' he added unsurely, 'it was all his fault.'

'I know,' I nodded. 'It was a minor thing – you're right.'

In the backseat, Animesh had shrunk into a corner. He looked preoccupied – and pale. I turned around and grinned at him.

'If Kisle had been here we could have let him loose on that fat guy. He's got that wiry toughness, Kisle – like a boxer.'

Animesh didn't smile. 'Did you hear what he said, when he saw us go?'

'No.'

'He said: "I'm going to kill you."'

We were silent for the rest of the drive. After I got back to the apartment, I switched on the television and watched a pointless three-hour-long Hindi movie from start to finish. I was trying to forget the incident as quickly as I could.

If I had known what was to come, I wouldn't have bothered.

9

'HE SOUNDS LIKE Santa Claus!'

That was Gitanjali's delighted response, when I told her about Ibrahim. 'It's a serious thing,' I insisted, but though she made some formal noises of concern, neither the court case nor the gang at the park seemed to have bothered her much. I was surprised. From this commonsensical girl, I had expected a properly grave response to the movie's enemies. Perhaps I had caught her in a jovial mood – or perhaps the bad news just didn't stick. Soon she was talking about other things.

'You're totally sold on Prashant,' she teased. 'You're more interested in his movie than your work.'

'I'm just helping from a distance.'

'Distance my foot. He told me there's a meeting in your flat this Friday. The "core team" is coming over?'

'Well yes,' I was sheepish. 'I've got him using the buzzwords now. I've told him this will democratise the process.'

'Then why am I not invited?' she clamoured.

Gitanjali had only a minor role. 'We're not *that* democratic,' I laughed.

We were starting work on the match-fixing episode – I mean, of course, the 'sting' that Ali Khan suffered in the West Indies, which, more than anything, had helped to turn his fame into notoriety, and to keep it that way – until his eventual redemption in the World Cup semi-final. It was interesting to me, because Prashant had a take on it I hadn't heard before. It also marked the first occasion I did any real work of my own on the movie.

There were six of us on that windy Friday evening: Sheila, Madhav and Vivek were getting their first look at No. 504. Animesh and I had tidied up before they arrived, but the getting rid of clothes and newspapers and leftover food only makes for a certain rudimentary neatness. The essential thoughtlessness of the arrangements remained, and while the boys didn't care, Sheila couldn't conceal a judgmental twitch of an eyebrow.

She sat beside Madhav on the sofa; Vivek was opposite Prashant on the takhat; Animesh had taken a chair to a corner and I was on my feet and occupied. Outside, it looked as though a storm was on its way, and the windows clattered to and fro until I hurried them shut. The trapped moist breeze settled cosily about the interior.

'Here's what I have in mind,' Prashant began. He was sitting very straight and alert. As he spoke, his earnest eyes sought us out, each in turn.

'The undisputed facts are that a man calling himself Dinesh Singh and claiming to be a bookmaker telephoned Ali during the warm-up match against Barbados, and offered him $50,000 to get out under ten in both innings of the first Test match.

'This was their conversation. Ali said: "That sounds good." Dinesh said: "When can I meet you?" Ali said: "Why do you need to?" Dinesh said: "Don't you want to? Should I consider it done?" Ali said: "There's no need to meet." He put the phone down.

'That was all. The next day the whole thing was plastered in three-inch headlines over the front page of the *Express*. There wasn't any Dinesh Singh; there was just Shekhar Sen, making his name at the time as a sting specialist.

'Ali Khan didn't really have an explanation. He said his words were being taken out of context, but that first line he'd said was damning. It was his tone: he'd sounded positively enthusiastic.

'So, an official inquiry was started, and of course, before it could be finished, Ali had hit a double century in the Test match. Eventually, he was only reprimanded. But the general perception was that the Board had shoved the whole affair under the carpet to save face. Shekhar Sen certainly never let it go. He kept bringing up the incident in the series of columns he wrote after that – all the way up to his piece in the *Express* when Ali retired.

'Now I've spoken to Ali about this,' Prashant said lightly, and everybody looked at him.

It hadn't ceased to impress, that Ali Khan was involved in our business.

'And I've got a plan for the scene, to explain how it happened.'

Madhav frowned.

'We don't want to be putting Khan's version across – solely. Why not just show what happened in a neutral way? It's not as if we know the truth anyway.'

'That's true,' Prashant admitted. 'But we can guess. I want to float a theory.'

'Guesswork isn't professional,' the other boy grumbled.

'It's what will make our movie different from the run-of-the-mill documentary drama.'

'You just like guessing,' Sheila said candidly. 'That's all.'

'Well, listen,' Prashant pushed on hastily. 'This isn't even something Ali said. It's what I really believe makes the most sense.

'He was sitting on the beach when he got that call. His wife was there. It was the middle of the afternoon. Blue sky, yellow sand, lazy Caribbean music floating all around. He's just hit a good half-century in the Barbados game. He's a little drunk. He's at peace with the world. His phone rings and someone mentions fifty thousand dollars. Do you,' Prashant was smiling winningly at us, '*really* expect him to get on his high horse, whip up in an instant the right moral indignation and slam the phone down? Of course not!'

We were all doubtful – but listening. In his corner, I saw Animesh studying the carpet closely.

'So it's no wonder he made that comment. The problem with the sting is, it draws your attention to something so *trivial*, and it makes you take it so seriously. Some things are too simple and too fundamentally human to analyse. But when we *show* the scene, people will understand at once why he was – flippant – that's all, easy and flippant.'

Prashant had on a faintly smug smile now. I looked at Sheila looking at him steadily. It was a look that said she had no illusions about him. She whispered something in Madhav's ear, and they both giggled.

'So when are we going to Goa?' she asked casually.

'Goa?'

'If we don't go to Goa for this scene, I'm not doing it.'

'Me neither,' Vivek piped up. 'And I'm the star.'

The motion was carried. Someone suggested we order dinner, and a celebratory burst of thunder rattled the windows.

'Why don't you open that window, and then fasten it so it doesn't bang?'

I did as Sheila said. Immediately the tremor of falling rain broke upon our ears. The high wind carried no dust, and we let it blow about the room and worry the curtains and whip our loose clothes and spoil Madhav's immaculately-arranged hair. Sheila caressed that back into shape, under Prashant's disapproving gaze.

'I was thinking,' he said forcefully, 'we can ask Shekhar Sen for an interview.'

Vivek threw his head back, remembering hard.

'Shekhar Sen did the sting — and then he retracted it?'

'He didn't retract it,' Prashant explained. 'But he didn't want Ali punished either. Shekhar had some weird ideas. At least, they were weird then. Entertainment wasn't always the buzzword it is now. But he delivered Ali a whole series of back-handed compliments about what a great entertainer he was. And damning justifications about judging him solely by the entertainment he provided.'

'Oh yes,' Vivek nodded rapidly. 'He even wrote that cricket should seriously consider scripting its results. Didn't he say that Ali's walk in the semi-final was so dramatic, it might have been planned?'

'He said a lot of crazy stuff. Those two never liked each other.'

Suddenly Animesh spoke up. He had been busy stroking his ivory-smooth chin, and gazing now at the carpet, now at the ceiling, with his big, thoughtful eyes.

'What,' he asked decisively, addressing no one in particular, 'does "entertainment" mean?'

'What does it *mean*?' he went on in seeming agony. 'I've never been able to understand. You might want to teach somebody or bore somebody or praise somebody or hurt somebody — but what does it mean to *entertain* somebody?'

We all turned to him in surprise. Sheila looked at him gently.

'It means to give them a good time.'

Animesh retreated deeper into his chair, a scarlet flush staining his cheek.

'He's an . . . essayist,' Prashant apologised, then grinned — and in between shot at Sheila a look of the most heart-wrenching admiration.

He thought nobody had noticed; he caught my eye and saw that I had. Quickly I started speaking, to cover for his shame.

'I'll go talk to Shekhar Sen.'

'We could just telephone him,' Madhav suggested.

'No, he'll brush us off that way. He's a busy man nowadays. Besides,' I said, 'I know where he lives. He was my neighbour once.'

~

In my schooldays, Shekhár Sen had lived on the road opposite my house. He hadn't got a column then, so a lot had changed for him since, but not his address. It was a spacious home in the greenest, most sun-speckled part of the city. He lived a comfortable middle-class life there, with his wife and teenage son, and for all the annoyance his views on cricket had caused me over the years, I was a great deal more comfortable calling on him than I would have been calling on Arindam Yadav.

I went to visit him on a Sunday afternoon. The previous day I had phoned the journalist at his new office at the *Economic Daily* and had been told he wasn't in. But the secretary had noted my name and if I was ringing Sen's doorbell now, it was only because 'Vaibhav Kapoor' had rung a bell before. It made my task a little more delicate though; I was trading on my father's friendship, and that security wasn't mine to mortgage.

Shekhar Sen's pleasant remembrance of my childhood days in his locality faded very quickly at the mention of the movie.

'Ali Khan?' he grimaced. 'Why him? He's history, champ.'

He talked that way. We were sitting out in his veranda, looking at a small, well-tended lawn and overhearing a game of football on the television indoors.

The journalist had a plump, bespectacled face, appraising eyes, and a definite accent, derived from Oxford and Cambridge and all the seminars abroad.

'Nowadays,' he told me, 'young people are making films about so many important issues. And you guys are making a film about a cricketer. A forgotten cricketer.'

He was shaking his head all the while he was speaking. I started to change my forced smile into explanatory speech but was interrupted by a tremendous exclamation from within the house.

'Owen equalises!'

'Way to go,' Sen called back grimly.

'Cricket's not even the top game any longer,' he shrugged at me. 'You kids have choices now, and I'd say high-level football is just better television. Cricket's old hat.'

I tried to remind him of the many columns of newsprint he'd spent on the old hat.

'That was a long time ago. You know something,' he looked at me steadily from over the rim of his spectacles. 'I was trying to save the game. My take on it was its only chance of survival. Cricket had to become first and foremost entertainment – and leave behind the fuddy-duddy image. And I thought this Ali fellow might be able to do that.

'He talked the talk. He walked the walk. He had the swagger. He gave the finger to all the old-fashioned business. Religion was out, nationalism,' he used the term in a matter-of-fact way, 'was out. What mattered was only personal achievement and most importantly,' Sen raised his index finger, 'entertainment.'

'Do you think he was actually . . . guilty? I mean – of match-fixing.'

'Of course he was. How should I know anyway?' he added immediately. 'You know as much as I know, because you've read my stuff. I still believe that in that semi-final he walked because he'd been paid to. It was the most entertaining finish possible.'

'Why's that?' I asked impulsively.

'Because of course Australia should have won. You think we deserved to beat them? No way. Our players are a bunch of school kids in comparison.'

This was a confusing answer, until I remembered what Prashant had said the previous Saturday over lunch. Perhaps it was true that Khan's various critics had put their own, preferred spin on his walk, so as to convince themselves that he had shared their fetters. Sen's fetters, I supposed, were the colonial hangover – and money.

However, naturally, I didn't say this out loud. Instead, I goaded him gently.

'Ali Khan didn't agree with you, did he?'

Shekhar Sen grimaced.

'Ali Khan's a crazy chap. He doesn't agree with anyone, and never did. I always had trouble with him – even long before the sting. I suppose you remember that interview we did.'

I didn't remember, but Prashant had mentioned it in his letter to Khan. I knew it had been a bad-tempered affair.

'And during the sting, and of course long after. He sent me some wild letters when I published the article after the semi-final. He said I was tarnishing his legacy. The guy spends the prime of his adult life knocking about a piece of leather with a piece of wood — and then talks of his legacy! I don't believe there's any other explanation for that walk, when you know the man. The spirit of cricket nonsense never washed with him, I can tell you that much. You recall how he punched Alex Jones in New Zealand? Spirit of cricket, my foot.'

I made a non-committal murmur, but inwardly I demurred. Alex Jones was a well-known boor and provocateur and I remembered me and my friends being deeply glad when Ali Khan had knocked him out on the streets of Wellington.

'Anyway,' Sen was saying, 'I stopped being interested after that. That piece after the semi-final was the last piece I wrote on cricket. There are more important things to worry about.'

I suppressed a smile. Sen's expression was the paper-thin mask of superiority to which we all resort, when an old, fresh trauma must be passed off as long-since conquered.

I got to the point.

'Can we interview you, for our movie?'

He hadn't expected that. And I hadn't expected his reaction.

'Why do you want to?'

'We have a section on the sting — and everything that happened after that. We thought we could get your side —'

— I suppose it was a poor choice of words —

— 'my *side*?

'Listen, champ.' This time he wasn't being friendly. 'You guys are just kids.'

It was the old, familiar line of attack – used on this occasion for context.

'I don't do cricket writing any more. I do other things. I'm not interested in having my stuff on Khan raked up again.'

'We thought,' I said respectfully, 'it'd be important.'

'Well, it's not important. The whole *subject* is just not important. People are struggling to get three meals a day and you're talking about a *sportsman*.'

'We have some new ideas about it.'

He looked, for a moment, most amused. Then he stopped smiling.

'Let me give you some advice,' he said.

'I've been in journalism twenty-five years. The way to tell a story is to put your head down, get to know some people, start off on a small scale and work your way upwards – and not to expect that a few half-baked *ideas* will come to anything. When you're seventy and the whole world humours you, then you can tell us what you just think. Until then, it's the hard miles and the hard hours. You've got to understand –'

As I heard him speaking, something stirred within me. My heart still beat faster to the chant of the long, self-effacing, masochistic haul.

Involuntarily, my fingers closed around the arms of the wicker chair. Inside of me, I felt suddenly hollow. My face contorted.

'All right,' I interrupted desperately. 'All right! I understand!'

Brought up short, Shekhar Sen looked at me suspiciously. Then he hammered home his advantage.

'Well I hope you'll drop the idea now. In any case, I want you to keep my name out of the movie.

'Does your father know you're doing this?' he added. 'Just because you've got a few newspaper articles to talk it up, doesn't mean this will go anywhere.'

The sunshine in the veranda was growing oppressive. Inside, the football commentator was figuratively keeling over in paroxysms of excitement, and the pubescent voice of what I supposed was Shekhar's son was shooting out at us in periodic, painful shards. I got to my feet.

'Thank you – it was very useful talking to you.'

'I hope it was,' he said firmly. 'I take it you've understood me?'

'I . . .'

Then I pulled myself together, 'I'll keep it in mind.' I turned away from him.

'Hang on a second, champ.'

'Let me have a number for your friend, the director. You're all just kids,' Shekhar Sen repeated, 'but you have to be careful what you say. You don't want to go stepping on other people's toes.'

After I'd given him the number, he said a couple more circuitous, vaguely warning sentences, before I was finally able to leave.

This failed encounter I reported cursorily to Prashant over the telephone. We decided we'd talk about it later. In the meantime, still stinging from Shekhar Sen's generations' old rebuke and the looming image of my father, I plunged desperately into work.

~

When I surfaced two weeks later, my confused conscience placated for the time being with the penance of my toil, I called Prashant again.

He answered at the first ring.

'Vaibhav. You heard?'

'No.'

'The goons came again.'

'What?'

'They came again.'

At three o'clock in the afternoon on the previous day, three men had clattered on the latch of the gate of Prashant's house. The clatterer-in-chief had been carrying a short, heavy stick. Luckily or unluckily, nobody had been at home – except the servant, Rajendran.

They didn't believe that, though. From the house they went to the park, and finding that empty, they returned to leave a 'message.'

Rajendran had enquired whether they wanted paper and ink. In the best traditions of their profession, the men had told him they'd prefer blood.

'"But what about the paper?"'

'He actually asked them that?' I couldn't believe it.

'Yes,' Prashant laughed. 'He just . . . . stymied them.'

One of them had taken a step in anger towards the servant. The muscles on the man's forehead had been quivering with whatever violent emotion Rajendran had aroused – as he later recounted in exact detail.

However, they had left him unharmed. They had taken the stick to the Mercedes instead.

'I hope it can be repaired,' said Prashant. 'My dad never let anybody touch it – and now this. The only good thing is my old Maruti is still A-OK!'

He was trying hard to be flippant, but the quiver in his voice betrayed his trauma. Without delay, Animesh and I dropped what we were doing and drove over to see him.

That whole fortnight, the city's skies had promised rain. Every four o'clock, the premature dark and the billowing gusts of wind had had the children at my apartment itching to congregate in the open compounds. It had showered sporadically, but until now the clouds hadn't burst.

I was pulling my car into the colony gates when the first big drops splattered against the windscreen. By the time we had hurried under the roof of Prashant's summerhouse, the rain was falling in dizzy sheets.

In the secure interior, Ali Khan was waiting. He was wearing a black raincoat that was slick with recent use. He had his back to the garden, and all around his still head the water was streaming down the pane of glass, spreading and obscuring the vivid colours of the flowers outside. I nodded silently at him; he looked at me gravely from under the hood of his coat.

The door opened a crack. Prashant slipped indoors and pressed it carefully shut behind him. Then he turned to face us.

'It's no use,' he announced. 'My father went to the station, but the police say they don't know anybody who matches Rajendran's description of those men. I guess the men have impunity.'

He sat down heavily.

'I don't even know what they *want*. All right, they broke up the car — but why? What's their point?'

'We know their point,' Animesh said sagely. 'They made it very clear the last time in the park — they don't want the movie.'

'Even Ibrahim,' Prashant retorted, 'was willing to discuss it. Why don't they *discuss* it?'

The boy's face was dark with worry. I empathised instinctively. The stubbornness of a mob is something inhuman: it is the sort of animal incomprehension that reduces well-meaning people to disbelieving tears. I realised suddenly that I wasn't far from tears myself.

Ali Khan cleared his throat.

'They won't touch you, if I'm with you,' he said gently. 'We can figure a way out.'

'I think so too,' said Prashant.

They were looking at each other with a mutual, tender determination and it was worrying me intensely. How could it be right to have strangers vandalise your property without some systematic recourse – some assistance from a friendly, impersonal source? In my head I was still thinking 'police'; I couldn't adjust to the idea that they had washed their hands off the whole affair so promptly.

'What do your parents say, Prashant?' I said in a strange, choking voice.

'That I should ask my aunt to get the news out that the movie is off.'

I breathed deeply. With a certain relieved shame I put my weight behind that suggestion.

'Later you can double-cross them and go ahead anyway!' I added wildly.

Prashant bit his lip. Behind his spectacles, his eyes flickered distractedly. Then as I watched, he seemed suddenly to relax.

'It wouldn't feel right,' he said at last. His tone was uncomfortably reasonable.

'It wouldn't feel right because it doesn't feel necessary. Maybe it's because I didn't see the men myself but I'd feel like I'm second-guessing myself if I – if we stop now. It would be too . . . showy.

'And I'm sure this can be straightened out,' he continued aggressively. 'Half the problem is, these guys don't even know what the movie is about.'

I looked at Animesh for support, and then felt an immediate contempt for him. He was sitting at Prashant's computer. He had his eyes shut. For all I knew he was meditating.

Grimly, I went on.

'Shekhar Sen doesn't want his name mentioned. He doesn't even want the movie made.'

I told them the details of my talk with the journalist.

'According to Sen,' I concluded flatly, 'the whole idea of the movie is overblown and unimportant. He said there are many more worthwhile subjects around.'

I didn't hold anything back. I know that the giver of wounds is the enemy, and not the quoted critic, but I didn't like the way my apprehensions over the vandals were being disregarded. I meant to be unkind.

'He thinks we're flailing about and wasting our time.'

They took it well, Prashant and Ali Khan. Prashant chuckled.

'Shekhar Sen is just afraid that his prospective employers won't be thrilled at his tabloid past. He doesn't want it raked up. There's some politics there – my aunt was telling me.

'And his advice! Now that's what I call mean-spirited advice,' Prashant grinned sardonically. 'The idea behind it is to stop anyone doing anything.'

'Maybe he's simply realised that cricket is only a game,' I said stubbornly.

'I think,' Prashant gave Khan a friendly, knowing glance, 'that when someone spends all his best and most grownup faculties on a game, it can hardly be "only a game".'

'And look,' he added gently, 'there's always a "more important" subject. But if it isn't your subject, it isn't your subject. What are you going to do?'

He was enjoying the taste of his rhetoric. He liked the smack of forceful words. Prashant narrowed his eyes; his lips curled. The current of feeling that charged his response was still flowing.

'You know what, Vaibhav?' he said suddenly, with the most beautiful candour.

'No, I don't,' I smiled back at him -- he had that effect.

'There's a different rule -- for genius. That's what the Shekhar Sens of this world don't understand.'

Not even the elder man's presence tempered his enthusiasm. Ali Khan was regarding Prashant with raised eyebrows, but without scepticism. His experienced eyes were not immune to the other's vivid charm. Call it an appalling sentimentality, but I dare say he saw something of himself in the boy across the room.

A volley of wind sent the rain scything against the windows of the summerhouse. Khan raised the timbre of his voice above the battery outside.

'You three understand events better than any journalist I've known.'

'Why, thank you.'

That was Animesh. I gave him a look. Prashant replied indirectly, to deflect the burden of the compliment.

'I honestly think it's simply a question of getting it right. All our guesses and all our theories are fundamentally fine. Shekhar Sen's were fundamentally rotten. And of course we have to point that out. He doesn't get to decide who talks about his writings.'

'May I say,' said Khan, with merriment in his eyes, 'how glad I am that you chose my career as a topic for your talents?'

Outside, the downpour had not abated. I wished it would, because I couldn't hear myself think. This was all very well,

I told myself, this mutual appreciation, but how much more manageable was the decorous protest of the journalist than the blind violence of Yadav's men? Prashant had strung together a few uplifting sentences that disposed neatly of an intellectual attack – but the Mercedes was still a broken wreck. What good were pretty sentiments when your opponent had a gun? Slowly, my optimistic mood of the last five minutes began to sink.

'Vaibhav,' I heard Prashant say. My misgivings must have showed in my expression.

'Hey Vaibhav,' he said pointedly. 'It's going to be a great movie. You know that.'

I remembered later the next sentence he spoke.

'There's nothing to worry about because I can take all comers. It's all easier – it's all easier done than said.'

There was no grin then, and there were no dramatics either. It was a staggering thing, but I think he meant it as plainly as he said it. I waited, in the seconds just after that speech – for the apologetic laugh, the backward step that nine out of ten would have succumbed to. But it never came.

'We're going to Goa,' he reminded me instead. 'Goa!' he said again, and I smiled too. 'But when you say so. Some weekend? Or can you take a few days off? The rest of us are okay with anytime.'

'The sooner the better,' Animesh chipped in.

We discussed that for a little while. Eventually, we settled on the following Tuesday. My boss was going out of town then, and a 'personal' workplace like Wildlife Alert didn't work much without the person in charge.

All through the rest of the evening, Animesh and I stayed in Prashant's summerhouse, waiting for the rain to stop. In that time we talked about the upcoming series in South Africa, and then Khan started to tell us stories from his playing days. I barely noticed when the sun came out again.

And I don't think I would have noticed, not for a long while, if my phone hadn't beeped to break the spell. It was a reminder I'd set myself to call Anita that evening – I had made a resolution to call her more often.

That was the reason I left in a hurry. I said a quick goodbye, and by the time I was out of the door the other three had returned already to their conversation. So I didn't get a proper look at Prashant. He was giggling at something with his back to me, and I couldn't see his face.

Well, you can't legislate these things. It was how it was and I never saw him again.

10

LONG BEFORE I heard the news, another blow had set me tottering.

I had had bad moments before with Anita. But they hadn't been like this. When I went home that night and telephoned her, it wasn't anything in particular that she said -- I could have dealt with that. It was her tone. In a dispirited way, she told me how her day had gone, as though it was a chore. She didn't complain about any of the trouble she was having with her boss, and she didn't enthuse about the movie she'd seen last night. She just told me. There had been a suggestion, the previous week, that she might visit me in Delhi, but when I raised the subject now, she was vague and dispirited. I realised also that there were voices in the background. Before I knew it she was hanging up with a hurried 'catch you later'.

Afterwards, a dull and painful silence settled about me. Suddenly, strangely, I wanted her desperately. I sat, paralysed, on the edge of the bed, thinking hollowly that I should call her back. What would I say, though? We hadn't quarrelled. This dread feeling was new territory for me.

But I am no stronger than the next man. To consider calling is to inevitably call. Ten minutes later, I rushed for the phone and beat out the digits, hoping to catch her on my drummed-up emotional high. A woman's voice informed me that her phone was switched off.

I flung myself onto my bed and switched my laptop on. I put on *Kiss the Rain*. At two minutes and ten seconds it started to seem just trivial.

So I phoned Gitanjali instead.

'All it means,' she assured me, 'is that Anita didn't feel like talking. That can happen sometimes.'

'I know – but it was *me*.'

'Oh, stop it.'

'What? What?'

Gitanjali sighed.

'Just let her be.'

'But I don't even know how she's feeling,' I protested. 'Why isn't she coming to Delhi like she'd planned?'

'Listen,' Gitanjali's voice was kindly, calm. 'The biggest mistake you can make now is to try to ferret out how Anita's feeling. If she wanted you to do that, she'd have let you know. Right now, you've got to swallow your curiosity, and the next time you talk, maybe she'll be fine again.'

'What if she isn't?'

'Then you cross that bridge when you come to it.'

A pensive silence ensued. Then Gitanjali said:

'Why don't *you* go to Mumbai?'

'I . . . there's work.'

'I thought you were quitting work. You told me that last Tuesday.'

So I had. The previous week, my boss had suggested that I write fulltime for Wildlife Alert's monthly reports. This was a step-up in the professional hierarchy and superficially a high, but deep down, I had heard the alarm bells ringing. I knew that the longer I lingered in this job, the harder it was going to be to break free. And yet —

'It's complicated,' I complained.

'How so?' Gitanjali asked patiently. 'Would your parents object?'

'My parents,' I laughed mirthlessly. 'My parents would be thrilled. They'd like nothing better than for me to leave this crazy line and get a nice, cushy "company job". But see,' I insisted, 'that's just it. I don't want to do something conventional, just to please them. My parents treat me like some precious, fragile thing that will break the moment it's bent. They don't know what I'm capable of. I'm not . . . I'm not someone *ordinary*. I can bend!'

I could sense Gitanjali smiling. 'Yes you can,' she agreed. 'Just don't bend over backwards. Anyway listen — you could still take some time off, and go see Anita.'

A prickle of embarrassment crawled over me. 'I am taking time off,' I admitted. 'I'm going to Goa with Prashant.'

That weekend, I spent half of Saturday and all of Sunday at the office, finishing a proposal for a funding possibility that was on the horizon. This was more conscientious than my deadline warranted — but that date didn't factor in a jaunt to Goa. I had taken leave starting Monday, and I managed my work so I was almost finished by the early hours of Monday morning. Then I crept back home, waking late and unbothered several hours later.

Looking back at it now, I find I can remember details of that day that I normally never would. Perhaps this is because I have played it over to myself so many times since.

In the morning I drew aside the curtains, and let the sunshine come streaming into the living room. Almost anything looks good if you throw enough light on it, and in this bright flood, even our usual mess acquired a certain unabashed glory. The dust motes were dancing in the rays, and I was slipping into a familiar, peaceable mood – the college holiday mood, when there is nothing ahead of you but cheap food and more leisure.

This is all more so when you are coming off a recent burst of hard work. My mind was still flushed from the triumph of the completed proposal. For the time being, I was not assailed by any of my abiding worries – not my parents, not Anita, not even the guilt that in a day's time I was going to Goa, when I could have been going to Mumbai.

Animesh, groggy, and for once, my inferior in self-possession, was a fine target for my exuberance. When he emerged sleepily into sight, I sang a burst of a Hindi song at him.

'Kucch kar le, kucch kar le . . .'

'How's it going?' I threw a cushion at him. 'Are you packed yet? Got your swim things ready? It's Goa – look sharp!'

I was feeling light-headed.

'What's the matter?' I asked. 'Late night?'

He nodded. 'Movie,' he explained.

'Oh, really? What movie? And with whom?' I added significantly.

'The Legend of Zombie Central. With nobody.'

'Why am I not surprised?'

He shrugged. 'I liked it.'

I gave him a dubious look, and then, as I looked, an old curiosity roused within me.

'Hey Animesh – what are your essays about?'

He loped over towards the sofa and sat down in front of the television. He didn't turn it on. Of course, he couldn't relinquish the attention.

'At the moment,' he said, 'my subject is the confluence of personal and public lives.'

'Meaning?'

'Meaning: is there ever a contradiction between how someone is at home and by themselves, and how they are in the world outside? Does your work define who you are? Or is life what happens outside work?'

It was 11.30 a.m. We were both in our pyjamas. I, at least, had a job in life. I reckoned this kind of talk should remain confined to one particular time and place: the witching hours of the college years.

'Animesh,' I said gently. 'Why does that question occur to you? The answer, by the way – and it's the same answer to everything – is sometimes yes and sometimes no. A bit of both. The midpoint. I can tell you that without two minutes' thinking, and you'll tell me that after two months' thinking. *Your* life certainly mirrors your work,' I exploded warmly. 'Both bloody useless.'

They were harsh words, but my geniality took the edge off them. Animesh smiled good-humouredly.

'When I'm rich and famous,' he said, 'I'll be sure to remember you. Besides, I'm more useful than you think. I pass off as worse than I am, but that's better than the other way around.'

'It sounds manipulative,' I said primly, thinking suddenly of Anita.

'It isn't. Being criticised unfairly is no problem. But being praised for what you haven't done is unbearable.'

As usual, he had made the conversation too abstract for my taste. I was eyeing him uncomfortably. He met my gaze with a placid regard. He looked small and objectively insignificant, but his relentless egoism painted him in mysterious hues.

'You know what?' I said suddenly. 'You're like a girl. Girls like to make themselves difficult to understand. But men are supposed to act simply – and just say what they mean. Real men.'

'Real men?' Animesh raised an unperturbed eyebrow. Suddenly he sighed.

'The trouble,' he said distantly, 'is that everybody assumes they know all about men. Boys will be boys, they say, and they leave it at that. Women think only of women. Men think only of women. No wonder we finish up so misunderstood.' He looked at me wearily, 'You should be ashamed of yourself.'

I arched my neck in surprise.

'It makes you so vulnerable,' he went on, with the same air of grand tragedy. 'It makes you a pawn in other people's hands. It makes my job so much harder.'

'Your job?'

'My job – to set people thinking straight.'

'Oh, I see, so that's your *job*? Well, Mahatma, I'm happy to say I can relieve you the burden of saving *this* damned –'

'One second.'

I stared at him moodily, while he kept his hand raised and his head lowered.

'Your job,' I muttered bleakly, 'I suppose Prashant is one of your disciples, then? No wonder you're always so pleased with him.'

He was looking at his cell phone. Something in his expression made me pay attention. A certain stiffness.

'What is it?'

He didn't answer immediately. When he did, his tone was as usual again. In fact, it was more toneless than anything.

'It's from Gitanjali. I think it's a group message.'

'What does it say?'

I felt a telltale vibration.

'Wait, I think I've got it too.'

'It's about Prashant,' Animesh said quietly.

I remember now, how I felt at the precise moment that I read that message. It was with the growing self-consciousness, that this was one of the crises of my life.

'Prashant died last night. Accident at home. Please tell whoever you can contact. Trying to find out when the cremation will be – Gitanjali.'

But I cannot remember the moment after, because it was nothing, literally nothing. No sooner was I done reading, than there opened up a void in my consciousness, a pitch-black abyss that swallowed whole the march of my thoughts. It was only a minute later, I know, that was I coming to again, but my blinking, disbelieving eyes were trained on a different world.

Stupidly, my mind veered towards Gitanjali and away from the contents of her message. How had she felt when she wrote it? How odd to be communicating such shattering news in such an impersonal manner? Was not the word 'died' too stark?

'God . . .' I whispered. I stared at Animesh. Nothing more had struck home.

I shifted my eyes in the cheerful, streaming light, but I didn't notice the room any longer. I was concentrating on my own bewildered self. Amidst the jungle of feeble thoughts, one struck me as worth speaking.

'Should we go to his house?'

'I think – not yet. His parents . . . Let me find out what happened,' Animesh said distractedly, 'I'll call Gitanjali.'

There, in front of me, he dialled her number and began a short, one-sided conversation. In the time he was listening to what she was saying, I tried to collect my thoughts. I was searching my memory for some poignant image of Prashant; some snapshot of his signature smile, or the way he drove his car, or the fits of giggler that he always burst into.

I wanted desperately to worry the wound. But every hurt isn't a toothache. You can't size it up so easily, so quickly.

Animesh lowered his phone. I looked up at him.

'What did she say?'

'She doesn't know the details. He was found this morning slumped face-down on the floor of the summerhouse. They thought at first he might have fallen asleep there. He did, sometimes.'

I winced.

'Who found him?'

'His father.'

'His father called the ambulance,' Animesh went on wearily. 'But apparently, Prashant was dead already.'

'No, I mean,' I protested, 'what was the cause of death?'

Automatically, I was using the jargon.

'A hit to the head. They think he fell and hit his head against the ledge in that room — where he keeps his camera. They also think he was drunk.'

'Who's they?'

'Oh – the police. And the doctors too, I suppose. The cremation is at three o'clock.'

I looked at my watch. My heart thudded slowly. Three o'clock was just a few more hours. Just days ago we had sat and talked. Now, for the first time, I felt reality teetering.

'What a . . . thing,' I clenched my fists tight around my chair.

The crematorium was near Okhla. It was an electric crematorium; a phrase and an idea that made me shudder. We drove there along empty roads on a day shaping up as the last gasp of the dying summer. I cocked a disheartened eye at the shining blue sky; the unrelenting sun. In my bones I felt sick. Once, my mother had undergone a petty but worrisome surgery, and I had spent a night in a hospital's waiting room, watching gruesome scenes of blood and violence, flashing like nightmares on a wall TV. It was one of those modern 'news' channels that I had laughed at many times from my drawing-room sofa. But that night, the horror had taken me. And the same deep-set dejection, the same hopeless surrender to an alien world that had enveloped me then, I was experiencing now.

The crematorium walls were a dirty white, and high, like the walls of a fortress. I tried to turn into the main gate, but a crowd of people in what I registered vaguely as traditional dress – were they mourners? – had blocked the entrance. A gruff voice called out to me to move along – just move along.

We circled the place for ten minutes, trying to find a spot to park. I was growing tense with the idea that we'd be too late for the ceremony, if that was the word. Then, on the third revolution, a policeman appeared.

'Do you want to park?'

He directed me into an opening that I hadn't spotted before. I manoeuvred the car onto an elevated open space, where four or five other vehicles were already parked, including Madhav's Lancer. We got out and I looked down at a stone courtyard, steeped in sunshine, and milling gradually with slow-moving figures. I thought I recognised Gitanjali, and Roshan, and Vivek.

The policeman was by my side.

'You here for the New Friends case?' he said.

He was forty-ish, I suppose. He was plump, with thin hair, and thin lips pursed together morosely. Something unhealthy flickered in his eye.

'I know about that family,' he went on officiously. 'After all that Mr Padmanabhan has done – his son let him down.'

'What do you mean "let him down"?' I murmured rhetorically. 'It was an accident. Come on, Animesh, let's go.'

'It was an accident caused by him. Young people drink too much nowadays. Just the other day at Connaught Place, there was a car crash. Don't you read the papers?'

I closed my eyes and turned away.

'You're all too spoilt,' he called out disdainfully. 'You bring it upon yourself. God balances riches with calamity.'

He practically snickered then.

We left him behind, and started on the mud slope down to the courtyard. I was surprised at how much I was seething. It wasn't the policeman's general thesis, and it wasn't even his timing. It was the slur that had stung me.

'How could Prashant get that drunk?' I said bitterly.

Beside me, Animesh frowned.

'I've never known him to be drunk – at home, I mean. You remember his saying to you that he only drank in company?'

'For other people's sake,' I nodded. 'That's what he said. I didn't really understand what he meant though.'

'He told me once,' Animesh was smiling sadly, 'that a single unselfconscious drunkard pays for a whole company's self-esteem. Like a rich man can pay for their meal. But people like to feel superior even better than they like to feel wealthy.'

I shook my head deliberately – to clear it. We stumbled down the last few paces into the desolate crowd below.

The whole horrible affair lasted an hour and a half. In the beginning I didn't speak to anybody, and nobody spoke much at all. I think we were all waiting for the moment when Prashant's parents would arrive. Any pattern of behaviour that we struck up before then would be premature.

But I couldn't really look when they did come, except to stare at intervals in a stark, stricken way. His mother was sobbing. I'd never seen his father before. He was a short man with alert Keralite eyes and the same tense mouth his son had had, and the same confident gait too – but all that was only from memory. Apparent behind the controlled exterior was his lost and broken self. It was all worse than I had imagined it would be, and soon enough there was more wailing and more tears and more helplessness than my nerves could withstand.

That I didn't cry myself, was due only to Animesh. All through the congregation in the central hall, and the awful, hollow imperative of looking at the corpse – I had only a glimpse and I wanted no more – and later, when we stood around listening to the crackle of the electric operation in the adjoining room, I stayed with Animesh. It seemed the whole company was dissolving into tears and I felt the impulse of that dreamy, dire mood – but apparently he didn't. He just looked stern. So I held on too.

I say this not proudly, but as a matter of fact, and because it helps to explain why afterwards, when we all ebbed out into the early evening, I was still able to think.

Naturally, I had looked for how other people would react – I suppose that was a game everyone was playing. I had been surprised to see how powerfully affected Madhav had been, and how down in the dumps Roshan had looked. I had also noticed that Sheila wasn't around.

Gitanjali emerged, determined, ahead of me. Her eyes were quite dry.

'Hi,' she said.

I tried to gauge her mood. I realised she had been too involved with the organisation of that afternoon to partake fully of its emotions. It was an effect I was familiar with personally, albeit in happier circumstances.

'Hi,' I answered. 'Where's Sheila?'

'Oh, she's at home. She couldn't . . . take it,' Gitanjali explained, 'You know.'

I nodded.

'How're you then?' I asked her brightly.

She didn't answer. She shrugged slightly and I caught a certain wild plea in her eyes, just an instant before she reverted to a mask of composure.

'I got the phone call from Pravin Uncle at eight this morning. Prashant's father. I mean – was his father. I mean is – well, you know. I went straight over.'

Listening gravely to our conversation, Animesh intervened.

'Is his father, is correct. Because there's no such thing as an ex-father.'

I opened my mouth to chastise this flippancy, but I found, to my astonishment, that I wanted to smile. Gradually, then, our emotions recovered a semblance of balance. We walked aside to a corner of the courtyard, where the canopy of a gulmohar tree was keeping out the sun. Standing forlornly in the shade, Gitanjali clicked her tongue with disgust.

'It's such a stupid thing to happen. Such a *freak* thing to happen. And it wasn't even a fatal blow or anything. I mean, it didn't have to be. He didn't . . . die . . . at once. The doctor at the hospital said it took several hours.'

'Then he must have been unconscious,' I said.

'Yes. And if he hadn't been, he would have got help, and it would all have been *fine*.'

Her hard, small face slackened. She pouted unhappily. I took a half-step forward towards her, but she leaned fractionally away from me. The message was: I'm okay.

A grisly curiosity provoked me onwards.

'Did you go to the hospital too? Did you see what sort of wound it was?'

'Owww!' Gitanjali made a face, and immediately I stammered an apology.

Suddenly she gave me a steady look.

'There was no wound.' She jerked her head toward the crematorium wall. 'He looked just like he did in there. The doctor said it was all internal bleeding. Closed head trauma. He had a weak skull, you know – otherwise it might have protected him.'

I nodded. I had noticed, also, that Gitanjali was avoiding saying Prashant's name. Again, I had the sense she was putting up a particularly brave face. Of course, she was close to his whole family, in a way that the rest of us weren't.

Nobody spoke for a while, until she confided another moment of her torrid day.

'They had to break down the door.'

'How come?'

'Because it was locked, silly. The summerhouse was locked, the windows were bolted, and he was inside. And he didn't answer when Uncle knocked.'

'So,' Animesh said thoughtfully, 'he was alone inside. He hit his head on the ledge and he fell unconscious – and then after a few hours . . .'

'That was it,' said Gitanjali. 'How . . . *stupid* is that?'

I felt a brief burst of affection for her, and her inadequate, expressive vocabulary. Meanwhile, Animesh was still thinking aloud.

'If he was found alone in a locked room, then of course it had to be an accident. There's no other explanation.'

'Of course not,' Gitanjali looked at him, startled.

'I heard he was drunk,' I offered disingenuously.

She pursed her lips. 'That's what the police say.'

'You don't think it's true.'

'What? No – I was just . . . surprised.'

Then her face became earnest.

'One thing that did bother me was how the police behaved. They were so . . . rude. And indifferent. I mean, it was awful for Uncle and Aunty. They were more concerned about the stupid car.'

'What?'

'His old Maruti,' she said listlessly. 'It had some bumps and scratches.'

From the shifting group in the courtyard, an elderly lady in a faded green sari stumbled into the sun, with her arms half-outstretched and her eyes half-closed.

'That's his aunt,' Gitanjali whispered. 'I have to go.'

'Oh, I see,' I murmured. I watched the two of them embrace. It was strange to see Shanta Padmanabhan, Prashant's hitherto-unseen benefactor, so cruelly materialised.

Then my wondering gaze stiffened. Another figure was shuffling along in the distance, a little way apart from anybody else, looking this way and that in a bemused fashion. It was the figure of a man – an old man with an unmistakable flowing beard.

Animesh came up beside me, 'Isn't that –'

'Saeed Ibrahim,' I stared disbelievingly, 'Yes it is. What in the world is *he* doing here?'

11

IBRAHIM SAW US coming towards him. His grave eyes focused. As before, I noticed his pout, which now signified a deep disturbance.

'Ah . . .' he ventured, 'we met . . .'

'In the court, yes.'

'Yes.'

I waited for him to say something more, but he didn't.

He seemed taller now than I remembered. He was wearing a kurta that wasn't any kind I recognised; it had an earthy, authentic design, which, like his flowing beard, spoke deliberately of a certain pious rootedness. I found it oppressive.

'What are you doing here?' I demanded at last.

'I did not expect to be here.

'It's very difficult for me to be here,' he complained further. 'The body should not be disrespected.'

'What do you mean "disrespected"?'

Animesh leaned over.

'He means the cremation.'

'Oh!'

At that time, my ordinary inhibitions had no hold over me. I turned to glare at Ibrahim. I wanted to tell him off with a pithy denunciation, but my voice didn't hold. I finished up screeching.

'Nobody asked you to come. But since you have come, have the decency not to judge things you don't even . . . under*stand*!'

Angry tears pricked suddenly at my eyes. I swallowed a lump in my throat.

But I was glad to see my outburst wipe the self-regard from Ibrahim's face. With an effort, he affected an air of understanding.

'Death comes to us all, my son. Your friend was perhaps too good . . . The world is not so good.'

'I met him just yesterday,' he said. 'We had a very nice discussion.'

'You met him yesterday?'

'He called me,' the old man answered proudly, 'for a compromise.'

Ibrahim used the word lovingly – like someone patting a favourite pet.

'You mean,' I said, 'Prashant called you to settle your case?'

'That's right.'

I was surprised. Ill-advised as I had felt it to be, I had reconciled myself to Prashant's stated tactic of a blanket defiance to all the opposition the movie faced, and I suppose, inwardly, I had admired him for it. At this latest news, I felt a little let down – and then suddenly I felt very tired.

'Let's just go,' I turned to Animesh. 'Everybody's going.'

A few stray figures had disappeared through the gates, but the majority still hung about in many wretched pockets, spread out through the central hall and the courtyard where we were standing.

He ignored me. He was looking intently at Ibrahim.

'Did Prashant call you to his house?'

'Yes, he did. Your friend had good manners. He learned from his mistakes.'

'Why don't we walk up, sir,' Animesh requested,' 'to the parking? We can talk there.'

He had injected into his tone a wheedling plea that probably struck Ibrahim as properly respectful. I didn't like it, but I didn't have any more emotional reserves from which to summon up a response.

The weather closed in all around as I dragged my feet up the thirty feet of slope. By the time we reached the top, I was perspiring steadily in the muggy air. Experimentally, I touched the bonnet of my car, and it flared up against my hand. I turned wearily to look at Ibrahim. Just then he seemed to me about six feet tall.

All the same, he was waiting expectantly — even eagerly — to be questioned, in a way that took the authority of that looming figure, that kurta, the beard and those wrinkles, right away. My mood didn't permit me to think it then, but it was the one nice thing about Saeed Ibrahim's appearance, that it survived his getup. It was the reason he had been able to strike us as friendly the first time we had spoken at Tis Hazari.

'Your friend,' he was recounting happily, 'yes, he phoned me. He apologised to me. Said he was glad I had offered to discuss the case with him. Said he knew some people who don't bother to talk. They only want to fight.'

I exchanged a glance with Animesh. I thought of Arindam Yadav and the mob and the battered Mercedes.

'He said, could I come to his house and we could discuss the script? I checked my diary and I gave him a time.'

'*You* gave him a time?'

I looked sardonically at Animesh – but he was doing a good impression of hanging on the other's lips.

'I was free at three o'clock,' Ibrahim informed us. 'So I met him then – and we talked. Your friend's aunt,' he added thoughtfully, 'is a great name. A really great name. I did not know that.'

'What did you talk about?'

'Many things. About morality. We talked about the principles of morality. We talked about the cheerleaders in cricket and how wrong they are. We agreed a lot. He told me he was convinced by my plaint. He is a wise young man, your friend. He has a very wise head on his shoulders.'

I didn't bother correcting his tense. The content of Ibrahim's disjointed speech puzzled me. He was going on reminiscing.

'He admitted his mistake. He showed me the script. He even interviewed me for the movie.'

'I thought you wanted an injunction,' I blurted out, 'to stop the movie ever being made.'

Ibrahim glared at me as though I was a heckler.

'Today,' he continued sonorously, 'I had gone to his house again with the papers of my old suit against Khan. He was supposed to meet me there. Then I heard he was dead.'

'So you came here?'

'So I came here.'

The incredible suggestion was that Prashant should keep his appointment. In this dreamy, imbecile spirit had Saeed Ibrahim arrived at the crematorium.

'Mr Ibrahim,' Animesh was staring eagerly. 'This means that when you met Prashant – in the afternoon yesterday – he wasn't drunk.'

'Eh?'

'When you met him, he was not drunk?'

I gave Animesh a quick look. His young face was the very archetype of innocence: round cheeks, wide eyes and a self-effacing curiosity. But we see the things we suspect. The lawyer shuddered down the whole length of his frame.

'Drunk . . .' He gathered himself. 'Drunk!' he said again, fairly spitting the syllable. 'Don't mock me, young man! Don't use wrong words!'

I allowed myself a minor smile while Animesh hastened to explain that he hadn't intended to cause offence. But I wasn't really paying attention any longer. I had taken a few steps aside from the other two. Familiar faces still crowded in the courtyard, and I wondered if something else was going on down below.

A burst of sobs rent the air, aching, staccato gasps. Prashant's mother emerged into the sunlight. Her face was buried in another woman's shoulder. A fresh wave of bleakness washed over me.

'Maybe,' I said, 'we should be with the others.'

But the others were coming to us. Madhav, Roshan and Vivek were trudging up the incline. From a distance, Roshan tossed his head at me in a comradely fashion. Close up, he stretched his hand out for a brotherly clasp, the preliminary to a brotherly embrace. Animesh got the same treatment.

Madhav's features were like graven stone. It occurred to me how well he looked as a mourner; his natural rigid manner fitted the bill. Only Vivek, like me, seemed uncertain of what to do and how to stand and what to say.

Roshan had something to say.

'Listen. Hey – Vaibhav. I thought of something that we should really . . . *do*.'

'Yeah?'

'Yeah,' he said emphatically. 'We should do a tribute to Prashant.'

He used the word 'tribute' rather like Ibrahim did 'compromise' – as a term of art – only less warmly and more warily.

'What kind of . . . tribute?' I asked doubtfully.

Madhav explained.

'The movie about Ali Khan meant so much to Prashant. It'll mean a lot to his parents, too. We should see it finished. One of us can take over the direction.'

'Well – I suppose –'

'I trust the movie is being made?'

Saeed Ibrahim's voice cracked querulously. He was regarding us with a jolly half-smile that did not conceal his anxiety. Slowly, his brow furrowed, the wrinkles around his eyes deepened, and they started to smoulder with an almost threatening note, so keen was his curiosity.

'Who's he?' Vivek whispered.

I gave Ibrahim a withering look. 'He's nobody.'

We talked it over. I hadn't yet thought about the fate of the movie, but my first instinctive reaction to the other boys' proposition was a silent demurral. This instinct I considered ignoble, and so I tried to beat it down.

My second thought was –

'Does Ali Khan know? About Prashant?'

'You'll have to ask Gitanjali.'

'Let's go right now,' Roshan suggested brightly.

'Go where?'

'Go to Prashant's house and get the movie stuff,' said Madhav. 'Did anybody have the script besides Prashant? No, right? I didn't think so.'

One hour later, when the last cars were pulling out of the emptying crematorium, Gitanjali stepped delicately into my Maruti, and Roshan and Vivek piled into Madhav's Lancer. With Animesh in the backseat as usual, we set off after them, bound for New Friends Colony.

The roads were still clear, although rush hour was approaching. I imagined a thousand engines revving in every corner of the city, preparing to converge on my little vehicle. I drove fast, abnormally fast, as though I might escape not just the traffic, but the day's calamity.

'What a coup!' Animesh exclaimed.

I asked him what he meant.

'Ibrahim! Prashant played him perfectly!'

'A one-eighty-degree turnaround,' I agreed. 'But you think he really got Prashant to agree to change the script?'

'I think, in his mind, he got every single thing he ever wanted. What's a life spent knocking about the corridors of Tis Hazari, as compared to show business?'

'It looks like they had a comfortable chat too,' I grinned.

'Oh, Prashant always could pull out the moral young man card — because he really believed it too. Had *you* ever heard him going on about the IPL cheerleaders?'

'No.'

'I had,' Gitanjali was smiling. 'I remember telling him to shut up already. What's this about anyway?'

We explained it to her.

'That,' I concluded, 'is how to deal with a publicist. If you can't beat 'em, make 'em join.'

Maybe it was the feel of the car responding obediently. Maybe it was the air conditioner. But the drive was a space of its own; I felt strangely at ease, shielded from the relentless city and the unremitting spectres that wailed outside the windows. For a little while, the facts of life held their fire. I wanted to stay as long as possible in the interim between New Okhla and New Friends Colony.

'What I'm wondering now,' I said, 'is what happens if the movie *doesn't* get made? And Ibrahim doesn't get his fifteen minutes of fame. Will he file *another* case?'

'Why would he do that?' Gitanjali asked innocently.

'Because we all fight the way we know.'

Animesh and I chuckled lengthily. I swerved the car dramatically around a corner, and when we came up straight again I flung a rebuke at him.

'Hey Animesh — why do you use wrong words?'

He gave me a droll look in the rear-view mirror. Then he turned solemn.

'Because it's important to know what happened to Prashant. Was he really drunk? Did he really fall? I mean, I want to know.'

The eagerness in his voice was jarring.

'We know what happened to Prashant,' I said firmly. 'Everybody knows.'

When we reached our destination, the Lancer was already parked and waiting. Madhav and company were hovering near the gates, peering down the quiet lane for our approach. I was reminded of my first night at Prashant's house; climbing into Madhav's car; driving down good roads to dinner. Outwardly, the scenes were just the same, and yet, in their import, so different. I didn't any longer envy the privacy of the end of the lane, or the posh neighbouring dwellings of the rich. I didn't think of how nice it was to have so much separate space, and a park next door, or how pretty the darkening day became when the lights flicked on in the looming outdoors. I just thought of how lonely this white house looked.

We went straight to the summerhouse. The glass panes were intact and opaque; the designer wooden boards still shone dully; there wasn't a break in the roof. It was as compact and inviolate a hideout as Prashant had always liked it to be – except for the gaping hole where once had been a door.

The inside told a grimmer story. The furniture had been pushed against the walls. The floor was wiped and sanitised. The room was hot. Beyond the darkened glass, the flowers stood shrilly erect, because there wasn't the ghost of a breeze. My eyes wandered to the video-camera that somebody had put on top of the CPU, and then travelled further until they settled on the guilty ledge. I lifted my gaze from there, and met Animesh's. His mouth opened.

'How did they know what he hit his head against?'

'They inferred – from his position,' said Gitanjali.

'From the position of the body,' he nodded.

He had spoken without a trace of sentiment. I saw Gitanjali's eyes, contracting disapprovingly. I disapproved myself.

But there were other things to worry about. Sitting at the computer, Madhav was looking puzzled.

'Where's the movie?'

'There's a folder where he used to load the files,' I explained. 'It's in the My Documents folder. Here, I'll show you.'

A minute and a half later, I was frowning too. The folder wasn't there. I checked the Recycle Bin and it was empty. I did a search and nothing came up.

'Somebody's deleted it.'

We all sat around, nonplussed. Then Vivek had an idea.

'Try the camera. At least the shots we've taken so far will be on the camera.'

But they weren't. From the camera as well, the stored data was gone.

'Well . . . where's the script then? The hard copy of the script must be here.'

But in the bare room, there wasn't a scrap of paper.

After I'd given up hunting for the files, I turned the chair around and looked quizzically up at the five standing figures. One of them stepped forward.

'Let me see,' Animesh demanded.

'Go ahead,' I shrugged. He was humming to himself humming audibly. I caught Gitanjali's eye and held her gaze for the sake of it, as one does when trying to manufacture an understanding.

'We can write the script again,' she murmured softly, and in general.

Next to her, Roshan had begun fidgeting. Now he nudged her with his elbow.

'Is it cool to smoke?'

'In life,' she asked, 'or right now?'

He didn't like that, so he laughed heartily.

'You can go to the garden,' she said.

'Madhav, you coming? Vivek?'

Roshan was shifting his weight from one leg to the other, restlessly. Vivek nodded. Madhav didn't answer. Instead, he instructed Animesh with his usual precise, out-of-place politeness.

'I'll be outside. If you find anything, please say so.'

I understood their uneasiness. Tributes are all very well if they are quickly manageable; otherwise there must be sufficient feeling at the back to carry them through. Of course, Roshan's suggestion that we finish this movie had been offered in the same casual spirit as his invitation to smoke — it didn't involve rewriting a script. I supposed that this was now occurring to him.

The three of them had left the room when Animesh made his discovery.

'There's one new video file.'

'One *new* file?'

'It's on the desktop. You don't notice the obvious things,' he complained.

'Shut up.'

I was surprised at how harshly I'd spoken. I continued quickly, so as to leave my words behind.

'Just play that file and let's see what it is.'

Gitanjali drew the curtains. The fading sunlight dimmed further, and out in the garden, the newly-gesticulating figures of Roshan, Madhav and Vivek blurred into dreamy outline. I went to retrieve a chair and a stool from where they stood on top of each other, in a corner of the room. She came to help; she bent to lift, and I saw the strain springing to her forehead.

'Are you all right?'

'I'm fine.'

I gave her a few more concerned glances that weren't returned. Then the video started, and I stopped.

Prashant appeared on screen. He was sitting opposite Ibrahim, just as I had sat opposite him on my first visit to the summerhouse. The camera had a fixed, wide-angle, close-up view of the both of them. The picture was clear, so was the sound. Prashant was in a white T-shirt and jeans. Ibrahim was wearing black and white — the lawyer's garb minus the coat. Prashant was asking the questions.

'Had you a right to pass judgment on Ali Khan's lifestyle?'

'Certainly. Yes. Yes.'

It was amusing to see Saeed Ibrahim so rigidly formal – like an embattled politician facing the press.

'Is .that,' Prashant asked airily, 'because you have a moral responsibility to do so?'

'Exactly.'

'Because,' Prashant continued glibly, 'I personally believe that the less you judge others, the less you are a society. I mean, I personally can't stand people who cry persecution every time they're contradicted. Would you agree?'

'Of course. Yes. I agree.'

'But on the other hand – how can you be *genuinely* moved into filing a case against a name in the newspaper? Someone you don't even know. Let's get real here: aren't you just being a busybody?'

I was watching with a grisly fascination. Prashant was goading Ibrahim unabashedly. Gradually, the lawyer found his voice.

'Ali Khan was an immoral man. He hurt the feelings of the Muslim community. That is a criminal offence. The court has to decide,' Ibrahim finished vigorously and relievedly – this sentence, I guessed, was familiar ground.

'The court did decide.'

'I cannot comment on the decision. Ulterior motives were involved.'

The figure of Prashant shifted in his chair. I looked at him closely. His sparkling eyes attracted the attention rather more than the stiff gaze of his guest.

'Ali Khan never professed your faith.'

'It is not about professing. It is what it is. You understand?'

'Perhaps.'

At that, Ibrahim visibly preened. Prashant went on —

'But if you say he's an immoral man; then how do you react to what he did in the World Cup semi-final?'

'Eh?'

'The World Cup semi-final,' Prashant repeated patiently. 'His selfless act in that match – does it not indicate a strong personal code . . . a code of honour?'

I thought to myself he was probably doing too much of the talking.

'That one time maybe. But earlier, it was different.'

'He walked throughout his career. As a matter of principle. You must be aware of that.'

'I don't . . . watch cricket.'

'You don't even *watch* cricket. And you filed a criminal case against this cricketer. Was it just to get your name in the papers?'

Ibrahim's face started to contort. 'Who says that?'

'His only crime was that he thought for himself. Why does that bother you so much?'

'What nonsense!'

It was a child's face now, openly petulant, openly selfish. It struck me suddenly how little the old man's years mattered, when the time came to show their teaching. No length of beard could conceal that littleness of manner.

'This is what your critics say,' Prashant told him earnestly. 'What do you have to say to your critics?'

So he had critics now. It was a good move.

'To them,' Ibrahim pulled himself together. 'To them I say: I will uphold the honour of my community, no matter how much I suffer.'

'All right, sir. Thank you. It was a pleasure. I'm so glad you agreed to do this. I'm sure the movie will be much the richer for it.'

Prashant was prattling away, much longer than necessary, and with a running chuckle in his voice. The lawyer grunted in return. Now my eyes widened as Prashant got up and took two steps forward before bending to bring his head on level with the lens. It was only his face on screen now, vivid and grotesquely enlarged. For one instant he seemed to be engaging us in a private aside. His shining eyes and humorous mouth were asking that we share the joke. I almost exclaimed – then the video ended.

Gitanjali was the first to speak. Unexpectedly, she sounded a note of disapproval.

'Well! I think Prashant was pretty rude!'

'He was fine,' I stirred myself. 'He was just . . . enthusiastic. Animesh, what do you think?'

Animesh was silent. Then he sighed.

'I think he was high.'

'High?'

'Oh . . . *yes*,' said Gitanjali. 'Yes, that's him high – I knew something was weird about it. Weird and familiar!'

Animesh rose and threw the curtains open. Twilight was settling upon the garden. The flowers were shrouded in the growing dark, and the pomegranate tree stood in misshapen, twisted silhouette. I wondered where the other boys had got to.

'He was high – but not drunk. He wasn't drunk.'

A burst of conversation entered the summerhouse, followed soon after by Roshan, Madhav and Vivek. Gitanjali and I turned automatically and Animesh didn't even twitch.

'That's two big questions,' he was going on speaking. 'Why is all the stuff for the movie gone? And why would Prashant fall, when he clearly wasn't drunk? That's two big question marks over this "accident".'

Again, I felt a resentment welling up against him – and I understood now that it wasn't on my own account.

'Stop theorising,' I said firmly, with a deliberate eye on Gitanjali. She was looking at her lap.

He didn't stop. He added thoughtfully. 'More likely Ibrahim clonked him one on the head.'

Suddenly he snorted with grim laughter. I threw a terrified glance at Gitanjali. She was looking back at me and I was sure her eyes were wet.

'Animesh,' I said savagely. 'Come outside a minute. It's our turn to get some fresh air.'

12

I LED HIM all the way beyond the gates, so that we'd be well out of sight of the others. In the park, the white lights were glowing steadily, and one perched globe threw its damp flare across the fence and onto Animesh's innocent face. I stood him there, just at the point where the street that led to Prashant's house started to curve around it, and his old Maruti came into view.

'What're you trying to do!'

He looked at me, slightly surprised and no more. For a moment he didn't answer. When he did, it was with a calm counter-question.

'Do you think,' he said, 'that it is . . . unseemly to ask what happened to Prashant, when we should be grieving instead?'

I wasn't exactly sure what I did think. His suggestion was helpful.

'You're *speculating* too much,' I tried to explain. 'You're behaving as though this has happened to a stranger. As though it's something we're reading about in the papers. Prashant wasn't a stranger.'

But uncertainty crept into my voice, even as I spoke. If Prashant wasn't a stranger to me, nor was he to the other boy, and gently Animesh reminded me.

'It's only because he wasn't a stranger that I'm curious to know what happened. That comes first for me. If I don't know how he died, how can I know how to feel?'

'It's difficult for the others.'

'I'm only making it easier – for everybody.'

'You could be a little sympathetic.'

'I'm being me,' he said blandly. 'When something like this happens, people don't know how to react, and so they act. They mimic the expected emotions – horror, sorrow, tears. Now that's fine and normal and I understand it, but I don't have to be browbeaten by it.'

A faint note of resistance sounded in his voice – hinting also that there was more where it came from.

In spite of myself, I considered the question.

'Look, it had to have happened the way the police say it did. He was alone in a locked room. It's impossible that it was anything but an accident. How could anyone have . . . hit him on the head?'

'In that case,' Animesh countered, 'who did this?'

I followed the line of his sight. In the darkness around the corner, Prashant's Maruti gleamed dully. I had to look, because the damage wasn't apparent in passing, although it was apparent enough. The windscreen was a pattern of fractured glass, and the door on the driver's side was bashed in. When I stepped closer, I saw that a layer of dust had settled on every surface of the little car. It looked forlorn and forgotten by the side of the road – and we'd all sat in it so often.

I stared for a moment, horrified. 'Maybe Prashant banged into something. One of these days.'

Animesh shook his head darkly.

'It's not the first car in this house that's suffered.'

Back indoors, the mystery of the missing movie still had the others stumped – and apprehensive, lest the solution be made their responsibility. I tried to guess how they felt. Roshan was remembering what a bit role he'd had in the movie and how little he'd liked Prashant anyway, and how he could use a drink. Madhav was growing increasingly uncomfortable at how generous he was being with his time. Vivek was wondering what the other two were thinking.

'Fucking hell!' Roshan exclaimed suddenly. He looked around the room with groggy belligerence.

'Fuck,' he repeated. 'Fuck.'

'I've got to take a breather,' he informed us. 'You know – you guys – Prashant and I had our differences of opinion, but now this has happened . . . I don't know what to say. It's just so . . . just so . . .'

'Fucked up?' inquired Animesh.

Madhav got to his feet.

'I've got to go see Sheila,' he announced. 'I suggest we all take a couple of days to ourselves. To figure out where we're headed with the movie. But more importantly, to make our peace with what's happened to Prashant.'

You couldn't fault him on his manner.

'What about . . . Goa?' Vivek ventured.

'What do you think, you . . .' Roshan glared at him. He was enjoying the spurious responsibility of dictating the terms of our mourning.

'Don't talk about *Goa*! Fuck, man! My head is so screwed already!'

On the other hand, maybe I was being unfair to him. Maybe he really was that distraught. Either way, he left me cold.

Madhav coughed delicately. 'Can I drop any of you home?'

Vivek and Roshan said he could. Soon they left, and then, once again, it was just the three of us.

I was starting to feel restless. Outside, the night had descended, and indoors the tube light was on, but that was a grating, nerve-wracking illumination. When I pressed the switch and the summerhouse fell dark, except for the glow of the desktop's screen and what moonlight spilled through the entrance, nobody complained.

And it became easier to talk. Gitanjali was sitting on the floor with her chin balanced on her knees and her arms wrapped around them.

'It's so strange the files not being there. Who could have deleted them? You guys think somebody forced Prashant to delete them?'

She didn't wait for an answer.

'I mean, I know there were people who didn't want the movie made. But how could it . . . *matter* so much? It was just supposed to be fun. It was just a fun idea. It wasn't such a big deal. Not even for *us*. You *saw* that!'

I nodded. 'It was quite a solo thing.'

'I didn't really care myself,' Gitanjali went on sadly. 'I think that Prashant was the only one to whom this movie meant anything. I was like Madhav and Roshan. Even after that guy came down – Ali Khan –'

'Does *he* know what's happened?' I remembered to ask.

'I haven't told him. He'll see it in the papers.'

'He cared about the movie too,' I said softly. 'It's what he came to Delhi for. I think one of us should tell him.'

'Then you tell him.'

Her sudden curtness caught me unawares. I grew immediately flustered.

'Oh – sure. I know – I mean – you've had so much to do. . . .'

'*What* are you going to tell him?' This was Animesh.

'I'll tell him what's happened to Prashant. He can infer what he will about the movie.'

'You'll tell him Prashant had an accident?'

'What else?'

We looked at each other. Loudest in my mind was the caution that Gitanjali not be upset. I didn't want to put forth any alarming theories. So I was surprised when she spoke up herself.

'Do you think,' she said, 'it was something other than an accident?'

'I think it's a possibility,' said Animesh diplomatically, 'and I'm just –'

'Because you know – Sheila thinks that too.'

I looked at her sharply.

'Really?'

'Yes.'

'What does Sheila think?'

'Well, I called her,' Gitanjali shrugged. 'I called her and told her what had happened and she just said "Oh God", and that it's not what they think. Then she said she wouldn't be able to come for the cremation.'

'Then?'

'Then I called the next person on my list.'

Animesh stood up. Gitanjali and I watched him begin a steady, circular walk around the boards in the middle of the floor. His face was set in a determined expression. Midway through the third revolution, he reached a decision.

'Let's go see her right away.'

'She's with Madhav,' I remarked drily.

He threw a beseeching look at Gitanjali, who was studying him with a frown that was only an accentuation of her normal sensible expression.

'Gitanjali, can't you . . . arrange a meeting? Sometime soon?'

'I think Sheila could do without your interrogation.'

This had not occurred to him. His face fell. He was like an enthusiastic child all ready for play, brought up short by the reminder of holiday homework.

'Of course – you're right. She needs to recover.'

'Perhaps,' he went on hopefully, 'after a few days then?'

The faintest smile appeared about Gitanjali's lips.

'The two of you could come home tomorrow,' she offered graciously. 'Sheila's going to be there.'

'I'm curious about it too.' Her dark eyes were quite composed.

~

We drove home that night through terrible traffic and black polluted skies. In the moist heat, my shirt clung wetly to my back, and perversely I kept the window down, the better to inhale the dust. As I drove, I glared at the motorcyclists weaving their way across the lanes and inwardly I wished them ill – though I held my tongue from habit. Once, I nearly hit a man pulling a cart at a perennially-crowded junction. Twice, I braked hard in front of maddening pedestrians.

'It's like one of those computer games,' I said bitterly, 'where enemies keep springing out from different parts of the screen. At least there you get to shoot them.'

The bile was coursing through me freely. Then I said something I hadn't even known I was thinking.

'Prashant was a fool!'

Animesh looked at me. I continued furiously.

'He was! A fool! What's the point of *talking* to a guy like Ibrahim? The guy's a religious maniac! I mean, this country is full of them! You can't talk to them; all you can do is avoid them! You know what I think: I think anyone who's really religious – unless they're your grandparents or something – you should just *avoid* them.'

'Is that what you do?' Animesh sounded doubtful.

'Of course!'

There was a moment's silence while I took a careful turn under a flyover. Then suddenly Animesh laughed. 'You live with Kisle,' he said. 'The guy prays three times a day. His cupboard has more deities than shirts. Haven't you seen it?'

This was news to me. 'No,' I said, 'I never knew that. What's his – I mean which god does Kisle pray to?'

'Some lesser-known few from the three hundred million. You know what he told me his prayers give him?'

'What?'

'Peace of mind.'

I had to smile.

The rest of the way I drove in a relative calm. I felt better for my outburst, not because it had got my thoughts in order, but because it had put a stop to them.

Animesh, too, was silent, but he, I felt, was not convalescing. When we were close to home, I looked at him. He was still staring stoically at the road ahead.

'What are you thinking?' I said.

'I'm trying to think what Sheila thinks.'

That night, as we entered the gates of Akash Apartments, I fancied that I saw the silhouette of Mrs Ramdass standing at the downstairs window. Under her imagined eye, I felt my worries returning, like so many untreated afflictions. I ran them over in my mind – my troubled parents, my unforeseeable career, my girl – oh my girl . . .

Then, midway through this dire exercise, I suddenly remembered that I didn't have to go to work the next day. Goa wasn't happening, but my leave was still on. The weight of the eight long hours of the night lessened perceptibly, and just then, I made up my mind. I didn't have to think about my report, and I didn't have to think about Anita, and I didn't even have to think about Prashant. I only had to think of Sheila, and what she would say the next day. I only had to figure out what had happened the previous Sunday in the summerhouse.

Back in our living room, Animesh looked around, bleary-eyed.

'I'm going to bed.'

'Me too,' I said gratefully. 'We'll . . . do this tomorrow.'

I went to my room, washed my face and changed my clothes. I got into bed and under the sheets. Then I rolled on my side and shut my eyes and kept them that way, until it was morning.

~

At twelve noon the next day, Animesh and I took an auto to the Asiad Games Village, because I didn't know the way, and I didn't feel like driving. On the way there, I remembered the conversation Prashant and I had had about Sheila. This place we were going to was where he had fallen in love, and I seemed to see it now through the rose-tinted prism of his memory. My heart quickened unaccountably.

We had turned a corner from a typically dusty street onto wide and leafy avenues. Along the pavements were leaning trees that scattered the sunlight, and young people dressed for tennis. It wasn't a romantic place – there wasn't the manmade grandeur that makes for romance; in fact, there wasn't any grandeur at all. But it was neat, and it was comfortable.

Those were the great things about Gitanjali's house too. When I saw her living room, I was deeply glad that she hadn't yet seen mine. It was as careful as our apartment's was careless; and as warm as Prashant's was forbidding. I noted with appreciation the bookshelf near the window.

The rogue element in the room was Sheila. She had only smiled at us when we entered – given us each a sharply individual welcome – and then the smile had died out along the lines of her mouth and retreated into her unfathomable eyes. But it was enough to make her at once the most vivid object in sight. While Gitanjali was busy living up to her ideal of the hostess, Sheila stayed curled up on the sofa. In between the several visits that the other girl made indoors and out again, we talked politely about nothing. I mean, Sheila and I talked. Animesh crouched in silence – I suppose biding his time.

Somehow, the conversation veered to sport – I think it was the Asiad Games motif.

'I heard you used to swim,' I said.

I didn't mention whom I'd heard it from.

'I used to.' She rolled her eyes. 'It was all a long time ago.'

'I can't swim at all,' I told her excitedly. 'At least, I can swim with my head out of water. Does that count?'

'I can drive in my driveway,' she smiled back at me. 'It counts as much.'

'I hate driving,' I declared. 'I'm always driving, office and back, office and back.'

'Oh, but your job's so interesting. You have the most interesting job of all the people I know.'

This pleased me, but I affected disdain. 'Oh – it just sounds interesting, really. At the end of the day, all jobs are the same, aren't they? Just drudgery.'

'Don't say that,' she coaxed. 'I think it's really interesting. So, you like animals?'

'I . . . do.'

'I love animals. I used to have a cat once. Or it had me.'

'That's cats for you. Me – I'm a dog person.'

'I never understand why people compare. It's like there's some obligation to.'

'That's because it's a surrogate for men and women,' I replied boldly and I thought brilliantly. 'Everyone likes to talk about men and women.'

'Either way,' she smiled, 'the answer's the same. They're both nice in their own way. That's the truth about cats and dogs.'

Her eyes dilated at the end of the sentence. They weren't large eyes – she was no waif – there were even little lines around them. But they emphasised her every expression. I nodded heartily.

'I read a good line once,' I said. 'Dogs look up at us, cats look down at us. Only pigs treat us as equals.'

Sheila laughed. Gitanjali flopped down on a beanbag.

'I'm done being good,' she declared. 'It's self-service now.'

About then Animesh leaned forward from his comfortable chair. In the mellow space of our conversation he interjected –

'I think we should talk about Prashant. It's important.'

A frigid silence fell at once. Bluntly, he went on.

'I don't believe that Prashant had an accident. I think there was more to it than that. Sheila, what do you think?'

It wasn't just abrupt the way he'd started; it was odd, the way he'd taken her first name. I felt she was somehow slighted by that. Maybe she felt so too.

'I'd rather not talk about it.'

'You'd rather not – oh, see, Vaibhav and I were discussing it yesterday. And Gitanjali too.'

Now he'd named all the company. I had the feeling he was trying to engineer a sort of team meeting. I gave him an angry look, which he ignored.

'It seems we're all agreed it wasn't just a fall. So the question is: what was it? Sheila, you have –'

'I have no desire to talk about it.'

She said it as sweetly and as reasonably as if she was declining a glass of wine. Just at that moment, I wasn't sure where my loyalties lay, and then some helpful instinct provided the answer. Clearly, the emotional well-being of the arresting girl beside me mattered, in a way that the unseemly curiosity of this other stripling did not.

We stayed the whole afternoon and never mentioned Prashant once. When the sun started to dwindle, some spark in Animesh seemed also to die.

'I think it's time I left,' he told me coldly. 'I suppose you're coming as well?'

I was going to say yes – reluctantly – but I felt a warning gaze upon me. I looked up at Gitanjali. She had been quite silent and complaisant thus far, happy to join the conversation, without attempting to mould it. Now she shook her head just perceptibly. She told me, with her eyes, to stay.

'I'll stay,' I said impulsively, 'a bit longer. If that's okay with Gitanjali?'

'Oh sure,' she said. 'I'm feeling sociable, so it's your lucky day.'

Near the door, while Animesh swept out sullenly, she caught my arm.

'Go talk to her,' she hissed. 'Go talk to her alone.'

The next item was the premise, which Gitanjali supplied.

'I'm going to walk Animesh to the auto stand,' she called out. 'Or the bus-stop, whichever he prefers. I've got some things to pick up for my mom as well. I'll just be twenty minutes – okay? I'm sorry.'

'No, no,' Sheila and I chorused fervently. 'That's fine.'

The door shut. The evening sunshine gleamed off the shelves of books, dazzling me momentarily. Sheila's hair was brown in this light, and her white arms were delicately bronzed. As I watched, a succession of moods seemed to overtake her. She looked now content, now puzzled, now sad. The colour in her cheeks rose, and receded, and rose again. Her lips quivered, balancing a thought.

'Prashant used to talk about you.'

'We went to college together,' I answered automatically.

I was going to ask a question, then I thought better of it. I saw that she was going to tell me herself.

'He used to say how nice you were. I think you're nice too.'

'Thanks,' I muttered unsurely, blushing uncontrollably. Nice, I thought, was the purest compliment.

Visibly, she composed herself.

'I feel – I don't know how I feel.'

'None of us know,' I said, and then I thought maybe that was the wrong note – her case oughtn't to be generalised. 'I guess it must be specially hard for you.'

She blinked quickly, then flashed me a smile.

'I spoke to him,' she said, 'just that evening. He sounded so much better than usual. He was boasting.'

'About what?'

The smile disappeared, and now Sheila looked at me with her cool and steady eyes. I couldn't help a twinge of regret at how little I figured in that look – personally.

'You know that journalist, your father's friend. And that lawyer fellow. He called me and said he'd taken care of both of them. He was so kicked about it. He asked me to have dinner with him.'

'What time did he call you?'

'Oh . . . about five or so. Why?'

'No reason. So you had dinner with him?'

'We went to the Mediterranean restaurant at the Community Centre. You know it?'

'I know it.'

Her mouth curved suddenly, and I thought, for an instant, she was going to cry. She didn't; she turned whatever emotion had come to her into a frightening iciness.

'I guess he thought he'd make it three successes in a day. He was behaving . . . poorly. Strangely. You'll think me a monster, won't you?'

'No.'

'He wasn't even talking straight. He wasn't even listening to me. He was tripping over his sentences. I don't mind that if the man has just met me, because they're always so nervous. But I'd given Prashant so much time.'

'What could I do?' She pleaded angrily. 'You know he liked me?'

I nodded.

'Well, I told him no.'

Slowly, I nodded again. Perhaps, when I didn't say anything, she felt she had to explain.

'Prashant was always so clear about what he wanted, and he wanted it to be the same for everyone. His mind wanted to stamp out every notion, except the one. But a girl's mind isn't like that. Sometimes, I was open to the things he'd already decided were second-rate. Sometimes it hurt how . . . strident he was.'

'Like Roshan – he could never stand Roshan.'

A spurt of loyalty hit me. I set my face at the idea.

'Is there something between you and Roshan?'

If she was surprised or offended at my forthrightness, she didn't show it. I sensed that in this mood, she was willing to talk about anything.

'I didn't mind him – if that's what you mean.' Of course it wasn't.

'Roshan's a . . .' my mind gave out. 'He's –'

'He's quite idiotic,' she said coldly, 'just like the suggestion that I can't take care of myself.'

My mouth half-opened in protest.

'I like Madhav,' she informed me, 'and I liked Prashant, and, like I told you, I don't mind Roshan either. I liked them all at different times in different ways.'

'So . . . nobody was special to you?'

'I didn't say that. But now I see why you and Prashant got along so well.'

The cut of her crystal speech was something new to me. I felt decidedly inferior, and since I have never been able to conceal my emotions, my face fell. Perhaps she saw this and wanted to make it better for me. More likely, I think, she could not fully confide in anyone whom she did not fully have the measure of. And now she had mine.

'I'm feeling so bad,' she said suddenly. Her voice was low and rich, and pitched so you leaned in closer.

'When Gitanjali told me the news – I didn't know what to say. Was it so bad for him? I used to think he had stopped being hurt by me. I never thought it still mattered so much.'

As her implication dawned on me, my eyes widened.

'Maybe it was the shock of it. He was so over the moon on the phone – so cheerful. But later – after we met – he was changed. He looked terrible. I should have known.'

A thought steadied my swimming mind.

'He hit his head,' I said harshly. 'He only fell. It could have happened to anyone. You mustn't analyse it any further.'

Sheila's entreating gaze leaped suddenly outwards. Something maternal welled up in her eyes.

'You're so *nice*,' she breathed. 'You're so nice.'

Her face shone through the gently falling dark.

'You're sure he didn't . . . you're sure it wasn't me?'

'I'm sure,' I said firmly.

'Do you think,' she considered, 'I was the last person to see him alive?'

'I don't know.'

'It was past ten when we walked home. Oh – I must have been.'

A strange ecstasy showed in her expression. Again, I was reminded of an idea I had formed much earlier. Sheila was altogether too complicated for me. It was a comforting idea, because it allowed me to stop trying to understand her. I realised suddenly how fatigued I had become – just sitting there.

A soft volley of light came bounding into the room, and then Gitanjali closed the door on it. She was struggling under the weight of a full shopping bag. I got to my feet, and helped her ease it onto a table.

'Did Sheila speak to you?' she whispered.

'Yes.'

'And?'

'And you be with her now.'

I told them both it was a long way home. I gave Sheila my reassuring smile – the one I'd used many times on Anita. She took it and added her own indecipherable intimacy to it, and threw it back at me. I walked out of the house with my heart in a tizzy. The long, brutal journey home awaited.

13

IT WAS EIGHT o'clock by the time I reached the apartment, and I was dog-tired. When I had finished the interminable trudge up the stairs and to my landing, I paused to take a breath – and to listen. The sound of many male voices was bursting into the corridor, one after the other, like so many cheap firecrackers. It made me sigh. I figured I had energy enough for a brief chat with Animesh, but not for the kind of frenetic and aimless vibe that Kisle and Arjun usually gave out.

But there was nothing for it but to grit my teeth and push on through.

They were watching a game of tennis. Animesh had his chin buried in his palm; Kisle was twirling repeatedly a lock of the greasy hair that he was so proud of; Arjun had on a disinterested expression that was plainly a disguise.

'What match is this?' I asked. 'Who's playing?'

'It's some tournamen' in Italy,' Kisle was regarding the television with indulgent interest. 'I'm for the guy in the white shirt.'

'He's going to lose,' Arjun warned.

I frowned at the flitting pictures. I watched for a little while. It was obviously a close affair, with plenty of long rallies, and a full stadium, and pretty red clay. I liked the man in white too. I didn't follow tennis closely, but there was something about him.

'He's so good,' I said impulsively. 'Who is he?'

'The World Number Three,' said Animesh. 'But now his ranking is falling. The last three years he was fantastic.'

What had I been doing the last three years? I sat down like the others. Gradually, the spell of the competition pulled me in — and then under. I knew the basics of the game, but more than that, I knew who I wanted to win. There is only one prerequisite to complete immersion and that is it.

'It's been nine tournaments since he reached a final,' Animesh said softly.

I suppose becoming a fan is a bit like falling in love. It may not happen immediately, but you know immediately that it's going to — and before you know it, it has. My eyes focused on the tall, graceful figure. I liked the way he moved, and the swing of his strokes. His mouth was cast in a controlled and attractive petulance.

Soon, my heart was thudding. My throat was dry from the parched trip home, but of course, I couldn't get up for anything, because then my man would lose.

At a crucial point in the final set, my whole body shook with fervour. I screamed at the television set. All of us were like that, except for Arjun, who was trying hard to appear aloof. But it wasn't going well for the World Number Three. The stadium in Rome was as partial to him as our apartment — nevertheless, the wrong man was winning.

'He can't do it,' Kisle shook his head. 'He's too nervous.'

'He can do it,' said Animesh. 'He's only one break down.'

Later, he was match point down.

'He just has to get it back in play.' I was hoping for a miracle. I think at that moment I would gladly have suffered many things, if only he would win. That was the truth; the melodramatic truth – although one hour ago I had never even seen the man. But the backhand floated wide.

We shared a silent moment of defeat. I waited for my heart to make its painful journey back to the middle of my chest, while the leftover slag of my emotions drained slowly. Surprisingly, the first to make a comment was Arjun – and he was vicious.

'The dude's over the hill,' he pronounced firmly. 'He should just retire. He can't play any longer.'

'Shut up,' Animesh retorted. 'You didn't even have the guts to support him.'

'Why should I support anyone? I appreciate good tennis, and I'm for the guy who plays the best tennis. It's as simple as that.'

'It's as silly as that. It's like being brave after the battle.'

'Oh you're just bitter. Look at you, man. So much bitterness – just oozing out. Relax – it's only a game. Don't be so bitter.'

'I think,' Animesh said reasonably, 'you should tell yourself that.'

He paused for a moment, turning something over in his mind. Then he said:

'Those who give their emotions to what they watch, only have enough left afterwards for relief, or for disappointment. It's the fence-sitters like you who finish up, all eaten up.'

'Ah . . . shut it.'

Meanwhile, Kisle was steadily swearing – but unlike Arjun, his expostulations tailed off into a despairing smile. For my own part, I was simply feeling bad for myself.

'Why is it,' I complained, 'that nothing good ever happens when I watch?'

'That isn't true,' Animesh said patiently. 'You just don't remember.'

'It is true,' I said stolidly. 'Everyone I like loses. There's been nobody great in my time.'

'Those are two different things. Besides, the moment you like somebody, they start to seem vulnerable.'

'And if there has been anyone great,' I continued morosely, 'then I've always missed them.'

'You've just forgotten,' Animesh said again. 'You've even forgotten Ali Khan.'

He lowered his voice then, so the others wouldn't hear. Between ourselves, we carried on a hushed exchange.

'By the way, have you called Khan yet – about Prashant?'

'Not yet . . . I was hoping someone else would. Maybe he saw it in the papers?'

There had been a tiny report in a corner of the city page of that morning's *Hindu*. It reported the death of Prashant Padmanabhan, twenty-four, by injury to the head, from an accidental fall.

'I wouldn't bet on it. It's easy to miss – Kisle and Arjun missed it.'

'They don't read the newspaper anyway. Haven't you told them?'

'I was going to. But they were so into the match -- and I didn't want to make it awkward for them. Besides,' Animesh said innocently, 'your girlfriend asked you to call Khan.'

'My what?'

'Gitanjali – your girlfriend.'

'You've got a nerve,' I said quietly.

Somehow, I wasn't as angry about that crack as perhaps I should have been. In any case, the mention of Khan's name had returned me to the business at hand.

We talked it over in my room, and I didn't give any quarter when Animesh sulked.

'Why didn't you let me ask Sheila what I wanted? I went all the way to Asiad just so I could speak to her, and you didn't even drive and –'

'She didn't want to talk to you,' I reminded him. 'And I'm through with ferrying you around. But she did talk to me, so will you just listen?'

When I'd finished telling him what had happened, I summed up.

'I think what she was getting at is that Prashant might have committed suicide.'

'Killed himself?'

I winced. Suicide was the decent term.

'If he was found alone in a locked room, then it's either an accident – or it's suicide. I suppose suicide is possible. I don't know – I know he really liked her.'

'I know that too,' Animesh said thoughtfully. 'But even so. He just wasn't the suicidal type.'

'There is no suicidal type.'

'That's true,' he conceded. 'But what I mean is – he wouldn't kill himself over a . . .'

'Over a dame?' I said sarcastically. 'Prashant wasn't some tough guy Philip Marlowe. He was just a boy. And I'd say he took things harder than most.'

Animesh nodded. 'Well that's true. He took things so hard, he'd never let anybody know. I know this because the girl he liked before Sheila didn't work out for him either. And we all thought he wouldn't want it mentioned – and he was always the first to bring it up in conversation. That's how scared he was of having an Achilles' heel – socially, I mean.'

I grimaced.

'That's a little . . . masochistic.'

'That was Prashant,' Animesh shrugged. 'And why is the movie gone?'

'The movie?'

'Yes. If it was all about her — why were the movie files deleted?'

'Sheila did say he was out of sorts. Maybe he deleted it himself. Maybe he just did it out of . . . I don't know — some nihilistic mood. Maybe he felt his life had gone to pieces.'

'Maybe she is pretty conceited.'

'Hey,' I said, 'she's feeling terrible.'

I said it half-heartedly. I didn't really have any handle on her emotions.

'Look,' Animesh responded quietly. 'The more heartbroken Prashant was, the more he'd care about the movie. There's only one thing that heals your heart, and that's your work.'

'How do you know,' I was genuinely interested, 'what heals hearts?'

'Also,' he went on as though I hadn't spoken, 'who commits suicide by banging his head against a wall?'

'I don't know. It seems as good a way as any.'

I must have sounded particularly dejected. Animesh glanced up at once, and when I felt his inquisitive eye on me, I sighed.

'I think I'm still thinking about that tennis match,' I said. 'It just seems to make things — oh, even more hopeless — than they always are.'

He waited patiently, while I talked off my mood.

'Why can't you ever be satisfied? Just accept that he was drunk — or even if he *wasn't* drunk — that either way he lost his balance and hit his head and died. Or he was cut up about

Sheila and so he killed himself. Or *both*. It may have been a sort of death-wish.'

'The summerhouse was *locked*, Animesh,' I said vigorously. 'You think someone . . . murdered Prashant? He'd have had to be a ghost to walk through walls. And you think someone deliberately deleted the movie files? I can't picture any one of Arindam Yadav's ruffians pressing Shift Del at all the right places. And Sheila saw him at ten in the night, and he was perfectly alive. She was probably the last person to see him alive. So next you'll be saying *she* did it.'

'I'm not saying she did it,' Animesh replied smoothly. 'But why don't we have a chat with Shekhar Sen?'

'Why Shekhar Sen?'

'Because Sheila told you Prashant was boasting on the phone about how he'd taken care of Saeed Ibrahim — *and* Sen. I want to know whether Sen enjoyed that as much as Ibrahim did.'

This was a reasonable question, but it occurred to me that getting the answer was a thing easier said than done. Shekhar Sen hadn't exactly warmed to me on my last visit to his home. I didn't think he'd take kindly to amateur interrogation.

'He knows your father,' Animesh reminded me.

'I've already played that card. He's a busy guy,' I said. 'He's a sort of minor celebrity.'

Animesh gave me a tolerant smile.

'Minor celebrities are the most accessible of all people. They've thrown off the decent shyness of ordinary folk, and they haven't exactly got a paparazzi problem.'

'Yes — but they're accessible to their social superiors. Not to social nobodies like you and me.'

'They need us,' Animesh said confidently, 'for reassurance. Do we have his phone number?'

'Not his mobile ph —'

'His landline is good enough. He'll be home now.'

I watched with a certain grudging admiration, as the other boy fished out his cell phone. My way is to put off tricky phone calls for as long as possible, and sometimes forever. Looking at him now, a quick stab of guilt assailed. I remembered I had to call Mumbai, and Anita.

On the line, Animesh was introducing himself as a friend of mine, and a colleague of Prashant's. From where I sat I could hear both ends of the conversation. There was a faint crackle of static in the background and a boy's adolescent voice saying something inaudible. Then a gruffer speech sounded out clearly.

'Yes?'

It was Sen, properly peremptory. Animesh repeated his introduction, and when that was done he added —

'We were wondering if we could meet you.'

'What for? I've met enough of you already.'

'I mean . . . sir, perhaps you haven't heard about Prashant. He died on Sunday night. It's in the papers today.'

'Ohh . . .' The astonishment in Sen's voice was plain and obvious. 'Good God — I didn't know! What happened?'

'It was an accident. He had a fall.'

'Well! I'm sorry! I'm sorry to hear that. But —'

'We could really do with some advice. It's the first time we've tried anything like this, and so far, Prashant had been taking charge.'

'You want my advice?'

'Yes.'

'Regarding what?'

That stumped Animesh. He launched into a sort of paean to Shekhar Sen, the journalist. But Sen wasn't a fool for flattery —

at any rate, not a complete fool for flattery – and as Animesh didn't have anything faintly perceptive to say about his profession, we could both feel an unspoken impatience developing at the other end. It was rising steadily, threatening at any moment to interrupt – and hang up.

'On a couple of specific scenes,' Animesh said quickly, 'and also your thoughts on the . . . feasibility of the project as a whole. We won't take too much of your time,' he promised. 'Perhaps sometime tomorrow?'

'I have a book launch to attend tomorrow.'

'Perhaps after that?'

Eventually, we got Sen's permission to come by the India Habitat Centre the following evening, and, as he put it, to hang about until he was finished with everything else. Animesh claimed victory.

'Once I said the word "advice" he wasn't going to turn us away.'

'What exactly,' I inquired, 'do you expect Sen to tell us? It's obvious he was as taken aback at what happened to Prashant as you and I were.'

'He saw Prashant on Sunday, and you and I didn't. Let's just keep our ears open – and let him talk. And you'll drive, won't you?'

～

I still had misgivings. I hadn't enjoyed my last run-in with the journalist – his criticisms had a way of getting under my skin. He may have been my father's friend – or perhaps that was why – but Shekhar Sen knew how to hit where it hurt.

At least the IHC was a pleasant prospect. It is a spacious complex, just off the best-guarded, best-kept parts of town, where the judges and the ministers are given their homes. We drove there with nothing in the windscreen but shaded road, spreading leaves, snippets of sky and men in uniforms.

'Isn't this great?' I said, as we swivelled around another roundabout, to another broad, level, tree-lined thoroughfare. 'Compare this to the god-awful hole where we stay,' I said bitterly.

Beside me, Animesh looked unenthused.

'The problem with this part of the city,' he pronounced, 'is it has no charm. And you know why?'

I made a face.

'Because it's full of power', he continued serenely. 'The casualty of power is charm. Where there is power, there is not –'

'– charm, yes, all right. I find good roads and space to breathe very charming.'

'Not when they're backed by violence. No, you're just thinking of when you were six.'

'You'd prefer, perhaps, a row of slums?'

'Oh, any day,' he said impassively. 'Any day. If I see another policeman, I'm going to scream.'

After a little while, when our red-walled destination showed itself from in between the greenery, he said he felt better. A group of young people that I might have gone to college with were leaning on the gates and chatting leisurely, which was, it is true, something you never saw on Tughlak Road.

Once upon a time, I remember, I had walked through the disorienting compounds of the Habitat Centre and felt them to be exactly right. The lighted doors of a restaurant here, the dark mouth of a tunnel there, green lawns and red brick everywhere and a dizzying roof of glass, all flicked unobtrusively by the gaze that I rested on the girl besides me. That was Anita, many winters ago.

Today we made a beeline for the Convention Centre and stood about in the corridor outside Conference Room Number Six, waiting for the rubber-lined doors to give out their crowd.

'I feel like a fool,' I complained. 'Look at us – like a couple of groupies.'

Animesh only smirked. Inside, a well-known name was releasing his new book on the history of contemporary India. Apparently, Sen was vying for a teaching position at the other man's university – hence his presence in the cheering squad this evening.

I told Animesh the politics didn't concern me. I just hoped we could get this over with quickly.

It turned out that way. Fifteen minutes passed, and then we had our backs to the wall and our anxious eyes trained on the figures coming through. First an old, jacketed man wandered into sight, slow enough and swaying enough to keep everybody else in queue. Edging up close to him was a scowling woman in a fashionable sari, who seemed to me on the verge of shoving. When they were through at last, the exodus became general.

About the time I was considering going inside to look, Shekhar Sen strolled out. He was looking distinctly pleased with himself. I was afraid we'd spoil his mood, but when he caught my eye, he raised a vague hand in greeting and moved on, still smiling.

'Come on,' said Animesh. 'Before he starts talking to someone.'

We caught up with him just outside the main entrance, where the crowd thinned and frittered in various directions.

'Hey champ,' he nodded when he saw me. 'Awful news about your friend.'

I nodded as well. Sen, I thought, looked in good form. His hair, shampooed and coloured, was swept back confidently from his forehead, and his *eau de cologne* was clearly working.

'I had a chat with him just this Sunday,' he said. 'We had a bite together.'

'You met Prashant?' My ears pricked up.

'I had some things to pick up at Khan Market, and he said he'd bring the script over. I thought I'd straighten out this movie angle. I had some reservations, you remember?'

'I remember,' I said. 'I had . . . communicated what you told me.'

'Well,' Sen considered, 'I don't like to say anything now that I hear of this accident – how did it happen again?'

'He just slipped – and fell – and hit his head.'

'Well, I don't like to say anything now, but that script he'd got up needed a lot of work.'

'You saw the script? In hard copy?'

'Of course in hard copy.'

'Could you,' Animesh asked eagerly, 'let us know what you thought of it?'

In the fine evening air, Sen's nose wrinkled.

'Take out the whole section on me. That's what I told Prashant. He said he'd like to interview me, and I said I don't do cricket anymore, and I want to keep it that way. But in any case, that whole section is wrong – the narration is biased.'

'Biased?'

'Yes, biased. You've got to respect people's right to comment. If I had a certain opinion of Ali Khan, and a certain interpretation of his actions, who are you to stand in judgment over them? If

I say it's likely – likely, mind you, not proven – that he took money for walking in the World Cup semi-final, who are you to say he didn't?'

We fidgeted on the stone flooring. I nodded slowly. I didn't like myself for it, but I nodded all the same.

'You know what your friend answered, when I said that to him?'

'No . . .'

'He said he was interested in the true interpretation because it wouldn't be fair to Ali Khan otherwise. Your movie is based on blind hero-worship and you're talking about a true interpretation.'

Sen had worked up a good head of steam now. I guessed that he was re-enacting his conversation with Prashant – and this time, with our silence in place of Prashant's answers, he was working it the way he'd intended.

'People want to know how success happens, and how failure happens, and there's no more frequent and obvious success and failure than in top-level sport. It's the job of the journalist to interpret the sportsman. He gets all the fame and all the money, and so he better take all the scrutiny too. The searchlight is on *him,* and not on us. Your friend didn't seem to understand that. I got the impression he was more interested in showing up the critics than showing up the cricketer.'

I could tell, from the disbelief in Sen's voice, that this, to him, was the cardinal sin.

'Then I said to him: Fine, put out all the theories you like. Let them all coexist. That's all right, that's no problem. But don't judge the judgments of others. If you're going to make a movie about Khan, then say something about how good or bad Khan was, and not how good or bad were the people who wrote about him. Your friend said he couldn't do the one without the other. I tried telling him all journalism is really just interpretation and all that really matters is – is how well you write.'

I know now, that this is the unspoken ethos that permeates the work of many pundits. But at the time, I wasn't admiring Prashant for having drawn it out in the open – I was paying attention to Sen.

'And he kept harping about getting at the truth. Now I don't know,' Sen put his palms up magnanimously, 'what he knew about sports journalism in three weeks that I don't in three decades. But I never got into the kind of trouble you guys seem to have already. I heard about the court case.'

A new aspect came over his features then – one that was uncomfortably familiar. A new tone came into his voice, and I recognised that too.

'Don't mix,' he urged, 'with these elements. You're all well-brought-up kids. Remember that.'

He sought me out particularly. His warning gaze rested on my pleading eyes.

It was my own earnest face, looking down at me. It was my mind's own reprimand I was hearing. Sen went on, gravely, compassionately. He was speaking perfectly sincerely now – I could see that. I felt myself leaning towards him, searching out the emotions in his expression.

'And it seems you've got some right-wing ruffians on your tail as well. Prashant told me. He seemed to think it all quite funny.'

I tried to imagine how Prashant might have looked, when he'd said that. I pictured him – smiling with an inner assurance that I could not, for the life of me, fathom.

'That's because,' Animesh said innocently, 'he wasn't afraid.'

In one furious motion Sen and I turned on him. Animesh's cherubic face betrayed nothing. After a moment, Sen said stiffly –

'There are some people who don't have anything to lose. They can take chances. You both have a lot to lose. And so you can't. You can't meddle with people whom you do not understand. They are not your people and they never will be, and the best way of coping with them is to leave well alone. That's something you need to learn.'

I was listening desperately.

'One way or the other,' he added lightly, 'you need to learn.' He looked at his watch.

'Sir,' Animesh said hurriedly. 'What time did you meet Prashant?'

'I told you, didn't I? It was about noon.'

'Hey, he was a good guy,' Sen shrugged. 'We had a couple of drinks. He was well-spoken. I liked that. But – well, I've seen that attitude before. It's not an attitude that lasts. When I could see he wasn't paying heed to me, I figured I'd just fix things with Shanta. She and I go back.'

'Shanta?' I wondered. 'Prashant's aunt,' Animesh whispered.

'But now that I've met you boys,' Sen's eyes focused again in our direction, 'I suppose that won't be necessary?'

Animesh dealt with this point nicely.

'Can we come to you again, sir – in case we need more advice?'

'Well – sure. Call first.'

'We'll do that.'

'Good.'

When he had gone, I tried to gauge my mood. My nerves were thoroughly jangled. Shekhar Sen's last cautionary speech had struck home harder than I'd expected it to.

Animesh, meanwhile, was musing out loud.

'So Prashant had a busy Sunday. Shekhar Sen in Khan Market at noon, which is where he had a drink, Saeed Ibrahim at home in the afternoon, which is when he was a little high, Sheila at night in New Friends –'

– I found his composure off-putting.

'Who beat up the Maruti?' I interrupted. 'That's all we need to think about.'

I was certain of it.

'It's all very well for Prashant to play on Ibrahim's attention-seeking, and grin stubbornly at Shekhar Sen. But at the end of the day, Sen is right. You can't sweet-talk your way out of the path of a mob. It's not like any other opposition.'

'It's still only opposition,' Animesh said firmly.

'What's that supposed to mean?'

'I just think that Prashant was dealing well with the opposition.'

I sighed angrily. I didn't like being made out a coward. Animesh's unflappable manner was stoking my frustrations, and I spat the flames out at him.

'You talk a lot of stuff. The mob doesn't talk – it just strikes. First, it strikes the Mercedes, then the Maruti, then – Prashant. doesn't matter how well he was "dealing" with anything. starting to think you were right about this not being an nt. More likely, it was a lynching.'

nesh said nothing. We walked in silence through the unting night, and my first intense pleasure at shutting him up started to dwindle. Bickering with Animesh was not the solution.

By the time we reached the parking, I earnestly wished he'd say something. He did.

'All right then,' he nodded. 'Let's go to Prashant's house. Let's figure out what happened to his car.'

14

Bᴜᴛ ɪᴛ ᴡᴀs late. Too much time spent alone in a room in faraway East Delhi had made me regard any time past nine o'clock as stale for a new beginning, and it was already eight-thirty. Add to that, we were both strangers to the family, and I didn't see how we could simply land up.

'Call Gitanjali,' Animesh suggested.

'Why?'

'It'll be easier if she comes as well.'

I told him she wouldn't drop everything at a moment's notice. He told me it wouldn't hurt to ask. So I called – and discovered she was already there.

'The house has guests,' I informed Animesh. 'She says there was quite a big party not long ago, and it's only just starting to thin. She says we can come over, no problem at all.'

Given this assurance, I shoved down as unworthy my neurosis over the hour of day. The sacrifice was compensated by a lurid image of myself as a sort of action hero, strapping on my seatbelt for the next adventure. But altogether, I was nervous. The prospect of any social gathering always has me on edge. I always struggle to determine in advance the dynamics of the occasion, and on this occasion, I was struggling particularly.

'How come there are so many people there?' I asked excitedly.

'Of course there will be,' Animesh murmured. 'It'd be so hard for his parents if they were alone. Can you imagine how hard it must be for them — just to get through the night?'

I couldn't. It is hard at the best of times. What must it be like now?

I drove listlessly along the impersonal roads. In a mood like this, I understood the attraction of people over the attraction of crowds — what a small town has over a city. I stared warily at the grinding traffic and the looming grey horizon. Even the systematic red and green of the traffic lights depressed me.

'I want to talk to Prashant's parents,' Animesh was saying, 'and I want to talk to that other guy — what's his name?'

'Rajendran?'

'Yes. I want to talk to Rajendran too.'

I couldn't help a smile. The expression on Animesh's face reminded me of how a certain five-year-old cousin of mine looked when doing a jigsaw puzzle. It was the same fierce concentration, uninterrupted by the vagaries to which most people's minds are subject. As with the child, it was pretty to see.

'You think,' I said, 'that Prashant's parents also doubt it was an accident?'

'I think they're too broken up to have any opinion.'

'That's why it's our job,' he added.

I was already desperately affixing my best forlorn face when we turned into the familiar lane at New Friends Colony. But tonight, Prashant's house looked cheerful. The curtains were pulled open; the lights in the windows were shining vigorously. A mellow, enhancing glow had bathed the garden golden. So far, my visits to the house had been, more or less, a scurry to the summerhouse. It was going to be different tonight.

Directly I'd pressed the switch for the bell, I saw Animesh emerging from around the corner.

'Prashant's Maruti is still in the same place,' he said. 'Still in the same condition.'

Down the driveway came the click of a door opening. I peered over the gate at a silhouette that peered back. We stayed that way for several seconds.

When it seemed we might stay that way interminably, Animesh and I unlatched the gate ourselves. As we approached the still figure at the entrance, it resolved itself into the servant, Rajendran. Beneath the blaze of an overhead bulb he gave us a hundred watter of his own, then ushered us obsequiously through the door.

I stepped cautiously into the living room, hoping I'd see someone I recognised. But the brilliant light of the chandelier fell on an empty room. The full ashtray on the coffee table and the disarranged cushions on the sofa told that the party had shifted. A moment later I heard the patter of nimble feet, descending hurriedly.

Gitanjali appeared, smiling at us from over the wooden banister.

'It's great you dropped in. It's only relatives and friends of his parents. We've been telling stories about Prashant, and I'm a terrible storyteller, so now you guys can take over!'

'You'll stay, won't you?' I asked, alarmed.

'Half an hour more, maybe. They'll be glad to see you.'

Then her brow twitched suspiciously. 'Hey, how come you're here?'

But she knew that we were looking into things, and in any case it wasn't a secret. So I told her.

'We think whoever bashed up Prashant's Maruti is . . . the guy we want. We're trying to find out who did that.'

'The guy we want?' Gitanjali's smooth features creased softly. 'But you know what Sheila thinks – don't you?'

'We're not convinced,' said Animesh haughtily, 'with that explanation.'

'Listen,' I said. 'Are people talking about this stuff? I mean, the people who are here?'

She shook her head decisively.

'Nobody's questioning that it was an accident. Nobody, except the two of you. So,' she warned, 'be careful not to upset anyone.'

'Of course.'

'But tell me later,' she added firmly. 'If you find something dramatic I don't want to be left in the dark.'

The landing at the top of the stairs opened out into a carpeted lobby, which might equally have been a second drawing room. I liked it better than the first. It was a good deal less opulent, and more child-friendly, for which there was proof. An unattended boy in a sailor suit had paused his inspection of the surroundings to study the latest addition to them. I gave him a smile.

Prashant's parents were there, and two others – one gaunt figure in a half-sleeved shirt, and a woman, well made-up. When the child ran to her and she diverted him to the thin man, I understood they were a couple. Prashant's mother recognised me.

'We've met,' she nodded. I relaxed a little. She was smiling. She looked composed.

I sat down heavily on an empty chair. 'You must eat,' his mother insisted. The others already had, and I wasn't keen to, but I didn't refuse. I knew that cooking food and serving food and eating food was all part of the fix. It was reassurance that the world still yielded in the ways that it used to – that what had happened wasn't personal.

Two members of the kitchen staff brought forth a cheesy bake. While Animesh and I prodded our forks, we were introduced to the other couple, Mr and Mrs Kumar, architect colleagues of Mr Padmanabhan. Afterwards, it was suggested that we tell a funny story or two about Prashant.

'You're the young people here,' Prashant's father explained. 'You must know a side of him that we never did.'

The way it was done, there was no pressure – but just the same I was mortified. The truth was that I had no stories about Prashant. And that wasn't only because I hadn't known him in college – it was because he wasn't the type. I could recall plenty of rambunctious laugh-out-loud episodes involving my other classmates, and in my mind's eye, I even seemed to see Prashant in the mix. But he didn't figure directly. I suppose, even in those days, he was conscious of possessing a secret life all his own, with a self-knowledge the rest of us hadn't yet attained. It had gained for him a personal space that was rare in our college, but when you stave off the jibe, you also keep out the hug. You may not want either -- that's different.

I was relieved, consequently, when Animesh spoke up instead.

'I remember once,' he was saying thoughtfully, 'in the twelfth standard – it was the last day of school. The teachers had a farewell lunch for us. There was a funny incident that happened right after.'

We all arranged our faces expectantly.

'Right after it was over, Prashant and I decided we'd walk down to the market and have an iced tea. It was a novelty just at that time.

'It was a muggy day. There was a storm coming, and the wind was already pretty quick and exciting. We were both quite on edge and very excited ourselves. And we were talking about going abroad, and how it must be such a different world abroad. And he was telling me about a documentary he'd seen about Paris, and how washed and grand and uplifting the city had looked.

'Then, on the way to the market, there was an old woman lying on the pavement with a begging bowl. When we got closer she began to moan. It was a far cry from our Parisian paradise.'

Now Animesh was smiling a wry and knowing smile.

'And Prashant took two short steps and kicked her bowl straight into the road. It got knocked out of sight by a bus.'

My gathering grin fell apart.

'And *then* he was profusely apologetic. That woman was so shocked, she hadn't a chance to say a word. He turned his wallet inside out and shook all the money out in front of her. I remember, because I had to buy him the iced tea afterwards. He didn't have a rupee left.'

Whatever the story was, it wasn't funny, and Animesh was laughing alone. The couple with the child had managed a sickly smile, and Gitanjali and I exchanged bewildered glances. More worryingly, Prashant's mother looked troubled.

'Prashant was always so contrite,' Animesh explained. 'Suddenly impulsively offensive towards the things he didn't like – and then contrite, no matter who you were. It's a thing I remember about him. It was quite unique.'

I thought so too, but it was also a thing probably too complicated for the occasion.

Then I saw that I had misinterpreted Mrs Padmanabhan's expression. Her disconcertment had become a kind of elation.

'You are so right,' she said. 'Isn't he right?' Her husband nodded. She went on speaking.

'There are . . . aspects . . . between a mother and son, that are . . . bittersweet. It's hard for other people to understand. But it's only at the age that the child turns on the parent, that you see for yourself how well you brought him up. When he apologises to you, like he ought to to a stranger, that's when you know. He's grown up.'

She gave a little sob then, but her eyes were bright with happiness. Meanwhile, Mr Kumar was musing to himself. 'Prashant was emotional. Because he was talented.'

The implication was that the blame for any mood-swings lay with the artistic temperament.

'He was going to make movies,' I said, and then was startled to see his mother turning to stare.

'But I forgot,' she cried. 'You all were in the movie too!' We admitted it.

'One moment please. Just one moment.' She got up, and I watched her walk hurriedly through a curtained doorway in the wall behind. And no sooner was she gone, than Animesh turned to her husband. All this while, he had been staring listlessly into the middle distance.

'Sir,' Animesh began, 'I was wondering – how did the Maruti downstairs get damaged?'

'What?'

'The Maruti downstairs . . .'

'I wish I knew.'

The man's eyes clouded over. His mouth contracted miserably, and I felt, for a moment, the visceral waves of his suffering. Then he snorted.

'Whole colony is full of security guards and they all say they know nothing. Everybody here only cares for themselves. I'm going to have to hire a guard myself now. This fellow is a fool – doesn't do his job.'

I supposed he meant Rajendran.

'I don't know what happened,' he continued. 'Chitra and I weren't home. Rajendran says he saw no one around.'

'Aren't the police –'

'The police are impossible. It was the same story with the Merc. I've filed two reports and they've found nothing. I doubt they're even looking for who did it. I said: at least find the people who damaged the Merc, because you have a description. They say the description isn't helping. I don't know what that means, unless it means Rajendran can't see straight. Which is also possible.'

He trailed off with a dead laugh.

'There was trouble,' Animesh said gravely, 'with a group. There was a group opposed to Prashant's movie.'

'I know.' A grim, unhappy regret lined Prashant's father's face, 'His movie . . .'

Suddenly he burst out, 'Prashant was so stubborn! We told him many times – Chitra and I both – you need to think about your future! There was a great opportunity in the science ministry – but he was set on filmmaking!'

Beside me, I sensed the Kumars shifting uncomfortably in their chairs. In the meantime, their child had finished his tour of the perimeter. Under his parents' adoring gaze, he stumbled towards the centre of the room.

Mrs Padmanabhan returned, clutching a sheaf of stapled papers. She looked at us proudly.

'Prashant gave me this. It's the story for your movie.'

'The script?' said Animesh. 'When did he give it to you?'

'Oh – on Sunday. Well, he never liked my coming in when he was working,' she smiled weakly. 'But it was past ten. I had gone to check on him.'

'Why did he give it to *you*?' I spoke without thinking. Immediately, I regretted the question, but she didn't seem to mind.

'I've been wondering myself. Maybe he wanted me to read it. I had been prodding him with a lot of questions. He just said: "Here, take it." So I took it.

'He didn't look well,' she added unhappily. Again, she held at bay the suffocating sorrow that must surely have welled up in her throat. She controlled herself.

Looking at her, I felt a sudden admiration for her resilience. When I had first met Prashant's mother, she had greeted me with such trepidation, I thought her awkward and somewhat socially inept. And perhaps, in the ordinary stresses and strains of life, she was flustered – but in this tragedy she was calm.

'You will need this, won't you?' She was looking hopefully in my direction. 'You will need this to do the movie?'

Did she know her son's work had disappeared? That we were as good as not even started on his movie? I guessed not. Gitanjali answered, from behind my shoulder.

'Yes, Aunty.'

A little later, when Gitanjali got up to leave, we did as well. After I had said goodbye to the others, I shook the little boy's hand. 'He is always well-mannered,' chortled the Kumars, a picture of proud parenthood. Immediately, the timid thought occurred to me: Would their obvious joy not chafe against the other couple's bereavement? But from all that I could see the answer was no.

Downstairs, Animesh and Gitanjali huddled immediately about the dining table, poring over the script.

'Let me see,' I said.

Animesh tightened his hold on the papers. I gave him a scornful look. He ignored me, and said instead, in a self-absorbed way.

'Prashant had added a scene to this.'

'What scene?'

'The walking scene. Here, on these pages.'

'He did say he was going to. Will you let me see?'

I snatched the script from off the table. The first thing I noticed was the header at the top of the page.

'I didn't know he'd picked a title,' I exclaimed. 'I thought we were going to discuss that. I had some ideas!'

I squinted at the page. *Show Me a Hero.* I saw the small print: *And I will write you a tragedy.*

Then I read further. This is what I read:

'INT. *Visitor's dressing-room – NIGHT*
Camera pans slowly across empty room from right to left – across three sofa sets, a television, and a table. It lingers near doorway.

Khan enters, dressed in full cricket gear with the helmet under his arm. His hair is damp and his eyes are wet, but he walks in a no-nonsense way across the room and out of sight. Camera pans quickly to cover the movement.

Cut to:
EXT. *Visitor's balcony – NIGHT*
Balcony is empty.

(Sounds of a voice on a loudspeaker announcing, for the last time, the Australian victory and signing off. Voice fades from foreground to background.)

(Sound of a door opening)

Khan emerges onto balcony wearing the team T-shirt. He is smoking a cigarette. With his left hand, he scratches his chin. He grimaces in a general way.

Ramesh Chauhan, the sports psychologist, follows Khan outside.

Chauhan: That was well played.

Khan: Thanks.

Chauhan: It was swinging like crazy at the end.

Khan: McDermott has a funny grip.

Chauhan (with a short laugh): I didn't know you were a walker.

Khan shrugs.

Chauhan: I hope you're okay. I have to tell you, some of the guys aren't happy. People will –

Khan: I don't care.

CUT TO BLACK

I smiled suddenly.

'Where did Prashant think we were going to shoot this scene? Not the Wanderers Cricket Ground?'

'We could have done it on our terrace,' said Animesh wryly. 'The magic of the movies. But I wonder what was wrong with it.'

'Why should there be anything wrong with it? I mean,' I considered, 'I'd say the scene lacks drama, but maybe Prashant was trying to keep it understated. And besides –'

Gitanjali touched me on the shoulder.

'It's crossed-out, silly. That's what he means.'

I looked again. It was true. I hadn't given a thought to the diagonal line of blue ink that cut across the three pages of the walking scene.

'All right,' I declared. 'So he didn't like the scene. Before we were through, I bet we'd have been cutting plenty that way.'

'That's not all you missed,' Gitanjali was still staring at the printed sheets.

'There's a telephone number here – on the first page.'

So there was. It was a solitary number on the top right corner, with no name or address to go with it. It looked like the kind of thing you scribble down, for want of a piece of paper.

'It's written with the same pen as those lines,' said Animesh. 'Can you tell whose handwriting it is?'

'No,' I said. 'But I can tell it's an East Delhi number.'

'It's a man's writing anyway,' I added sagely. Gitanjali made a face.

'What makes you think that?'

'Because women write bigger and loopier.'

'Prashant wrote a loopy two,' she countered.

'Well then,' I said gracefully, 'this isn't his writing.'

We spent a contemplative five seconds staring at the non-loopy two. Animesh started to guess aloud.

'So, whoever cancelled out these scenes in the script is the same person that deleted the movie files from the computer. And the same person that attacked Prashant?'

'And the same person that left behind his number?' I said sarcastically, just before the lights went out.

Not all of them – it was the bright splash of the chandelier that had disappeared, leaving the living room only bleakly lit by a table-lamp in a far corner. But where we were standing it was dark, and then it got darker by a notch, and I heard the front door click shut.

This was all more annoying than eerie. I am the kind who burrows deeper into the blankets when there are bumps in the night, but with people upstairs and so much splendour all around, I did not hesitate. I walked over to the door, pushed the handle down and pushed the door out.

In the bright yellow driveway, Rajendran had retreated a few paces. Before he got much further I accosted him.

'Hey – why'd you switch the light off?'

'What, sir?'

The man quailed and then immediately began laughing in a fulsome, toothy fashion.

'I did not see you inside, sir. I thought: why waste electricity? Sir has often told me not to waste electricity.'

I figured he called everybody sir.

'Didn't you hear us talking?'

'I did not see.' He did not answer.

We moved towards the edge of the garden just ahead of the gate, so as not to be sidelined by the cars parked further. within. Rajendran was rocking lightly on his heels – back and forth, back and forth – smiling a slim, steady, accommodating smile. It was only a front. When the other two arrived, his manner changed.

'Sir, I want to ask your advice.

'Sir,' he continued, 'something bad happened to Prashant sir.'

A frisson of anticipation went the length of my spine.

'We know that,' I said slowly. 'We know he had an accident.'

'It was no accident, sir.'

My mouth felt stiff and its insides parched.

'Sir – he was killed.'

It was one thing hearing Animesh speculate. It was another, hearing this stranger speak. The less I know anybody, the more infallible I reckon them, and so the servant's words carried for me a weight far beyond their rational due. I looked at him with a wild surmise.

Animesh looked at him with a sharp query.

'What do you mean?'

'I mean – that somebody killed Prashant sir.'

Rajendran's voice was quickening and rising with a barely repressed excitement. It was disturbing to behold.

'What exactly do you know,' Animesh asked, slowly and lucidly, 'and why haven't you told anybody else?'

We were all staring at him. He took the first question first.

'Sir – very late on Sunday night – my watch is not working these days but it was very late at night – I heard the sounds of a fight. From inside the small house.'

I understood he meant the summerhouse.

'From inside the small house Prashant sir was yelling at somebody to go away. At the top of his voice. He used . . . bad words . . . very bad . . . like they say, four-letter words.'

'All right,' said Animesh. 'Then did you check who it was?'

'Sir – I was on my way out from the garage. I was going to check if the gate was locked. When I heard those sounds, first of all, I just listened. I stood in the driveway and listened until they stopped. When they stopped, then I did go to check. But Prashant sir's door was locked and the light was on. So I thought – let it be. I thought – maybe Prashant sir was talking on the phone to somebody.'

'That's a thought,' I muttered. 'You didn't hear the other person answering back?'

'No – Prashant sir was speaking . . . in a desperate way. He was using all kinds of insults . . . and threats. But I didn't hear the other person say a word.'

That dynamic was sinister. I'd once read of an animal activist and his girlfriend mauled to death by a grizzly bear in Alaska. The whole affair was caught on audiotape. According to the reports, it was all screams and exhortations at one end and at the other, just gentle, grim persistence.

'And you didn't see anybody coming out of the summerhouse? The small house?'

'No.

'That is why,' Rajendran's eyes widened dramatically, 'I think it was a phone call. Or else the person jumped across the wall from the garden straight onto the road. Otherwise, I would have seen him go to the gate. I was standing in the driveway,' he repeated.

'Was the gate locked?' Gitanjali asked sharply.

'No. I had forgotten to lock it. I did, after that.'

Animesh was shaking his head with a kind of wonderment.

'Rajendran,' he rebuked. 'If you heard this, and the next day Prashant – Prashant sir – was found dead, then *why didn't you tell the police?*'

'The police were not interested. They said: if the door is locked from the inside, it has to be an accident.'

'So why are you telling us now?'

'Who can I tell? Not sir and madam – they will be so upset. But it seems you people also think it was not an accident.'

'How do you know what we think?' I frowned.

'I heard you talking inside,' he said calmly.

'So you *did* hear? Just now –'

'Oh, forget it,' Gitanjali interrupted. 'That hardly matters.'

Animesh remembered something that did matter.

'I wanted to ask you, Rajendran,' he said. 'What happened to the Maruti? You were here all day on Sunday. You must know who damaged it. Was it the same men that came the previous time?'

At this, the servant visibly blanched. He turned his eyes towards Gitanjali, perhaps for support, but her gaze was more penetrating than either of ours, so he gave that up and settled instead for his own two shoes. Then he recovered, with a set of questions of his own.

'Sir,' he said. 'Sir, is it possible for me to stay in this house all the time, the whole day? Do I not sometimes need to go out – for shopping, or meeting somebody?'

Now his voice was charged with the indignation that is known to every worker, everywhere.

'I do all the work of the house. The other staff come and go, but I am always here. Such a big house and I do all the work. But I'm not a security guard. Am I supposed to keep a watch on the gate all day?'

'When,' Animesh asked peaceably, 'did you go out?'

'Maybe six-thirty. Maybe seven. I told you, my watch isn't working. Before then, I know for a fact that the Maruti was untouched, because I had seen it. And after that, I never saw it again. Until the next day.'

He looked around defiantly. 'Is any of it my fault?' he challenged.

We said nothing.

'You are young people,' Rajendran went on, suddenly impassioned. 'You may not know the ways of the police. But I know. Straightaway, they blame the servants!'

The idea of the peril that stalked him filled his features with a fearful indignation. In the diffused light of the outdoors, his weak mouth convulsed agitatedly.

'I am going now,' he announced, and turned away without a second look. Having unburdened himself of his secret, I supposed he wanted to feel relieved, not guilty, and certainly not any longer involved.

I watched his comically slight figure dwindle down the driveway, past the cars, into the garage.

'That guy,' I said, 'is not straightforward. He's not direct.'

'He's just a little afraid of responsibility,' Animesh suggested. 'So he's transferred it to us. That's okay.'

'It's not okay,' I said emphatically.

How could it be okay? There were systems to take that responsibility, were there not? Then again, I reminded myself, this was New Delhi, not New York.

'It doesn't mean,' said Animesh, 'that he was lying.'

A little controlled wave of excitement went rippling through me. I breathed in deeply.

'At least now we have some concrete proof of foul play. And I think the best thing to do is to call that telephone number we found. It's the only proper lead we've got.'

'What are you going to say, when you dial it?' Animesh was looking sceptical. 'It could be absolutely anyone. And I mean anyone.'

'Also,' he continued doubtfully, 'these facts don't fit. Let's say, whoever beat up the Maruti came between six and seven p.m. – when neither Rajendran nor Prashant's parents were at home. But Prashant's screaming happened in the dead of night. Until now, I had thought the attack on him and the attack on his car were one transaction. It looks like I was wrong.

'So,' he bit his lip, 'I don't know. I can't figure it out. I think the best thing to do right now –'

Gitanjali interrupted him.

'The best thing to do right now is to go home.'

To my surprise Animesh nodded.

I gave them both a disappointed look.

'Well aren't you two curious –'

'My dad,' she said evenly, 'will hit the roof.'

'Your dad?'

'Yes. I told you he worries.'

Suddenly, Gitanjali sighed.

'You have nobody to go back to. You're lucky.'

'I have nobody to go back to.' I sighed as well. I didn't think I was lucky.

And I didn't know I was wrong.

15

Mrs RAMDASS WAS waiting.

It wasn't her night of the week, and our rent wasn't due, and she hardly ever called just to say 'Hello'. But she was there now – ensconced on our sofa at her usual spot, if you can call half-a-metre a spot; channel-surfing maniacally, to quell the agitation that danced about her features. An open newspaper lay discarded beside her.

When we entered, she gave us a wild look in which there showed both gratitude and admonition – rather the look of a mother. Which only goes to show how superficially similar are the best and the worst.

'I've been waiting here an hour,' she exclaimed. 'Where *were* you?'

'What's the matter, Ma'am?' Animesh asked politely.

For a moment, she glared daggers at us. Then I saw that it was only a cover. Her eyes widened. Her mouth quivered. She sat back heavily, and the lines of worry deepened on her forehead. ·

It was an uncomfortable thing – to see Mrs Ramdass so reduced. I felt much better when, with an effort, she recovered herself.

'Why did you children not tell me?'

'Tell you what, Ma'am?' Animesh was continuing his choirboy performance.

'Tell me about your friend!' she thundered. 'The boy who used to keep coming over! It has been two whole days and you did not tell me! What was his name? I've forgotten.'

'Prashant Padmanabhan.'

'Yes, Prashant, the boy from Kerala. What is this I am reading in the newspaper?'

'It's really sad.'

'Sad!? It is . . .'

Her whole frame shuddered. This was, after all, a mother.

'It is horrific. It is shocking. He was just a child.'

We stood before her, deliberately calm, with a tranquility that balanced her disarray and wouldn't have been possible without it. But I still didn't see what she'd been waiting one hour for.

A grimace passed across Mrs Ramdass's face. She asked the million-dollar question.

'How did it happen?'

'It seems,' I said carelessly, 'that he fell and hit his head.'

At that, she pursed her lips. In her position, confronted with the news of a stranger's misfortune, I would just have shaken my head quietly at what a ruthless world it is. But where I would have thought of machinery, Mrs Ramdass thought of motives.

'That's only what this newspaper says. That's only what the person who wrote this paragraph says!'

She wasn't one to believe everything she read. She wasn't one to believe anything she read. In common with most people that never leave their homes, Mrs Ramdass's mind was forever on the move.

'I don't believe it,' she declared. 'Does a young man of twenty knock his head against a wall and just – die?'

'Twenty-four,' I corrected. 'And he had a weak skull.'

'There is not one quotation in this piece,' she went on critically. 'Whose opinion is it based on?'

'There is one,' I remarked mildly. 'There's a quote from the inspector.'

'Chheh!'

Folds of sari shifted about the folds of her flesh. From Animesh to me, her gaze stayed steadily scornful.

'The inspector does not want to investigate. And why? Because your friend was not an important person. Just like the boy who was killed in Dwarka last month and they said the servant did it and they never investigated. And then they found that the poor servant was murdered, too.'

I was starting to get irritated. It was presumptuous to expect us to pander to her theories. It was presumptuous to expect us to theorise in the first place — that we had been doing so was beside the point.

'Whatever it is, Mrs Ramdass — Prashant is dead. We know that much. And I guess none of us know any more.'

I also didn't like that we should both be standing around, while she sat on our sofa.

'Animesh,' I said, 'what's the time? It's pretty late, isn't it? I think I'll turn in. Will you switch off the lights?' I added brutally. I made a move for my door.

To my immense astonishment Mrs Ramdass — sobbed. Not on and on, but once indisputably, and once was enough stop me in my tracks.

Like the heroine of her favourite soap, my landlady's moods seemed to alter by the minute. This latest was the most disturbing. It was a kind of hysteria that she had struck up.

'Oh God,' she wailed. 'Oh God!'

'What happened, Ma'am?' Animesh asked tenderly.

'It's bad,' she cried. 'And now your friend is . . . dead!'

'Something happened,' she confessed. 'I have a terrible feeling about it.'

'It's probably nothing,' said Animesh, who couldn't possibly know. 'But what was it?'

'One man had come looking for your friend last Sunday.'

'Oh?'

'There was a man that came that evening. I told him where your friend lived.'

Animesh lowered himself onto the takhat. The television was still flickering frenetically in the background, but the sound was muted. Mrs Ramdass made a sobbing sound again. I noticed, however, that her eyes were quite dry. Now she was staring at us sullenly, expectantly – like an injured child demanding to be looked after. I asked, with just a shade of brusqueness –

'How did you know where Prashant lived?'

For an instant, her eyes glistened in an unholy way.

'I know where you three used to keep going. New Friends *na*? I looked him up.'

'I always keep an eye on my tenants,' she said defensively. 'You know, in Pune they do not accept lodgers who are . . youths? It is because you are at an age where undesirable activities come easily.'

I winced.

'I wouldn't call myself a "youth," Mrs Ramda –'

'That's sensible, Ma'am,' Animesh assured her. 'Who came on Sunday?'

At 6 p.m. on Sunday evening, about the time Mrs Ramdass had finished her climb upstairs and settled down for her serial, the doorbell had rung. She answered it.

'He was . . . maybe forty, forty-five,' she recalled. 'Healthy. Not sickly like you two. Blue shirt. No moustache.'

But even as she opened the door, a strong current of caution had warned her to slam it shut. I understood part of the reason why.

'There was no phone call. The guard at the gate never called to say who was coming. They are supposed to do that for every visitor.

'And also . . .' she shook her head. 'There was something about him. Not friendly.'

'Well, what did he want?' I asked.

'He said there was a boy from Kerala who lived here, who owed him money. I told him there was a boy from Kerala, but he didn't live here.'

Here she broke off and looked at us guiltily. Of course, she had said more than was strictly necessary. Then again, conversation isn't cross-examination, and I couldn't see much to blame.

'I just thought,' she explained, 'that if he owes somebody money, I should assist.'

'Assist whom?' said Animesh. She ignored that.

'He made me describe your friend.'

'Made you?'

'Asked me to. But he was very determined. He said he'd been trying to track him down for weeks. I said the boy I knew was a medium boy with glasses.'

This rudimentary description had been good enough for the stranger. Armed with Prashant's New Friends' address, he had left.

'Did he tell you his name?' I asked excitedly.

She shook her head. Then she asked, with a most unusual timidity –

'Would he have . . . hurt your friend?'

'I wouldn't think so,' I said. 'You shouldn't worry. He was probably just some guy Prashant knew.'

'Mrs Ramdass,' said Animesh quietly. 'Did the man tell you why he was owed money?'

She nodded.

'He said there was a car accident.'

It all came together then. A puffy, paunchy, clean-shaven man. A fast intersection. A heavy Sumo. Prashant hadn't stopped – and the other man hadn't let it go. It was weeks ago – and he hadn't let it go.

I looked at Animesh, and I saw that he'd made the connection too. Now I recalled all too distinctly the final threat that we'd left behind on that deserted stretch, when Prashant had stepped on the accelerator.

I'm going to kill you.

'I think you boys are right,' Mrs Ramdass was saying. 'It is probably nothing.'

We looked at her blankly.

'Now that I have told you what happened,' she continued, 'I can see how harmless it was. This man probably never even went to your friend's house that day. Such traffic, no?'

'It was Sunday,' I said tonelessly. 'There wouldn't have been traffic.'

But she wasn't listening any longer. She was the second person whose conscience we'd successfully assuaged that evening, and I didn't think either Rajendran or Mrs Ramdass deserved to sleep easy. When Animesh said he'd walk her downstairs, she was so much herself again as to take the chaperoning for granted. He motioned to me with his head that I should follow as well. Unwillingly, I did.

Outside, alone in the lit courtyard, I faced Animesh.

'It's *him*,' I hissed. 'The man in the Sumo!'

'I know.'

'How did he know Prashant was from Kerala?'

'I suppose, from his number plate. He has a Kerala number plate.'

'We've got the man,' I proclaimed. 'We've got the murderer.'

Animesh looked at me steadily.

'So now you're convinced it was a murder?'

'Well everybody seems to be,' I said. 'You – and Rajendran, and now Mrs Ramdass too. And this guy was a road-rager and they'll do anything. I bet he's the guy Rajendran heard Prashant yelling at.'

'And don't you see,' I went on excitedly. 'It explains why Prashant's Maruti is all bashed up!'

'It doesn't explain much else,' said Animesh. 'But let's check at the entrance. The guards must have noted who came that Sunday.'

We made our way towards the guards' booth. As we walked, there loomed all around us the lighted windows of the eight-storeyed towers, and for the first time in four months, I felt their metropolitan charm. They stood about us, humming and murmuring with interior life, sending a flutter of the city out into the night.

The effect ended dramatically at the gates that held out the shadowy main road. In the guards' booth beside them, the sleepy habitual was slumped over his metal chair. I prodded him awake.

He was a hapless, long-suffering thirty-something called Vinesh. He recognised me.

'What is it?'

'Vinesh, I want to ask you something.'

'Go ahead.'

'A man had come to my apartment on Sunday evening at six o'clock. Did he sign the register?'

'My apartment is No. 504,' I added.

'I know that,' the guard mumbled. 'Nobody came,' he said half-heartedly.

Animesh started to turn away but I caught his arm.

'Nobody came?' I gave Vinesh a knowing look. He smiled sadly.

'Let me think.'

'A fat man in a blue shirt,' I jogged his memory. 'Maybe he was driving a Sumo. He probably parked it outside.'

The game was up, and Vinesh simply shrugged.

'You told me yourself not to take the register too seriously.'

This was, unfortunately, true.

'So I let him in.'

In my early, jittery days at Akash Apartments, I had resented the frequent intrusion of telephone calls informing me that one or the other member of Arjun's 'marijuana mates' was at the gates. I had the least visitors among the four of us, but I seemed to be answering the phone the most. So I had decided to solve that problem at its source.

With no results, until now – or so Vinesh would like me to believe. But I didn't want to argue.

'Okay, I'm not complaining. But what I want to know is, what did the man say to you?'

'He said that he was looking for the boy who drives the black Maruti. I told him there's only one black Maruti in these apartments. Then I told him where to find you. He was a nice man.'

The guard's idea of a nice man, I knew, was a man who was nice to him.

'Why?' he went on sleepily. 'Is there a problem?'

'Yes,' I said. 'I want to find that man.'

'Well, I can't help you there.'

Those were his favourite words. I knew from experience.

'I can't help you there,' he said again with relish, 'because he was out almost as soon as he was in, and I don't know where he came from or where he went.'

There was no more blood to be had from that stone, so Animesh and I walked around the grounds instead, trying to take stock of things. The perimeter of the compound took us along the sidelines of an empty basketball court, through an ornamental park with a solitary, romantic children's swing, behind the brightened windows of the ground floor kitchens, past the parked cars; out again to the gates. The moon was up; it mingled with the high lights to charge the air with an unfamiliar glow. Again, I felt that I was seeing all this as never before.

'Can you imagine,' I said wonderingly, 'that anyone could obsess so much and so long over a scratch on a car? It's . . . frightening.'

'It is,' said Animesh. 'These child-men always are frightening. I think there's a certain kind of person, the very homely kind, that never learns to take care of his possessions, because he's never learned to value them. So he treats the safety of a car with the same amateurish jealousy that he treats the fidelity of a woman. He's the guy who's only really comfortable with the things he can take for granted – like his Ma.'

'Poor Prashant,' I shook my head, 'He must have got a shock when this . . . apparition – came knocking on the door.'

On our second approach to the park, Animesh pulled out his cell phone.

'Who're you calling?'

'That number we found.'

'Well that's what I sugges –'

'Shhh,' he frowned hard at me. I watched his thumb flick over the keypad.

I heard the 'Hello' at the other end. It sounded three times – each high-pitched, and the last irritable – then Animesh disconnected. He hadn't said a word.

'It's him.'

'Who?'

'The driver of the Sumo. I know the voice.'

'Are you sure?'

'It's an easy voice. It's a tinny voice.'

I'd heard it too, that night on the road, and I couldn't tell. But Animesh was confident.

'All right,' I agreed heavily. 'You know the voice. So now we know –'

'That he did visit Prashant. And left his number.'

We looked at each other. Animesh had on a thoughtful pout.

'Now we effect a rendezvous.'

'This guy,' I told him, 'is definitely a madman and most likely a murderer. I'd rather not parley with him.'

'We don't know anything yet,' Animesh objected. 'He's just the logical next step in the investigation. Just like Ibrahim, and Shekhar Sen. We take it coolly – until there's some reason not to.'

'Isn't there already?'

'No.'

'Well, what are you going to say to him?'

He was already punching out the number again. I strained to listen to the conversation. It was hard in the outdoors, with the ambient drone of late traffic and the blustering breeze. But I managed.

'Hello?'

'Hello.'

'Who is it?'

'I'm a friend of Prashant Padmanabhan.'

Animesh's voice was calm. For a little while there was no answer. I was waiting for the click at the other end and the bleating of the cut line.

'Ah – yes! How is Prashant?'

He couldn't have faked that. I'd once had a conversation with a rich, elderly spinster whose lost cat a boy from the office had picked up, just by luck. She had asked after my boss in the same tone of eternal gratitude. He couldn't have faked it.

'You left your number with Prashant,' Animesh ventured neutrally.

'Yes I did. Has he got the cap already?'

'Has he got it?' The voice on the line quivered with excitement.

Animesh gave me a bemused look.

'The . . . cap? The cap? Ye-es.'

'Oh thank you. Thank you. This is . . . great, sir. Thank you, sir!'

The road-rager murderer was calling Animesh sir. Neither of us had any notion what he was talking about, but in his obvious thrill at whatever news Animesh had just communicated, he wasn't bothering with our *bona fides*. I suppose he simply assumed we were Prashant's agents – Prashant's 'men'. There is that culture of cronyism.

'When can I take it from you sir? I am so grateful.' He sounded it.

'One moment, please,' Animesh said neatly.

He put his hand firmly over the phone and held it an arm's length away.

'What should I say?' he whispered at me.

'What the hell is *he* saying?' I whispered back.

Animesh made a face at me. He swept the phone back to his ear.

'Where is a good place to meet? We are in Patparganj –'

'So am I,' the other man said eagerly. 'I am in Navroz Apartments.'

It was four kilometres down the road.

'Well then, Mister . . .' Animesh fished.

'Seth. Praveen Seth.'

'Well in that case, Mr Seth, how about right now – at the Indraprastha Community Centre in twenty minutes? Outside the Nirula's?'

'Done,' said Mr Seth delightedly. 'Will you please communicate to Prashant my best wishes and heartiest gratitude?'

'We'll see you there,' Animesh assured him instead. 'Goodbye.'

He put the phone back into his pocket.

'That,' he said crisply, 'is that.'

'You mean we go right now?'

'Uh-huh.'

It was past eleven o'clock. Ordinarily, I would have berated Animesh for setting up such a late appointment, but on second thoughts, I didn't. Like him, I didn't want to put this off. I suppose he was simply enthusiastic, but my reason was different.

My reason was that I had to go back to work the next day. The old, sapping routine was only hours away and I wanted to pack in as much of this surreal state of affairs as I possibly could, before it all came crashing down and Prashant's death became just another grim episode in the brown succession of days.

However, it didn't seem likely that Mr Seth would have any answers for us. He didn't even know the question.

'It's completely inexplicable,' I declared aloud. 'He went to New Friends all set to put the wringer on Prashant. And now he's *thanking* him — for what? Did they discover they were long-lost family?'

'And the bit about the cap,' Animesh said drily. 'I didn't understand that either.'

'So how do you propose to do this? He doesn't even know Prashant is dead.'

'Look,' Animesh considered. 'Judging from that conversation, I'd say he's got nothing to hide. Which also makes him harmless. At the same time, it *was* his number scribbled on the script and he *did* go see Prashant on Sunday — so there's a good chance he knows something that might help us. We can be as candid as we please. Sure, he's in for a big shock. Big deal.'

In such an emboldened spirit did I wheel out my trusty old Maruti. The Community Centre was just opposite the road from where the other man lived. For him, it was a two-minute walk. For us, it was a five-minute drive. Along the sparse roads, I tried, literally, to put the pedal to the metal, but a stray, strolling cow, and a veering cyclist prevented that from happening. Still, we were at our destination with ten minutes to kill — if Seth was on time.

16

THE MONGREL DOGS had lain down for the night, but behind the half-closed shutters of the general stores, there was still activity. The fourteen-year-old boys that kept the businesses going were still doing three things at once and shouting at each other, and being shouted at by the invariable grey-haired shopkeeper, which was the usual for all concerned. A throbbing Esteem crunched up the gravel approach to one such establishment and tried to place a late order, which was first rebuffed, and then, after negotiation, allowed; meanwhile, the music kept bursting through its windows. Another big car that I didn't recognise, parked not far from where we stood, made a three-point turn in three seconds and roared away into the night.

I looked about the dusty, garbage-strewn, stench-filled compound. I was only glad that it wasn't deserted. Seth had been a darling on the phone, but my strongest memory of him was still the sinister one on the road, and I didn't fancy a lonely rendezvous with a quiet ball of rage.

Beside me, Animesh was jiggling his head as though there was a song playing inside it.

'Vaibhav,' he said suddenly, 'we shouldn't tell Seth about Prashant – until he's first spoken freely.'

'What makes you think he'll speak freely?'

'We can get him to.'

'I'll watch you.'

We both peered down the road. For many minutes it remained empty, save for the occasional car.

Then the figure of a man came into view. He was crossing the narrow divider between the lanes.

When he came up the slope that led from the road to the marketplace, I could see the excitement in his short and twitching strides. When he got a little closer, I could see the rest of him. I hadn't gotten a good look at him that night on the road, but I remembered enough to recognise the face.

It was a broad-cheeked, full-lipped, slit-eyed face. The eyes didn't have to be that way; they were probably nice eyes – they had nice lashes – but the burgeoning fat underneath bunched them up. It was the kind of face that flicks very easily from bonhomie to brutishness. At the moment, a juvenile enthusiasm was writ all over it.

Soon, the rotund figure had made its way to where we waited. The man was wearing a pink T-shirt and blue jeans, and he was breathing heavily.

'Ah,' he proclaimed gleefully. 'You are –'

'Prashant's friends,' Animesh nodded. 'You must be Mr Praveen Seth?'

'Of course, of course. He has not come himself? Prashant has not –'

'He couldn't.'

'Oh – I see. Yes, he must be busy. He is a very remarkable young man.'

I frowned slightly. Animesh smiled slightly. The man coughed.

'Have you got the cap?'

'You do remember,' said Animesh casually, 'we've met before.' Pleasantries before business, was the unsaid admonition.

'Really? I'm sorry. I don't remember.'

I was quite astonished at how deferential Seth was being.

' 'We were on the road,' Animesh reminded him. 'We were in the Maruti when you were in the Sumo. There was an accident — don't you remember?'

'Oh,' the fat man fairly blushed. 'Oh yes. But I didn't know you both were in the car too. I only saw Prashant.'

'I was in a bad mood that day,' he added quickly. 'Something had happened in the office.'

He grinned then — sheepishly. Animesh grinned as well.

'What I didn't understand,' Animesh went on cheerfully, 'is how you met Prashant again, after that night?'

'Didn't Prashant tell you?'

'No.'

'He *didn't* tell you?'

'No.'

Someone once said, plausibility is a matter of style, and Animesh had hit just the right note of unconcerned matter-of-factness. That may not have sufficed to stop Praveen Seth wondering why we didn't know this basic detail. What did suffice was his obvious, overriding pleasure at the opportunity to recount the story once more. I figured he must have bored many people with it already.

'It happened by chance,' he said. 'Mind you — I believe that what is meant to be, is meant to be.'

Animesh was looking at him in an admiring way. Encouraged, he continued, in a voice that was thick and charged with emotion.

'I went to New Friends as Prashant's enemy. I ended up his saviour. And I was rewarded for it.'

'His saviour?' I didn't see how.

'Oho – he was in big trouble.' Seth shook his head gravely. 'He was going to be beaten up. Badly. . . . There were five men against two. When I got there, the Maruti's windscreen was already smashed. Prashant was shouting for them to stop. See, I wasn't going to get involved, I'll be honest.'

'You just figured,' Animesh smiled, 'that someone else was doing your job for you.'

'Yes,' Seth was quite earnest. 'Yes, you could say that. But then I saw who Prashant was with. Then I realised my mistake. Please understand,' he said apologetically, 'I didn't know that Prashant . . . knew Ali Khan.'

His eyes brimmed over. He started to say 'Sir' again.

'Sir, I had never imagined I would some day see Ali Khan in the flesh. Let alone talk to him! Your friend made that possible. I am forever indebted to him. When I saw Ali there and those ruffians around him, sir – I did not think. I just went and gave one of them three tight slaps.'

'They're all cowards,' his beady eyes shone in triumph. 'They cannot deal with anything unexpected. They fled.'

'Can you describe any of them?' Animesh asked innocently.

'Four young chaps – all good-for-nothings. The one I slapped was older.'

'He had a moustache?'

'Yes. Yes. You know him?'

'There'd been some trouble before,' Animesh admitted. 'Did they hurt Khan – or Prashant?'

'Absolutely not,' said Seth stolidly. 'I came in time. Nobody hurt Khan.'

'Or Prashant?'

'Nobody hurt Khan.'

'Or Prashant?'

'Or Prashant.'

But it was quite clear to whom Prashant had owed Seth's good offices. The double misfortune of Yadav's men and Seth's revenge had been averted at one lucky stroke – Prashant had been judged by the company he had kept.

Now I understood what it was that was shining in Praveen Seth's eyes. It was loyalty – or more precisely, it was the raw material of loyalty. It was something coarse. It wasn't honed. I suppose it wasn't even preferable to the thing I instinctively contrasted it with, which was the jaded glibness of Shekhar Sen. Just at the moment, it made me smile. Deep down, it was disturbing. What could you say about a man who waited weeks to beat up a boy over a scratch on his car, and then became his debtor for life because they had someone in common?

'I see,' Animesh was nodding vastly. 'So you saved them. What time was this, by the way?'

The flesh beneath Seth's T-shirt shifted as he squirmed – with pride.

'6.40; 6.45. And sir, how could I not save them? How could I have held back,' now his voice trembled, 'when Ali Khan was there? In my family, we did not eat dinner the days he was batting. I used to be just too tense. I did not have an appetite.'

This was scarcely believable – but if true, then powerful testimony indeed.

He would likely have gone on rhapsodising if Animesh hadn't interrupted.

'What happened after the other men left?'

'Oh, we talked. I cannot describe what an honour it was just to talk – to Khan.'

'What did you talk about?'

'About the movie Prashant is making. It is a great idea. It has my full support,' he assured us. 'Then, when I was leaving, he promised to get me a cap – from Ali himself. An autographed India cap. An autographed India cap,' he repeated fondly. He beamed at us.

'Can I have it now?' he asked. 'You have got the cap?'

Something in our eyes must have alerted him. For the first time in the conversation, distrust crept into his voice.

'Have you got the cap?'

The long charade had played out and there was nowhere to hide. Animesh and I exchanged glances. I clicked my tongue, and he gritted his teeth.

He was impressive. I was afraid we were playing with fire, but Animesh remained composed.

'We haven't got the cap today.'

'You haven't?'

'There's been a problem. I'll tell you. We'll try and get it soon.'

'*Accha.* . . .'

It surprised me, but Praveen Seth didn't seem to mind that we'd lied to him before. I suppose the autograph was still a favour and the giver of a favour is allowed some leeway. Perhaps he was also used to a tradition of social compromise, where nobody ever said exactly what they meant and nobody expected them to.

'Prashant is dead,' said Animesh unflinchingly.

He summed up the horror in a few swift sentences, and then having dropped the bombshell, began immediately to clear up the mess.

'We thought you wouldn't talk to us if we told you in advance what had happened to Prashant. I'm sorry – but I have to do everything I can, to learn as much as I can about that Sunday.'

'Oh, my God . . . oh, my God!' Seth was truly horrified.

'It is shocking, isn't it?'

'Oh my God . . . I can't believe it!'

'Police have given up. But we haven't. Thank you,' Animesh gave him a searching look, 'for your help.'

By throwing ourselves on the side of his astonishment, and drawing him into the inner circle of our investigation, Animesh was making him feel almost like an ally.

There followed mutual commiserations and – apropos the cap – an assurance from us to him that we, too, had Ali Khan's ear. When Seth finally left the marketplace, still groggy with disbelief, I took a deep breath. Animesh turned to me.

'You really must call Khan! You've been putting it off.'

I had been – and my way of getting over mental blocks is to do it all at once. So right there in the Community Centre, at 11.30 at night, without rehearsing any speech, I called Ali Khan.

It was a short conversation. He hadn't heard – at which I felt a sharp twinge of guilt. He said he'd been trying to get through to Prashant. We didn't talk about the movie. I was going to tell him we'd recovered the script, but before I could, came the click at the other end.

'He's just shocked,' I told Animesh. 'Everybody's shocked.'

'Not everybody.'

When we got into the car, I disagreed.

'Yes – everybody! We've spoken to every single person Prashant met that day. The only proof of any violence was the bashed-up Maruti – and now even that's explained. And Praveen Seth has turned out to be a complete sheep in wolf's clothing.'

'Except for Rajendran's hallucinations,' I went on bitterly, 'it's all as mundane as the police said it was. Or else Sheila is right. You certainly are not.'

Animesh was smiling in a tense, private way.

'What's so funny?' I asked.

'I think,' he said, 'that the most mundane part of it is actually those hallucinations. I think I know what that fight Rajendran overheard might have been about.'

I was only half-listening. A fast-moving truck had just roared by on the road below the marketplace, and having barely braked in time, I was concentrating on letting my Maruti roll safely down the slope. Back on level ground again, I relaxed.

'Well, tell me then. What do you think? You think it was somebody on the phone – like Rajendran does?'

'No, I think it was his mother.'

'Very funny,' I laughed.

'I mean it.'

'Right.'

'I mean it.'

He said it with such conviction that I ceased grinning. He wasn't smiling any longer and there wasn't any laughter in his eyes. I tried to prod him in the right direction with a further little chuckle of my own.

'It was threats – and four-letter words,' I reminded him.

'I know.'

'You don't use threats and four-letter words,' I said gently, 'to your mother.'

Animesh had folded his arms across his seatbelt. He was hugging himself close. He looked small and cold, but his voice was strong.

'Rajendran was standing on the driveway when he heard Prashant shouting. He didn't see anybody leave the summerhouse. Nobody approached the gate.'

'Which means,' I pointed out, 'that the person either jumped the garden wall or was at the other end of a telephone. As Rajendran said.'

'Or went inside the house. Straight from the living room, and straight back.' .

I shook my head firmly.

'From what he overheard, Rajendran inferred that Prashant was talking to his *murderer*. His murderer. Not his mother. You can't confuse the two.'

'She told us,' said Animesh placidly. 'Prashant's mother *told* us that she went to the summerhouse. Past ten o'clock – which squares with the late night time Rajendran was talking about. She even told us Prashant didn't like her coming there. . . .'

'It's a mother and son thing. Like she said herself, some things are hard for other people to understand. Although,' he added neatly, 'I disagree there.'

As I listened, my mind harked back to the odd episode of the ice-cubes in the orange juice and Prashant's tirade at his mother, the first time I'd sat in his living room. Doubtfully, I told Animesh –

'I'd once heard him flaring up at her for . . . for really no reason at all.'

'Well, there you go.'

As the idea became more plausible to me, I found myself even more astonished.

'But . . . four-letter words!?'

I was quite shocked. Prashant had always struck me as unusually well-spoken.

'Sure,' said Animesh. 'Why not? Curses don't have to be punctuation. They are actually intended to blow off irritation.'

'He hardly used insults with *us*,' I said. 'How could he with his *mom*? Was there some . . . problem between them?'

'I don't know, Vaibhav. I don't know the details. It was probably nothing in particular – just everything generally. At our age, it's tough, isn't it, to be nice to your parents?''

I was quiet – I neither agreed nor disagreed. As a general question, I had simply never considered this.

'Because you don't know any longer who's taking care of who,' Animesh went on, 'because you can't just rely implicitly on your parents, like in the past. Now you have to judge them, and sometimes they're right, sometimes they're wrong – and when they're wrong it feels like betrayal. So the tension builds.'

I worried my lower lip, thinking it over.

'Oh, come on,' Animesh rolled his eyes. 'You know it's not *so* shocking.'

'And I'm sure of it,' he continued with conviction. 'It matches perfectly with the way Rajendran described what he heard – Prashant going on and on, and no response from the other person. That's them fighting in their own two styles – him arguing desperately, and his mother ignoring him. And perhaps that's why she liked my story about how nicely Prashant used to apologise, after an outburst. I guess you don't want the last memory of your child to be a temper tantrum.'

We were home already. I made a quick decision and drove straight past the gates. That startled Animesh.

'Hey,' he protested. 'Where are you going?'

'For a spin,' I said lazily. 'What do you want to go back for, anyway?'

The truth was I knew that the closer I got to my room, the closer I would feel to the next morning – and work.

'I want to go back,' Animesh clamoured.

I mollified him with congratulations.

'This mother theory,' I told him, 'is what they call thinking out-of-the-box. I'm impressed. How did it occur to you?'

'Oh,' he tried futilely to pass it off as nothing, 'I don't know. It just did.'

I waited. Five seconds later, he explained happily.

'It was ever since I mentioned Praveen Seth and what a homely sort he must be. It got me thinking of how diametrically different a person Prashant was. I realised they'd both go mad about some things – just different things. And if Mother was the one idea Seth could never protest against – then that's exactly what Prashant would struggle most with.'

'That was my train of thought,' he explained. 'That was –'

'Yes I see,' I stopped him. 'It's a neat train but the last station is the town of Anti-Climax.'

I was being abrupt, but I couldn't help it. I couldn't help but feel depressed. If Animesh had never started speculating about the way Prashant had died, I would have been fine. But to build up the idea of a murder, and then to have it seemingly supported by evidence, and then to have that evidence dissolve – that was a joke. I hadn't noticed it happening, but I realised now what a mental and emotional investment I had made in the business of figuring things out. If the business was a non-starter, I was the loser.

I reached for the radio. Beyond some catchy, lifted Hindi tune and abominable hip-hop, I found a more obscure station where Frank Sinatra was singing *I'll Never Smile Again*. I let that play.

'So let's get this straight,' I said. 'The damage to Prashant's car was by Yadav's men, who were then chased away by Praveen Seth before they could hurt anybody. Praveen Seth himself forgot all about vengeance and became a buddy. The yells that Rajendran heard were all in the family – if you're right in your guess. Until after ten o'clock, Prashant was very much alive. Ever since then, he was locked into his summerhouse.'

'But he wasn't drunk,' said Animesh. 'He wasn't drunk like the police were happy to settle with. A couple of drinks with Shekhar Sen was all he'd had.'

'Maybe not drunk,' I agreed. 'Still – if you're alone in a locked room there's only so many ways to go. And murder isn't one of them.'

As in my mind, so on the road, I had reached a dead-end. Patparganj is full of such blind alleys that culminate in wilderness and shrouded dark. Usually, the sight of endless untended plains and a murky, dirty horizon makes me yearn for home and hearth. Tonight, I swivelled the car around, and slipped it into gear, and sped off in a further unfamiliar direction. Tonight, I was determined to keep driving.

Animesh, I could see, disapproved of that decision. He retreated into thought.

'Prashant met everybody,' he said softly. 'Everybody that wanted the movie shut down. Shekhar Sen at noon, Ibrahim at three o'clock, and then the mob in the evening.'

'And survived all of them,' I pointed out.

'I suppose. But why is the movie deleted? And why did he discard the script?'

And then suddenly it was clear to me. When you'd eliminated the impossible, and so on and so forth –

'There's only one explanation,' I said quietly, 'and that's whether you like it or not. It explains Prashant's foul mood on Sunday night, and the fact that he didn't look well, and that he yelled at his mother, and that he wanted to be alone. .It explains his tossing aside his work. It explains how he died although no one was around.'

'When you consider that Prashant and Ali Khan and Praveen Seth seemed to have chatted happily about the movie at 6.45 – and then at ten o'clock Prashant cashes in his chips and hands the script over to his mom – well what happened in between?'

My passenger opened his mouth to answer, but I didn't want to be waylaid.

'Sheila happened,' I said quickly. 'He broke down over her. I understand that. I guess you don't. You don't know any girls, do you, Animesh?'

Faintly, he bristled.

'I don't need to,' he said dully.

In hindsight, I understand what he meant. But I am slow-thinking, I am conservative, I did not guess his secret then. It was buried deep in him, overlaid carefully by his mysterious, selective reticence.

Instead, I chuckled.

'It is important,' I laughed at Animesh. 'Because that's what this is about. This is about love. And you're out of your depth.'

Now, of course, I am sorry I said that. But I didn't care then. I was thinking of other things. The reckless night, the aimless drive; the razor-sharp music; was making me bold.

'Prashant was a confident guy,' I continued strongly. 'I guess he was pretty cool under pressure – at his work. But there's nothing that undercuts a fellow's confidence more than a girl. The bigger a guy's ego,' I said with perverse pleasure, 'the swifter it punctures. Prashant's was big.'

At this stage, Animesh produced some murmurs of disagreement, which I ignored.

'And that evening he'd inflated it particularly. Remember he was boasting to Sheila on the phone about how deftly he'd handled Sen and Ibrahim? Well, I guess she showed him.'

'He may have been good and brave about his movie. But he wasn't so hot on the girl front, was he?'

I almost quoted Roshan, from a long time ago.

'"For all his supposed smartness, he still can't get any".'

Animesh was saying something to the effect that we'd discussed this before, and that I knew he didn't agree.

'I have another idea,' I heard him say. 'I think – well, do you want to know?'

But I had already stopped listening. I didn't know how they had sounded out loud, but the verbal shots I had been aiming at Prashant were ringing ever more half-heartedly between my ears. I had been talking about him with a desperate superiority, and all the while an inexorable shame was settling around me.

Why? Surely I wasn't doing so badly myself. Tomorrow was bound to be a good day at the office, with my report done well before time, and my boss ceaselessly impressed at my ability to make the right noises on paper.

And if I was going through a bad patch with Anita, well, it wasn't the first time.

Those thoughts didn't change my mood. They heightened it. Now my head was swimming. My ears blushed and tingled. There was a dry taste in my mouth. I can only compare the sensation to what I used to experience in my college classes, especially in the early years, but in some measure, all the way through, when, after keeping shut for a long while through a discussion on a question that I knew I had the exact, the perfect answer to, I'd finally raise my hand – and wait, trembling, to be called upon.

About then, a number of thoughts took shape in my head.

I was twenty-three years old.

Prashant was dead.

Work was guaranteed to nobody.

Love was guaranteed to nobody.

I had a job. I had a girl.

I had to keep them.

I held that thought. I had to keep them.

I had to lose them.

I drove slower. Going fast, you don't get a sense of movement. Going slow, you can listen to the tyres. Going slow, you don't hate the potholes. They just wriggle you around in your seat, and that's a nice feeling.

'Can we go home now?' Animesh requested. I turned my head in his direction.

His expression was hesitant – and confused. He was prepared to hear no.

I gave him a warm, gracious smile.

'Of course,' I said.

I drove us home. By the time my head hit the pillow, my rebellious mood had slipped right off, like the girls' gowns do in the movies. So there was work the next day. That was fine. I wasn't trying to escape.

And I wasn't going to surrender. I felt quite at peace, even cheerful. My only conscious thought was that something momentous was on the cards, and that no matter what happened, I could take it in my stride.

I was partly right.

17

THE NEXT MORNING, which is always the best judge of the night before, was confusing. Many times in the small hours I'd written foolish, sentimental emails to people I barely knew, only to wake up kicking myself. On more than a few drunken midnights I had told myself I was going to change the world, and then decided at 11 a.m. in the streaming sun that it was doing all right as it was. I was used to having my eye-openers in the dead of night and looking away in the morning light. That was normal. But waking up today, with a strange sense of calm and a strange sense of mission, was not. I wasn't in my comfort zone. I wasn't sure how I ought to feel.

Patparganj was perfectly sure. Quietly, it mocked me with the usual traffic jam and a specially blazing sun. Was I a changed man? It giggled.

At Wildlife Alert, it was a slow day. There was a rumour that the boss would not be in, although it was normal for him to arrive late, sometimes as late as six in the evening. Nevertheless, something told our receptionist that Mr Bhairav Chopra would prefer to rest upon his return from Hyderabad.

'A man does not like to work,' he explained, 'when he feels he has already done his quota.'

Undoubtedly, the receptionist was generalising from his own case. His name was Surender; he was a stout, cheerful shirker, full of homely wisdom and impish humour. Today it seemed that half his mind was occupied with commiserations on my ruined trip to Goa and the tragedy of Prashant – in that order and without a trace of irony – and the other half on predicting our boss's likely movements. Sitting at my desk with nothing to do, I spent the morning marvelling at his antics.

It was a useful buffer for my otherwise wholly serious thoughts. I knew that now was the ideal time to have that conversation with Mr Chopra. I was going to give him two weeks' notice – and I was willing to go up to a month. Not more than that, because if I didn't do this' quickly, I wouldn't do it at all.

In such moments of decision one seeks out a sounding board. I was considering Santosh. He was a relatively new boy – he'd only been at the office a week longer than I had. He was a researcher, just like me but not as good – and that was important. Since the whole object of consultation is to receive support for what you have already determined to do, an equal in experience and an inferior in ability is the right man for the job. I pictured myself giving Santosh a few terse lines on Life and Getting Ahead, and him nodding, thoroughly impressed. I suggested we have lunch together.

On the road behind our building in Jangpura was a rudimentary market with the food of two dhabas to choose from. One I had considered tasty and cheap, before Surender had assured me it was oily and too expensive. The other was so incomparably cheap that we'd all agreed it wasn't a bit oily. That was where we went. I gave our order to the towel-toting specimen who was making his rounds. Then I leaned back on the metal bench, in a dark corner of the dingy interior, and stretched my arms out luxuriously.

'So, Santosh,' I grinned at him, 'you haven't told me your plans.'

'My plans?'

'Yeah – your plans. For life,' I reminded him.

He was a bespectacled boy. He had combed hair and a careful accent. He studied me for a second. I kept my smile up.

'I want to do what sir does.'

'Sir . . . Chopra sir? Well that's good.'

'I guess,' I added with an air of knowingness. 'I guess if you have that dedication to a cause –'

'Of course I do,' he said abruptly. 'Why else would I be here? None of my classmates are doing anything like this.'

He was a law student. I suppose this was pretty out of the way.

'They all jumped on the bandwagon,' he went on thinly.

'The bandwagon?'

'The big money bandwagon. And my friends from school,' he was warming to his subject, 'are all either engineers in the US or investment bankers in London. They're all the IIT-IIM crowd.'

'Yes. It's funny you mention –'

'But, I said, "what's the point?" What's the point of doing something just for the security of it? Here, I have an opportunity to work with people who really believe in what they are doing and are really making a moral difference to the lives of other people.'

'You mean animals,' I offered weakly.

He gave me a strange look.

'No, I mean people. It's people's attitudes that are responsible.

'None of my friends would ever eat at a place like this,' he went on passionately. 'Except for kicks. As though they were tourists. But I say: this dhaba is the real deal.'

'Well I don't know,' I said innocently. 'It's not exactly charming. I mean, frankly I much prefer . . .'

'This is where India eats,' he insisted, 'and this is what India eats.'

When the food arrived I winced at the fate of a billion people. For a little while I nibbled moodily and tried to collect my thoughts. I hadn't bargained for such forcefulness. Certainly not from a nondescript boy like Santosh. On the other hand, I suppose they are right: it is always the quiet ones.

With an effort, I raised myself up to a cool vantage point.

'I might be considering my options,' I told him casually. 'In life,' I said earnestly, 'you have to consider your options.'

Again he looked at me – blankly. It was impossible to tell what he was thinking. I forged ahead.

'I'm thinking of leaving.'

'What?'

'I'm thinking of leaving.'

'Oh really?'

'Yes,' I said eagerly. 'This has been a good experience but I don't see myself in this line forever. I'm actually thinking of studying something.'

'Studying what?' he asked point-blank.

'Well,' I squirmed. 'Maybe – management. I'd like to do a management degree. And then just see where that takes me. You know.'

He didn't look like he knew. For a few moments Santosh said nothing. He had his gaze turned down towards his plate. He was chewing hard, and frowning hard. I started to dislike him.

In a flat tone, he asked:

'How will sir manage?'

'Sir?' I laughed unhappily. 'Sir will manage. Everyone will manage. I'm not indispensable. The graveyards of the world,' I joked, 'are full of indispensable people.'

A pair of cold eyes regarded me from behind glinting spectacles.

'This means,' said Santosh tonelessly, 'you're going to get a high-paying job'.

'I hope so.'

'I mean,' I added quickly, 'that's not the central idea, of course –'

I let the sentence go. My companion was glancing calmly up and down the dhaba.

'Let's ask for the bill,' he suggested.

'Well I mean,' I squeaked, 'I haven't made my mind up yet. I'll probably think about it for a while.'

'Of course,' he said, with supreme indifference.

I must have cut a disconsolate figure, when I trooped indoors after lunch. In front of the desk at the reception, I found Surender doing a jig.

'Boss is not coming,' he sang aloud. 'Why the long face, sir? Boss is not coming,' he pirouetted away unconcernedly.

'How do you know?'

'He phoned. He will come in tomorrow -- but not today. When the cat is away – the mice will play.'

He proved it with a scissor kick in the air. He really was a character.

So that was that. The little speech I'd been rehearsing since the morning would have to stay in storage. What a pity, I said to myself. But it was no use. A flood of relief overwhelmed me. So much so, that with a little coaxing, I might have joined Surender on the impromptu dance floor.

This was all wrong, and I knew it. I tried to shoo the happiness away by pitting it against shame. Then, while those two tussled, a certain *sang froid* settled about me. So I hadn't managed to quit today – so what? It wasn't as though I had chickened out. And besides, whatever be the case, it wasn't worth thinking about. Nothing much was worth that.

The 'live in the moment,' *carpe diem* mood was still my dominant mood, when at about 5.30, I left the office for the day. Surender was put out at my early exit – usually I stayed till seven or eight – because, as is often the case, his own chief vice was also his pet peeve. When it suited him, he cast himself in the garb of the office watchdog, without whose barks and yelps the whole establishment would fall apart.

'You're leaving already?' he said with astonishment.

'Yes.'

'Boss might phone,' he warned.

'I don't care,' I informed him. 'See you tomorrow.'

It was that time of day when the sun begins to lose its edge, and the sky turns pale and mellow. It wasn't rush hour, and I wasn't in any hurry. My Maruti pushed on at a steady pace. The road flowed past languidly. I rolled the windows down, and felt the breeze slipping by. I gazed dramatically at the rolling clouds on the far horizon, and let myself bask in the sepia-tinted evening.

After a few kilometres, before the bridge that would tip me over into East Delhi, I pulled over to the side of the road. I phoned Gitanjali. My state of mind seemed to me so interesting and so enlightened, it deserved to be shared.

'I've left work early,' I announced when she answered. 'It's such a nice day, isn't it?'

'It is nice,' her voice agreed.

Usually, I check to see if the other person doesn't sound distracted – on this occasion I didn't.

'I just realised: I've been taking things too seriously.'

'Yeah?'

'Yeah. I mean: whatever will be, will be. That really is true. I don't need to do anything drastic. And frankly, nothing is so serious anyway.'

'What are you talking about? Anita?' She guessed. 'How is Anita?'

'Fine,' I exclaimed. 'Everything's fine. I mean, nothing is *perfect*. But why get het up about it? These are minor things. I've just realised –'

'Hey listen,' Gitanjali interrupted. 'Can I call you later? I'm a little busy.'

'Oh . . . sure.'

I felt a surge of irritation.

'What're you busy with?' I leered.

Her steady voice flowed back at me apace.

'I'm with Sheila. She hasn't been too well.'

'She hasn't been well?' I said absently. 'Why, what's the matter?'

'Nothing new. Just Prashant.'

'Prashant? I thought she seemed pretty okay with Prashant.'

'Oh she is.' Gitanjali had her attention elsewhere – I could tell. 'But still – you know. I'll talk to you later. Bye.'

'Bye,' I answered automatically, just before the phone went dead.

Dissatisfaction crawled up and down my insides all the rest of the way home. A host of unworthy criticisms of Gitanjali welled up within me. Why couldn't she take it easy, on such a lovely day? Why beat me over the head with the Mother Teresa act? Her cutting short my call seemed to me a kind of admonition. And the conversation until then, a kind of condescension. I was still fuming to myself when I reached the apartments.

It was during the short stretch from the parked car to the stairs that I became aware of Kisle sprinting up behind me. He was clutching in his right fist a cheap plastic bag that clinked every time it swung.

'Vaibhav,' he slowed a little as he got closer. But he was still walking quickly. I had to quicken my own pace to keep up.

'Hey,' I said. 'What's the hurry?'

'Ali Khan is upstairs.'

'Ali Khan?'

'Yes!'

'One second – just wait one second, okay?'

I brought him to an unwilling halt.

'Ali Khan is here? How come? Who called him?'

'I dunno. He rang the bell fifteen minutes ago. I couldn't believe it.'

'And there was nothing in the house,' Kisle looked at me accusingly. 'You keep the fridge too bare.'

This explained the bottles in his bag.

'Why did he come?' I asked urgently. 'Does he want to meet me?'

'I dunno. But he's here. With the rest of us.'

'Us?'

'Animesh, Arjun, and me.'

I felt cheated. I felt like the boy who brings the bat and ball, and then finds himself sitting out of the game.

'According to you,' I told Kisle bitterly, 'Ali Khan was selfish and untalented and couldn't win us anything. So why are *you* so thrilled to see him? You don't even respect him.'

I was growing increasingly agitated with every sentence. Kisle just shrugged.

'Well?' I demanded.

'Don't waste ma time,' he said dismissively. 'I gotta go.'

For a nerve-frazzling instant I almost punched him. Then I pulled myself together. I tried on a superior smile. I had to tug at the corners, but eventually it fit.

'Ali Khan has come,' I said firmly, 'to meet me.'

We walked upstairs together. In the last several metres to the door, I darted ahead of the other boy, which was childish, but I didn't care. It was important that I should enter first, and look at ease. I'd walked into our living room a hundred times before, but today felt unfamiliar. I wanted to be ready.

When I popped my head indoors, two cheerful faces looked up in my direction.

'Hi Vaibhav,' Animesh said happily.

'At last!' said Arjun, but that was for the booty Kisle was dragging in.

'Is there any beer?'

'Of course.'

'Great. Mr Khan,' Arjun explained with uncharacteristic shyness, 'said he'd like some.'

It was a quiet, intimate scene, and those were two words I didn't associate with No. 504. Animesh and Arjun were seated side by side on the sofa, which had happened before, but their eyes weren't glazed over from staring at the screen ahead, which was the difference. Ali Khan had the comfortable chair besides the television, and no competition from it. Physically, he was in a corner of the room, and figuratively at the centre of it. There was something in the angle at which the other two sat that established that fact.

'Hello Mr Khan,' I nodded eagerly. I was a little out of breath.

He was wearing a loose shirt with the sleeves rolled up, and a pair of well-worn trousers and worn-out sandals. The footwear was brown; the rest was cream; the impression, overall, was of a Jazz Age specimen with a blue-collar sensibility. His hands rested casually on his thighs, and if there had been a surface of the right height in the right place I think he'd have had his feet up. His head was cocked back a little way, and the whole of his face and neck caught the dazzling, dying sun.

I sat down opposite him.

'It's good to see you, sir,' I told him earnestly.

'And it is good to see you too,' he answered graciously. 'We were just . . . talking.'

His voice was languid as usual – almost a drawl.

From the sofa alongside, Animesh leaned towards me.

'Not about Prashant,' he said in a low tone. 'Or the movie. Just cricket stuff.'

I was glad. I was through with the forensics and I wasn't in any mood to discuss the film. I was a fan. I liked this straightforward dynamic much better than the alternatives.

I think Khan did too. When Kisle and Arjun had finished bustling about the room and we all had a drink to sip at, he told us of his infamous run-ins with Alex Jones in New Zealand.

'The fellow had bad breath,' Khan complained humorously. 'People don't think of that when they say I overreacted.'

Loyally, I said that I'd always despised Jones.

'Most people did,' Khan agreed, 'including his teammates. But I am interested in what you boys think of it. Sledging, I mean.'

Sledging, or the business of verbal intimidation on the playing field, is the sort of stock controversy that swims, for the most part, safely beneath sight, and raises its head only occasionally above water. On such occasions, people invariably point at it -- as they will at anything that breaks the surface. A trout will do; the Loch Ness monster is not necessary.

At any rate, those were my views. I regarded the practice as no big deal. It was all part of the game, and I said so.

Arjun agreed.

'We all do it,' he pointed out. 'It's not just some Australian thing. Or some Western thing. Even when we play cricket in the courtyard, we sledge each other.'

Arjun and I were being consciously provocative. This wasn't Ali Khan's opinion – we knew that. Everybody, who had seen him walk off the field when the umpire refused to reprimand the fast bowler Jones for what he'd said, knew that. Khan hadn't got any support for that protest then, or since. Ordinarily, I'd have satisfied my instinctive desire to please, and given him mine now.

But something in his manner encouraged me to say what I really thought. He wasn't bitter, or hurting, or nursing an old wound. He was giving us a free rein, and the assurance that our most candid broadsides would not bother him a bit.

Meanwhile, Animesh and Kisle were quiet.

'What do you think, Animesh?' I prodded him.

After a moment, he replied flatly --

'I don't know.'

'Kisle?' I asked.

Kisle shrugged. He raised a bottle of beer to his lips. I don't care was his answer.

'Well, anyway,' I repeated stoutly, 'I think it's all part of the game. It's just a way of getting a winning advantage. And it's fun to watch.'

Khan's lips curled into a wry smile.

'I'm sure you know that I don't agree. I'm not surprised, mind you. In your position, I'd probably have the same opinion.

'It's just,' he continued gently, 'that there's a world of a difference between an amateur and a professional. I know that -- because every professional was once an amateur, and I used to trash-talk as much as every other kid. And celebrate as wildly when I won and sulk as sullenly when I lost. All that changed,' he chuckled, 'when I decided to really do this thing.'

Suddenly he sighed.

'I don't want to rant. But it seems to me the game is becoming more amateurish by the day. I'll tell you boys something, listen.'

About then, I gave Arjun an apprehensive look. His attention span was meagre, and I was afraid it was almost up. If it had been me or Animesh holding forth, he'd have long since been squirming and shifting and screwing up his face with impatient lassitude. Perhaps it was Ali Khan's superior years; perhaps it was his superior charisma. But at the moment, he was listening.

Khan dropped his voice -- and gave it an edge. He was speaking quicker now.

'Everyone says the difference between amateurs and professionals is that amateurs play for fun and professionals play to win.

'The truth is that amateurs play to win, and professionals play for a living! Not for money -- for a living! When I decided to become a professional cricketer, it meant that cricket was going to be the thing that taught me life. That's the standard to which I held it. That's the standard to which the businessman, and the journalist, and the government bigwig and every other hanger-on, does not hold it. The fans -- well, the fans used to understand. But they can be fickle.'

He shook his head firmly.

'Sledging is a corruption. Just like ball-tampering. Just like match-fixing.'

Just like match-fixing — his tone never altered. I was impressed.

'I always understood that,' he was still speaking. 'I never treated the sport as a circus. I took it seriously, the way it's meant to be taken. I learned from it.'

I was beginning to feel a tiny bit uncomfortable. There was a hint of wildness now, in Ali Khan's voice. Listening to him was like sitting in a very smooth, very comfortable train and enjoying the speed, and marvelling at the speed, until it occurs to you suddenly that it is going a little too fast.

The front door slammed, although no one had touched it. While we had been listening, the weather had been changing, and I'd hardly noticed it happening.

It had gotten overcast. The last glimmer of sunshine was almost snuffed out.

I jumped up to switch the tube light on. Against the enveloping murkiness, the steady white made the indoors surreal.

Already, outside, the wind was fairly swirling. Through the windows, I could see the trails of dust and litter flying between the apartment towers. The air smelled dank and humid. It wasn't raining yet, but there was rain all around.

'Where did this come from?' I called out eagerly. It had happened so fast.

But it was romantic weather. At times like this people's faces look bright. Their eyes become wide. Their talk turns dramatic. More foolish and happy things are said in the few minutes of a storm than in all the other hours of the day.

A vast clap of thunder sent a thrilled exclamation scurrying through the room. Ali Khan's voice rang out over the elements.

'Winning and losing is something in the heart!'

I stared at him, astonished. He seemed oblivious to the raging weather; in fact it was spurring him on. He was still seated with the same easy grace, but his countenance, like the sky, was heavy with foreboding. The windowpane by his head was shivering continuously. He never glanced at it, but his voice grew more urgent and more intimate. I found myself listening again – this time unwillingly.

'Most people,' he said, 'worship success. They *worship* success. Everybody looks for a king. Everybody looks to anoint somebody. They want to know who's the winner, who's the champion, the number one, the superman. And in sport, more than anything else, it seems so easy to know.'

His face was dark with an inexplicable anger. Only the eyes flashed and the lips moved.

'It's all untrue. It's all an illusion. There are no miracle men. The wins and the losses come from the rules and the rules don't come from God. Winning and losing at sport is just the same as winning and losing at anything else in life. It's about what you know, not what the people think, and not what the scoreboard says!'

I watched on, mesmerised by Khan, but also embarrassed for him. It wasn't what he was saying, but the unexpectedness of it. I'd expected a light, anecdotal session, not such a lot of wisdom.

'The toughest thing in sport is to keep at bay the spurious adulation and the spurious criticism. I learned to do that!

'I learned to do that!' he repeated emphatically. It was as though he was daring us to deny it.

Finally, he relaxed. Slowly, the rigid cast of his features softened. He drew back his long legs and exhaled heavily, like a man with a load off his chest. Another far-off rumble sounded, and then came the excited hollering of children running down the corridors. This time Khan's ears pricked up, like mine. He'd come to.

'I guess I shouldn't go on and on,' he said. 'You boys must be bored.'

'Oh, no,' I demurred. I looked at the others.

Animesh didn't catch my eye. He'd barely said a word so far, and he wasn't saying anything now. He was in his own world, as he often was.

But Arjun was through. Already he was fiddling with his cell phone.

'I have to go do some stuff,' he informed us.

Kisle didn't even bother with excuses. I suppose that, of all of us, he'd had the most disappointing time. He wasn't fond of talk, and he didn't follow the language very well. I don't know what his idea of hanging out with a famous cricketer was, but at the moment he was simply sulking into his Kingfisher. He took it with him into his room.

A moment later he was out again. In the bottle's place he was carrying a rolled-up poster.

'Please autograph this,' he requested dully.

It was an action shot of Ali Khan, following through from a square cut in a Test match in Barbados. It was an old picture, carefully preserved. I did a little double take. I hadn't thought

Kisle had much goodwill for Ali Khan; I thought he reserved it all for his own favourite, Shashikant Choudhury. Now I understood that, for him, becoming a fan meant taking a place in the whole cricketing family, and one had to be kind to one's poorer relations too.

When he was gone, Khan grinned.

'I'm out of practice, signing autographs. I used to do it all the time. I don't even remember the last autograph I gave.'

Animesh cleared his throat. For the first time in a long while, he spoke.

'We met somebody,' he said, 'who said you were going to sign an India cap for him.'

'Oh – yes,' Khan nodded. 'Some Seth.'

'Praveen Seth,' Animesh agreed. 'You met him at Prashant's house – this last Sunday.'

'I remember.'

'I was wondering – how come you were at Prashant's house?'

'What?'

'How come you were at Prashant's house?'

'Because . . . he wanted to talk about something in the script.'

'What exactly?'

There was no answer.

'What scene exactly were you discussing?'

I gave Animesh a sharp look. His tone sounded, to my ears, needlessly peremptory. Already he'd succeeded in nipping Khan's good humour in the bud. The cricketer's lined features were resuming a grim aspect.

A few moments of silence followed. The rain had started to fall, and the temperature was dropping. I drew my arms around myself, hugging myself tight.

Animesh's eyes were still trained on Khan. Twice I saw him open his mouth as if to say something, and twice he changed his mind. He seemed to be waiting for the other man to speak.

Finally, he reached a decision.

'Sir, what brings you here today?'

'Nothing really,' Khan grunted. 'I found out about Prashant, of course. Vaibhav had phoned me.'

I liked that he remembered my name, and I smiled. But my smile disappeared as Animesh continued.

'Did you come here for a reason? Did you want to say something in particular?'

'Animesh,' I tried to hush him. But he was bent on ignoring me. His eyes were opened very wide now and I was astonished to see a trickle of perspiration running down his cheek. When he spoke again his voice was shrill.

'Or did you just come to give us that speech?'

Ali Khan raised his head. The proud eyes fastened on Animesh.

'I'm sorry if I bored you.'

'You didn't bore me. I was just wondering –'

'When the rain stops – '

'– why you felt the need to make it.'

'When the rain stops,' Khan said in a controlled tone, 'I will leave.'

I was appalled. How swiftly the mood of the room had soured – and it was all Animesh's fault. At the moment his face was contorted horribly. The contortions continued, and then another vile sentence spewed out inexplicably.

'It's actually not even drizzling. If you want to leave, you can leave right away. Nobody's stopping you.'

Khan said nothing. Only the muscles in his face moved. The rest of his body seemed welded to the chair.

I watched in horror while the two of them regarded each other. It wasn't a staring match. Animesh was blinking at a rate that would have done Bambi proud, and yet, all the while, his eyes kept glowing with an unnatural confidence. On the wall, above the television, the clock kept ticking.

It ticked fifteen times before someone spoke. Khan, to my great surprise, was addressing me.

'Vaibhav.'

'Yes?'

Then he seemed to hesitate.

'Yes?' I repeated.

When he spoke again, his voice was distant and impersonal.

'Why did you not tell me sooner, that Prashant had died?'

'Oh I don't know,' I said sheepishly. 'We were involved with things. Actually,' I explained, 'we didn't think it was an accident. We though there might have been somebody that . . . well . . . that murdered him.'

'And what do you think now?'

'Now,' I looked doubtfully at Animesh. 'Now, I think it was an accident after all.'

'You were right to begin with,' said Khan. 'Prashant was killed.'

I was taken aback. I grimaced confusedly. 'You know that – for a fact?'

'I do. And if you'd told me sooner, I'd have told you who did it.'

'How would you know?'

'Because I did it.'

18

I FELT A UNIVERSE crashing about my ears.

'It's true,' he said.

In my mind, I was an outsider, watching in. I could see my body freeze on the sofa, and a bemused, experimental smile push its way out on to my lips; then fade away into confusion. I saw Ali Khan's eyes burning with an unearthly ecstasy. I saw Animesh's gaze dimming, as he started slowly to nod.

I heard distinctly the wind lashing the steady drizzle against the living room glass. It came in bursts, like a child's fists beating on the window, pleading to be let in.

The spell did not break at all once, even after Khan sighed. But my whirring thoughts focussed. A maelstrom of sensation gradually receded, and the cream-white figure on the chair leaned forward.

'You see,' he was saying, 'it was a shock to me as well.'

'What happened?' I managed. My voice sounded to my ears deep and calm. It was another step into reality.

'Your friend is perceptive,' Khan said evenly.

I looked at Animesh. He was quite composed now. His face had stopped the mad twitching of a few moments ago.

'I only guessed,' he said to me frankly. 'If Mr Khan hadn't come over himself; I don't think I would have.'

'Guessed . . . guessed what?'

He didn't reply. He turned to Khan.

'Was it – I don't know – was it about the scene?'

'Yes.'

'What scene?' I asked.

'The World Cup semi-final scene,' Khan answered quietly. 'Prashant and I had a . . . quarrel over it.'

My mind was racing: the World Cup semi-final scene was the walking scene – those three innocuous pages of script, with the mysterious blue line crossing them out. What had that to do with anything?

'It wasn't there in the script that I'd read. I didn't know he planned to include it. I would never have agreed to the movie, if I had known.'

Suddenly, Khan's face was severe again. Flint had entered his eyes for the space of these seconds; he was telling us through pursed lips.

'I could never allow it.'

'Why?' I exclaimed.

A strange turmoil showed in his expression. I pressed on.

'That scene was *flattering* to you. Prashant's take on it was that you walked because you thought it was the right thing to do – just personally. Not because you were falling into line with authority. Not because you'd taken money. Prashant wanted to do the right thing – and get the right –'

'Well, he did not.'

'What do you mean?'

Again, Khan was at a loss for words. I looked to Animesh for assistance, but he was no less baffled than I.

'What do you mean?' I asked again, 'Aren't you proud –'

Ali Khan raised his hand. He had collected himself. I stopped speaking.

'No,' he said. 'I'm not proud.'

The long, internal struggle was over. Beyond the windows, the rain was still falling apace, but a stray shaft of sunlight gleamed through the glass and onto Khan's face. He was talking freely now. Only the tiredness in his voice betrayed the effort that went into it.

'The reason that I walked in the semi-final is not what Prashant thought it was. And it isn't what anybody else thinks it was. The reason I walked is just that — I was too afraid to stay. That's the truth and I'm quite sick and tired of hearing the lies. You think it's flattering. I tell you it's unbearable.'

'Too afraid?' I said.

He looked at me beseechingly, as if willing me to understand. It must have shown on my face that I did not, not one bit.

Khan smiled then — an unhappy smile, full of memories.

'We only needed five to win. Just five runs. Everybody in the ground expected me to do it. And when I looked around the field, I couldn't see a gap. McDermott — McDermott used to swing it too much. I kept seeing visions of the Australians celebrating. I kept thinking of how many times we'd lost games at the last gasp.

'When they appealed, I was praying the umpire would give me out. All I wanted was to be out. I knew, if I stayed I had five more balls to face and still five to get, and my whole body was shaping up in defence on every ball. I was telling myself that I was going to play and miss all five. I was going to be humiliated, if I batted any longer. I had been out of form, for all those months, and there was too much pressure. I hated the pressure. I could never handle the pressure.'

I could never handle the pressure. I felt the layers of illusion peeling away.

'And when the umpire didn't put his finger up – that's the reason I walked.

'Even though,' he said, 'I never did nick that ball.'

I stared at him. My mind went careering back to that hushed summer evening in the hills, and all our breaking hearts. He hadn't been out.

He hadn't been out.

Again I turned to Animesh, whose face was a mask of no expression.

'You're the only two people I have ever told this to,' Khan was saying. 'Apart from Prashant. And I'm telling you because I want you to understand why I behaved the way I did – with Prashant.'

Neither of us spoke, but Animesh's gaze hardened. As I waited for Khan to continue, an irrational fear caught at my throat. I realised, suddenly, that I was afraid – afraid for Prashant. In listening to the event recounted, I felt like a horrified bystander watching it take place afresh, in front of his helpless eyes.

'Prashant had called me that Saturday night. He said he had something new in the script that he wanted to discuss. I told him I could come over on Sunday. I reached his house at about 6.30 on Sunday. I was just in time for those men.'

Here, Khan broke off. He asked in a friendly way.

'You remember those men? The ones who'd come to the park?'

'Yes,' I said, though the day in the park felt a long time ago. 'We know what happened. Praveen Seth told us.'

'All right.'

He went on, unperturbed.

'After the men left, and after Seth left, I read the scenes that Prashant wanted me to. I told him immediately that I didn't want the semi-final episode touched, not even in passing. I told him the only reason I'd given him the go-ahead to make the movie is that I thought his focus was on other things. I said I wouldn't allow the shooting, if he didn't agree.

'He was . . . surprised.'

Another stab of sympathy made me wince. I recalled what a happy pair of collaborators Prashant and Ali Khan had looked, even through the tough times, when Yadav's men had threatened to smash the project through. Poor Prashant, I thought to myself; how taken aback he must have been to find his own, his dear champion, turning on him from out of the blue.

'He asked me why. I said it was none of his business why. Then he said that he couldn't let me dictate terms to him.'

Khan raised the palms of his hands up to around the middle of his shirt, and held them there. He looked at us wearily.

'I tried to talk to him. I tried to tell him I had personal reasons for not wanting that scene included, which I didn't want to share. But your friend didn't believe that.

'This is not an occasion for justification. But for explanation, yes. I didn't like the way he talked. He looked so cocksure of himself. He wasn't interested in what I had to say. What he kept insisting was, I wasn't to tell him which scenes to include, and which to exclude.'

Khan stopped heavily just at that moment. I looked at him with a quick, rising hatred. My eyes took in the taut legs, the broad chest; lingered on the swell of his arms beneath the sleeves of his shirt. He gave off an impression of luxuriant power under a tense garb of self-control. This was a big man. This was a strong man.

Something Shekhar Sen had said came floating into my mind.

'"... a crazy chap ... doesn't agree with anyone, and never did."'

The words choked in my throat. My mouth twisted unhappily.

'So you just ... *hit* him? How ... brilliant of you.'

He was just the same as the others. How wrong Prashant had been; this was no enlightened rebel. Saeed Ibrahim, Praveen Seth, the invisible Arindam Yadav – Ali Khan. They were all the same. Use the wrong words, take the wrong tone, show a little irreverence for the wrong thing – and prepare to face the wrath of these hulking infants. I looked at Khan, despising him from the bottom of my heart.

He seemed to read my mind. That confused me.

'Try to understand. I liked Prashant – we liked each other. I liked that he wasn't obeisant. That he trusted his own thought. That he didn't think anybody else in the whole world his better.

'But sometimes,' he went on softly, 'when all the stars do their worst, and you're in the wrong place, at the wrong time, then the same quality in a person that attracts you to him turns you against him. You see, Prashant could be stubborn. Just like me. You won't deny that.'

I didn't say anything. But I was listening.

'He had already made up his mind, that I couldn't have a good reason for not wanting that scene. And that's what I resented. He was so sure he knew everything there was to know. These things happen in a matter of seconds. He walked up to the table where I was reading, and pulled out the script from under my eyes – and I swivelled and hit him with my fist.

'It was a harder blow than I had intended – I hadn't intended anything. I thought it had only shaken him up. I thought I'd only got his attention. So that he would finally listen. After that, I told him what the truth of the semi-final had been. I just told him – I didn't wait for his reaction. And when I left the summerhouse, he wasn't even holding his head – any – any longer –'

A pathetic plea shone in Ali Khan's eyes. I felt a lump in my throat. Bravely, he finished.

'Believe me, I never knew that it had killed him, not until last night when you phoned. I didn't know he had a . . .',

He paused. I swallowed hard.

'. . . a weak skull,' I said tonelessly.

'Yes.'

I looked about the room – anything to look away. I couldn't tell if it was still raining or not – perhaps it had slowed again to a drizzle. It was uncommonly silent. The only sounds were the soft, periodic rumble of traffic, and the whistling of the wind.

Very quietly, Khan continued.

'It seemed to me that you two were closest to Prashant. That's why I came here. Maybe I talked too much. It was only because I'd like you to think well of me. I'd like you to know that I do know a few things – just like Prashant believed I did.

'Only – try to understand that it is hard to be continually remembered, it is hard to be continually praised, for the single most shameful moment of your life. It was the idea of that happening again – when I only wanted to forget about it. . . .'

'We'll have to tell the police,' I said harshly.

'No, you won't.'

Outrage gripped me once more. Did he think a fine speech and a frank confession were enough to get him off the hook? What were we supposed to do – forgive him?

'Wait a minute,' I heard Animesh say. 'Wait a minute.'

He was looking at me with a troubled expression.

'If the police get to know . . .'

He drew his lips back with a sudden urgency. *Just imagine*, he was saying.

I tried to imagine. If the police got to know . . .

. . . it would mean the end of life as Ali Khan knew it. It would mean, perhaps, an arrest, a charge of manslaughter, the dirty, grime-soaked courtroom life stretching on for years and years of indifference and inhumanity. Without doubt, it would mean spiralling back into the public eye, stripped this time of every vestige of good repute. If the full story ever emerged, as it was bound to, sooner or later, it would mean denunciation as a coward who had let his country down on the world's biggest stage. Every two-bit journalist and critic would get his licks in. It would be open season on Ali Khan – and there would no changing that, ever. There would be no recovery from that onslaught.

It would finish the man. All that – for one moment's temper.

It was a staggering idea. I caught at the arm of my chair to steady myself – literally caught at it.

Again, Khan said:

'You won't tell the police.'

My brow furrowed. A word of protest rose involuntarily to my lips; then died.

'I'll tell them myself.'

Animesh flinched. 'Have you thought of what will ha –'

'I'm not the thinking kind,' Khan said humorously. 'This is not a quandary. This is easy. There's only one correct thing to do.'

'Your reputation . . .' I murmured.

'Can deal with this.' Then he sighed.

'It's all a mess at the moment. Let the truth emerge – what happened to Prashant, why it happened, what really occurred in the semi-final. I don't care what people say about that. It will be a relief to set the record straight. You don't know how it eats you up, when you let the lie survive, the way I have.

'And as for the rest, I will take it as it comes – take my life into my hands,' he said wryly, 'and tell the truth as I know it, and after that, who can tell what will happen?'

He smiled sadly.

'Who ever can tell? All I know is, nothing's hard if you stand – and stand – and face it.'

'No,' I said suddenly. 'You can't give yourself up.'

'Why not?'

'Because Prashant wouldn't have wanted it.'

A proud light flashed in the elder man's eyes.

'I don't give a damn.'

I fell silent. My mind was a tumult of thoughts that I couldn't pin down. Khan got to his feet.

'I'll get going,' he said. 'Sorry I forgot the cap.'

'What?' said Animesh.

'The cap for Praveen Seth. That funny man. I don't know how I'll get it to him.'

'Oh.'

'Maybe he won't mind.'

'Yes. Never mind.'

The front door closed behind the man in white.

That was my last glimpse of Ali Khan. Since then, like everybody else, I have only seen him in the burst of flashbulbs, an image on the screen, a photograph in the papers, facing down an uncertain fate.

But in the living room that night, I had no thought of the future. Every space was sealed, and I felt suddenly ill. The physical need to breathe in fresh air had become overwhelming. I staggered to my feet.

~

Animesh followed me, out onto my terrace. We stood against the railings, alone with the night. The raindrops were still streaking the sky.

The rain had transformed the place. Tonight, the cars glided along the glistening road, soundless, except for the muted murmur of the engines and the swish of tyres deferentially treading water. In the homes across the road, the windows were shining, and on the wet tar, the reflected red and yellow quivered brightly. There was colour, and there was quiet. The air smelt clean and heady, with that peculiar headiness which assures that the storm has passed.

Gratefully, I took it all in. For a little while, it seemed to me this weather was sufficient; all-embracing; exclusively deserving of my mind's surrender. Then a thought intruded.

Ali Khan had killed Prashant.

I repeated the sentence to myself, until the numbness had gone from the idea. Until I was able to consider it. On Monday morning, I had heard of Prashant's death. On Thursday evening, I knew the truth of it. Just four days – four days waking and subsiding on the same bed, with this dark magic in between.

From the view outside, my attention dragged unwillingly to the small individual beside me.

He was looking in the same direction that I had been, but he wasn't looking at anything. Animesh's dark eyes were clouded over. The rain dripped off his hair; it had streaked his cheeks and left tiny droplets glistening along the length of his lashes. I say the rain, because I suppose it was only the rain, but I don't know for sure.

'Hey,' I said. 'What a night.'

As I watched, he nodded once, twice, dreamily. Then he tossed his head and breathed in hard.

'I know.'

He looked at me – his eyes focussed.

'I know,' he said again.

'You never told me,' I chided gently. 'Why didn't you tell me?'

'Tell you what?'

'That you had guessed about Khan.'

'Oh, that.' Animesh's lip curled a fraction. Slowly, as I watched, he was resuming his equanimity.

'I would have,' he said distantly. 'I would have told you yesterday. Except you didn't seem interested.'

And now, as I thought back over the matter, a host of inexplicable points occurred to me.

'It still doesn't make sense,' I said carefully. 'I still don't see – I mean, Prashant had dinner with Sheila. He met his mom late at night. This was all after Ali Khan had left. How could –'

'Because,' Animesh interrupted, 'the blow wasn't immediately fatal. That's what the doctors said, remember. It took several hours. There's a way to be killed even when you're alone in a locked room, and that's if you're hit before. That never occurred to the police, but I had it in my mind from the very beginning. Especially after we'd disposed of the drunken fall idea.'

'But,' I stared at the other boy. 'If Prashant was hurt – even before he met Sheila – then how come she never noticed it when they did meet? I know there wasn't an injury – but surely there would have been something.'

'Of course there was,' Animesh said. 'And of course she noticed. Only she didn't interpret.'

'Meaning?'

'Meaning, Sheila told you herself that Prashant was behaving strangely. That he wasn't listening; wasn't speaking properly. She put that down to the force of her presence. He looked bad. And depressed. She put that down to the emotional blow she'd dealt him. Just like you did. Except that I thought – maybe that's putting the cart before the horse. Maybe he was depressed at dinner, not because of what happened there, but because of what happened before. Maybe he wasn't talking straight, because he wasn't thinking straight, and maybe he wasn't thinking straight, because he'd been hit on the head.

'It's a symptom of damage to the brain – and that's what Prashant died of.'

'That idea,' Animesh continued, 'occurred to me as soon as you told me what Sheila had said. Even though,' he added pointedly, 'I hadn't heard it firsthand, because I hadn't been present.'

'If you had been present,' I told him acidly, 'she wouldn't have said a word. So thank your lucky stars.'

'You were just overawed by her.'

'You were just too clumsy for her.'

'Have it your way,' he said demurely. 'But once I thought of that, I wanted to find out whether Prashant had been in a fight that evening. I figured it had to have been in the evening, because he was obviously fine when he met Shekhar Sen at noon and Ibrahim in the afternoon. Any time between when he called

Sheila on the phone at five o'clock, all cheerful and boastful, and when she visited at night, and found him a wreck.

'Whenever the Maruti got damaged was, I thought – we both thought – the likely occasion for Prashant to have got hurt. And when we spoke to Rajendran and he said he'd been out of the house at six-thirty or seven, so the car might have been vandalised then, it seemed to fit. Of course, Rajendran also told us about the late night quarrel in the summerhouse – and that didn't fit.

'Then we got to know about Praveen Seth. Seth said categorically that he'd been present during the attack on Prashant's car, and that Yadav's goons hadn't touched Prashant. I asked him, remember, and that's what he said. So that possibility was ruled out.

'And when I realised that it must have been Prashant's mother, not some unknown murderer, whom he'd shouted at late at night – well then it all came down to the one man whom we hadn't spoken to, and the one meeting we knew nothing of. And that was Ali Khan, after Seth had gone, before Sheila came. Exactly the time I was looking for.'

'But you didn't guess,' I suggested, 'what had happened between Prashant and Khan? I mean – the reason why –'

'No,' he admitted. 'I had no clue. I mean: how could I know? I just guessed something had gone wrong – something to do with the movie. But when Khan showed up, without a reason, without an invitation, the very day after you'd told him Prashant had died – it just seemed . . . I don't know – the compulsion of a guilty conscience. It just seemed to me, he'd come to confess.

'Of course,' Animesh added innocently, '*you* assumed it was all an accident.'

'Well,' I replied harshly, 'that's what any sensible person would assume. Why believe the worst?'

'Not the worst,' he shook his head. 'Just the most satisfactory. Hey, the movie files were deleted. The walking scene was scratched out. Prashant had surrendered the script to his mom – why would he do that? I mean, these things had to have an explanation. If he died by accident, what was the explanation?'

'What is the explanation?' I asked suddenly.

'Oh, I suppose he was just – I mean after what happened with Ali, he must have been . . .'

'. . . shattered,' I said thoughtfully. 'So he said: to hell with it.'

'Yes.'

'I'm so useless, to hell with my movie.'

'Yes.'

I clicked my tongue.

'Poor guy.'

'Yes.'

'Poor bloody idiot.'

'Yes.'

Another thought occurred to me – an incredible thought. 'He never even told anyone.'

'What?'

'We thought he must have lost consciousness after the hit to his head. Otherwise, surely he'd have got help. But he was conscious. He could have told Sheila what had happened. My God – he had dinner with her! He could have told his mother. He just . . . didn't!'

'I know.'

'Why on earth would –'

'I suppose –'

'What?'

'I suppose he was embarrassed.'

I shook my head incredulously. Animesh went on in a tired voice.

'Embarrassed that he'd been so totally wrong about the scene, about Ali, embarrassed that Ali had argued with him, embarrassed that Ali had struck him. He didn't want to admit to those things. Maybe, he never realised he was dying.'

Could it be true? Fragments of Prashant's ebullient speeches played back in my mind.

'"There are those who take care of other people, and there are those who need to be taken care of. I've always felt like I'm the first kind."'

'"I've got to be all-comprehending, all-forgiving. There should be nothing that can throw me off-balance."'

'" . . . I can take all comers."'

It must have been true. Perhaps Prashant would have confided his failure to me, or to Animesh, or even to any stranger. We could have talked about it at arm's length — we could have joked about it on terms of easy equality.

But he couldn't confess to the girl he loved, who didn't love him; or to the parent, to whom he was always a child. His pride was not so flexible that their pity would not lame him. His pride would not bend, and so it broke.

'I think,' I said viciously, 'he deserved what he got.'

The words buzzed about my brain, angry and frantic. But when their frenzy had faded, the calamity remained. What had he done? Failed to allow that the hero he championed had demons of his own. But what had he got?

I looked up into a gentle gaze. 'He was brave,' Animesh was saying. 'He fought hard for the movie. Even right up to the end, the only thing he lost to was himself. His own sense that he'd been beaten. And that's the hardest enemy there is.'

The hardest enemy there is; I knew that last thought was true. Now Animesh was going on, quickly, earnestly –

'Look at it this way: Prashant was proved right after all. He always believed that the truth of events does matter. Interpretation isn't like Shekhar Sen thinks it is – a question of glibness. Interpretation isn't some dubious, scared enterprise. It isn't a farce. There is a bedrock of reality and the task is to walk it, no matter who or what is trying to push you off your feet. You have to keep in touch, and losing touch has consequences. Prashant paid them. He paid much, much more than them.'

I grimaced. There remained a part of me that wanted only to denounce the boy and then stamp on his grave. His attitudes were not mine, and they never could be. I made a flurried list of all Prashant's foibles: his foolish drinking, his loose, grandiose talk, his indiscriminate emotional candour, and most of all, his irrational, light-hearted confidence that the world and everyone in it was on his side after all.

He had lacked entirely the wariness that I considered the stamp of growing up. He didn't seem to see that we live among enemies – that everyday, we walk among people who are not like us; who do not like us; between whom and us there can never be more than an uneasy impasse, based on the timeless principle of Live and Let Live – or Live and Let Die, whatever be the case. You don't make conversation with a beggar – and certainly not to say no. You don't invite a fanatic lawyer to your house – and certainly not to argue with him. These were spectres that belonged to the locked attic of the mind, far from sight where they wouldn't assail too much. Was it right to clean out the attic, turn each ugly artifact to the light – and then, with still more temerity, without fear or favour, to put each in its place?

I was pretty sure I knew the answer. I'd known it months ago, hadn't I, when I first set up house in Akash Apartments, and resolved to put my head down and grit my teeth and carve out my own cave in this chaotic city. I ought to be able to shake Prashant's influence right off, and get back onto the grooves on which, for better or worse, my life still ran, while his did not.

And yet here I was, with my mind on fire.

Angry sounds floated up from the street below, cutting off my reverie. The soothing effect of the rains had given way to a snarl, that was precipitated by a car that had broken down in a pothole full of water. As the blare of horns filled the night air, I thought to myself, I'd be driving down that road tomorrow. From over the cacophony, I heard Animesh saying —

'Are you going to work tomorrow?'

'What?'

'Are you going to work tomorrow?'

'Of course. Why wouldn't I?'

'I thought you were quitting.'

'Did I tell you that?'

'I think so.'

Had I told him? I didn't remember.

'Well — I don't know.'

'How come?'

'I just don't.'

'I suggest,' he said gravely, 'that you make up your mind.'

I looked at Animesh. He was looking very serious; very wide-eyed and solemn. He looked like a child waiting for good news, fully expectant that I would do the right thing. There he stood, this unfathomable boy who liked only to see things go right.

I see now that it wasn't only Prashant's influence working on me. I see now that this story hasn't been all about Prashant, after all.

I didn't say anything to Animesh then, and I didn't say anything to myself either. But already, I felt the slow stirrings of anticipation. I knew, subliminally, that the moment of decision had passed; that the conflagration in my mind had ceased, and the embers were still glowing.

~

A fortnight later, on a dim October evening, I walked with Gitanjali down Asiad's broad and empty roads. The change of season was upon us, there was winter in the air, and in the mellow darkness, a promise of renewal. Beneath our shoes, the dry leaves of autumn burst and crackled, and as the mood of the moment surged through me, I wanted suddenly to tell her what great things I was going to do.

The previous Thursday, I had left my job. My boss had been good about it – he'd even made a joke about wishing he had studied management himself, and then maybe he'd have been able to keep me. When we had finished talking and it was over, I could hardly believe how swiftly it had happened. That was the end of my daily commute to Jangpura. Just like that, I was free – free to start on something else; something, perhaps, that I was meant for.

And now, in the quiet of the approaching night, my voice was low and eager.

'After the degree,' I told Gitanjali, 'anything's possible. Who knows, maybe I'll be a sports agent – we have no good ones in this country, we hardly have the concept. I'll nurture and protect

290 / ADITYA SUDARSHAN

the Ali Khans of this world. I could become a kind of pioneer, someone tough and tender and wise and rich and –'

'And delusional,' she grinned. 'Congratulations on quitting. Your parents must be so pleased.'

I gave her a long look. 'You know that doesn't matter. If they're happy, then good for them. It's coincidental. But it's not the reason why.'

Gitanjali sighed. 'An MBA – you've sold out, Vaibhav. And I had such hopes for you.'

We walked on, smiling. Now, at last, I wasn't bothered by the thought. Was I treading the beaten path to quick money and comfort? Only if there was a rule that you had to make a show of suffering before you made a show of success. And if there was that rule, well, then I reminded myself that there was a different rule – for genius. Except that I didn't say genius. I said everybody.

For long moments my thoughts floated, undisturbed, settling at last on the old, abiding subject.

'Prashant,' I wondered aloud. 'What will happen to his movie?'

'We'll finish it, won't we?'

I said nothing. The truth was, I had meant the question rhetorically.

'Isn't it important to finish it? For his sake? For his parents' sake?'

I looked at Gitanjali's small and grave face and I felt a stab of tenderness.

'Oh, Gitanjali – the movie was always Prashant's baby. Not ours, and not his parents' either. Without him around, there isn't any point. We'd only end up with something half-hearted.'

'It would be something to remember him by.'

Her voice was cold, but more than that, it was unhappy, and I understood she wasn't looking for an argument. She was looking to be told. So I tried.

'Letting the movie go isn't − it isn't the same as letting his memory go. Listen,' I added, flushed. 'What was the movie anyway? *Show Me a Hero*, wasn't it? Well, he already did. It's already finished. I've seen it − and I don't need to again, because I've understood it. Once and for all.'

She didn't reply, but I had meant that little speech. The seconds passed; I listened to the rhythm of her stoic and suffering breathing. We turned a corner, into another deserted stretch of road, lined with shapeless, shadowy trees. At the end of this lane was Gitanjali's house. Consciously, I walked slower, that the minutes may linger.

'I have some news.'

'Tell me.'

'I'm not seeing Anita any longer.'

Gitanjali looked up, surprised.

'Since when?'

'She phoned me a week and a half ago. But when she broke it off, I knew she was right to.'

In the silence that followed, I was aware of Gitanjali's dark eyes, watching me worriedly.

'I'm sorry,' she said softly. 'But remember, Vaibhav, Anita was the first and the first is never the last. When people grow, sometimes they grow apart.'

I laughed then, so she should see that I wasn't looking for consolation − that I had a happier motive in mind.

'I know,' I said. 'I know what happened. It had reached a point where I couldn't tell her anything nice -- and she couldn't hear it from me. It had come to a stage where all that was left was a mutual pity. Anita and I went from infatuation to disillusion, but we never had the comfort of love.'

'That's . . . well put.'

'It's thanks to you.'

'What do you mean?'

I stopped and turned and held her gaze.

'The only reason I understand that comfort – is you.'

Around me, as I said the words, I felt the night contracting; the murky skies were swimming close, the lights of the houses dimming and glazing, and in the trees, the wind receding. That the end of one long romance should culminate in the birth of another, and the fires of disappointment forge a finer love – surely, that was only fitting. In the pit of my stomach there lunged a precarious hope.

'Be specific,' I heard her say.

'What?'

Gitanjali's lips were quivering at the corners. 'Be specific. Do you mean to say that you're in love with me?'

Her voice was steady all through the sentence. I opened my mouth to say the emphatic *yes*, but instead it stayed open, and I found I hadn't said a thing. I looked at Gitanjali's wry, challenging smile and it seemed to see right through me. I felt sheepish and confused, and belatedly defiant.

'Don't laugh,' I protested. 'It's true.'

'Is it really?'

'Well – why not? You're . . . the nicest girl I know.'

'How many do you know?'

'Listen – I mean it!'

She sighed tremendously.

'We're only friends, Vaibhav. You know that.'

'But how can you be so certain? You haven't even considered –'

'I'm certain,' she pushed back a lock of hair in a matter-of-fact way. 'You're not my type. And I'm not yours.'

'What are types?' I demanded. 'I don't believe in types.'

I was arguing, neither from conviction, nor from desperation, but a certain offended disbelief. I couldn't quite stomach how swiftly my fancies were being brought to earth.

'Your beliefs don't change the facts.'

'I could make it happen! We have so much in common.'

'Yes, we do. That's why we like each other. And no, you couldn't.'

Then she smiled.

Pretty soon we were both smiling.

At the gate of her house, she swivelled determinedly and I followed, scratching my head.

'It just seemed right,' I explained. 'You know – me getting to know you just as I started to lose Anita. I just assumed you'd fill the void.'

'It's okay,' she laughed. 'I understand – I think. Life doesn't work so neatly, though.'

For a little while, I thought that over. Like the sheer side of a mountain, the fact stared me down. It was undeniable, and venerable, but it was also hurtful. I asked her frankly –

'What am I going to do? Anita isn't coming back.'

'But that's the way you wanted it, remember?'

'I don't know. She was the only girl I've ever been in love with. And I thought it would last forever.'

'Everybody does.'

'But I'm lonely.'

We were silent for a bit. Later, when I was leaving, Gitanjali said:

'It's better to be lonely than lost.'

I think she was probably right. I'm sitting here at my desk in my room, in the same old No. 504 with Mrs Ramdass at the television outside, and the groaning traffic on the road below. Everything looks just as it did when I first arrived, and no nicer than before. Nevertheless, it is home.

And I'm not afraid now to say what I think of it. I have learned not to stifle my opinions, but to let them play out as they will, alter as they please, take me where they would. If, today, a young man came knocking at my door, charged with the passion of his thoughts and the courage to run with them, I wouldn't blanch at his ambition, or doubt his wisdom, or fear for his life. I'd cheer him on.

Tonight, when I look out of my window, I see clearly. The sky is black as ink. The moon is a silver orb. Tomorrow, perhaps, a grey haze will dull the horizon, and my sight will dim and flounder. And yet, all the while, there rises before me a healing mist of a single constant shade. It is diffuse and fragile, but it is there, more than anywhere, that I know I must look.

It is the future, the promised land, always the colour of roses.